I
DON'T
Wanna
BE RIGHT

Also by Alisha Yvonne

Lovin' You Is Wrong

I
DON'T
Wanna
BE RIGHT

Alisha Yvonne

www.urbanbooks.net

This is a work of fiction. Any references or similarities to actual events, real people, living, or dead, or to real locals are intended to give the novel a sense of reality. Any similarity in other names, characters, places, and incidents is entirely coincidental.

Urban Books
74 Andrews Avenue
Wheatley Heights, NY 11798

copyright © 2005 Alisha Yvonne

ISBN 1-893196-32-1

First Printing March 2006
Printed in the United States of America

10 9 8 7 6 5 4 3 2 1

Submit Wholesale Orders to:
Kensington Publishing Corp.
C/O Penguin Group (USA) Inc.
Attention: Order Processing
405 Murray Hill Parkway
East Rutherford, NJ 07073-2316
Phone: 1-800-526-0275
Fax: 1-800-227-9604

In Loving Memory of Corry L. Richmond
29 June 1974–10 September 2003

A Letter to Corry . . .

    I haven't seen a day when I don't think of you. You are never forgotten and will forever live on in my heart. I can feel you smiling on me—what an incredible honor to have an angel such as yourself watching over me. I'm blessed beyond belief.

    Get you some rest now because we've got a whooole lot to talk about when I see you again.

Love,
Sis

P.S. Please put in a good word for me. Really don't want no trouble at the Gate.☺

Acknowledgements

To my mother, Rhonda Brown: Your support is worth platinum in my heart. I can't tell you the number of times I've heard people say how much they admire you and how you have my back. Your shining light helps encourage me to keep pushing on. Thanks for everything. I love you.

To my father, Charles Brown: You've always looked out for me and supported me no matter what. Thanks for loving me, and I love you, too.

To my siblings Donna L. Smith, Gregory Savage, and Ronald Byrd: Thanks for always being there. I love you, and I couldn't ask for a better set of siblings. ☺

To Donna Harvey, Kay Sikes, and Albert Finch: I couldn't have done it without you. Your feedback on this story helped me to get through. Thanks for your dedication and for believing in my work.

To Tomeka Lark: Thank you so much for reminding me to let my light shine. Your pep talk was what I needed when others were trying to bring me down. Your spirit is beautiful, and I hope we remain friends.

To friends and family (Uncle Barry and Aunt Penny Clark, the Tutwilers—Benjamin, Paul, and Martin, Sherita Nunn, Kendal and Eric Hubbard, Royce Willis, Deborah Tuggle,

Lillie Garrison, Julie Cummings, Angela Bonner, Tonya Samateh, Audrey White, Pam Small): I'm excited that so many of you care. You have come out of the woodworks with support. I'm extending an open invitation into my heart so you can see just how overjoyed I am. *Uncle Barry,* I think of you constantly. Please know I love you. Aunt Penny, you are an angel. Thanks for your hospitality, and for just being you. *Sherita,* I'm proud that we are friends—thanks for all you do. *Uncle Ben* (Benjamin Tutwiler), I OWE YOU! *Royce,* I'm saying it again, you're the man! *Uncle Paul* (Paul A. Tutwiler), you were one of my first inspirations for the written word—now publish that book! *Kendal,* best friends don't come packaged better than you. *Grandma* (Lillie Garrison), you mean more than I could ever express. I'll just sum it up with I love you!

To some very special online and local book clubs (R.A.W. SISTAZ, Memphis-RAW, ReadInColor, Sophisticated Souls of Learning, Women In Sisterhood, Women Seeking Knowledge, Uchefuna, GFI-Mphs, Black Women Empowered Through Reading, The Literary Ladies, and Unique Women Social Club): What can I say to such a wonderful group of people? Your support is every author's dream, and I thank you all for helping mine come true. Girl Friends Inc-Memphis, I'm waiting on the next party . . . and please remember to bake me some macaroni and cheese. ☺

To Urban Book's staff and my fellow supportive authors (Carl Weber, Roy Glenn, Robilyn Heath, Keith Lee Johnson, Thomas Long, LaJill Hunt, Cherlyn Michaels, Cydney Rax, Eric Pete, David Williams, Regina Neequaye, Margie Gosa Shivers, and the entire Urban Books family): Did you ever know that you're my heroes and everything I'd like to be? In case you all didn't know, here it is written in black and white—you light up my literary world! Much success to all of you.

To anyone I might have forgotten: Please charge it to my head and not my heart. I appreciate everyone who has been a part of my success.

Chapter One

A Man Scorned

Maybe if I hadn't been the cause of Momma's death, things would be different for me today. There isn't a soul in this world who can replace Ma. Well, there is one who closely measures up: Holiday Simmons, the woman I've grown to love more than any other, is like a breath of fresh air. But now the time has come that just as my mother had to die, I will claim Holiday's life.

I had always thought my hands were meant to be used lovingly toward women, but after a stage of loneliness, hurt and anger, I learned I could use my hands to do some dangerous things. I came to know love with Holiday like I have with no other, and I refused to share her or see her happy with someone else.

I needed Holiday, but she just didn't get it. She belonged to me. I tried to tell her there was no sense in fighting fate. We were destined to be together.

When I first met Holiday, I knew there was something special about her. Her long legs are the sexiest pair I've ever laid eyes on. They're toned, and they totally complement the rest of her body. I've always been in love with Holiday's smooth brown complexion and her satin-black, Indian-looking hair. The days I'd see her let it flow were few and far between. For some reason, she seemed modest about wearing her hair down. Holiday has eyes that give new meaning to the word *ebony*. Although they're the blackest of black, they give off enough light to brighten every man's heart. There is so much more to her. I've never been able to put my finger on all that lures me to her. There's an attraction I feel toward her that goes far beyond her beauty.

Holiday lived by her own philosophies, and she somehow managed to get me to understand her reasoning in life. Just about everything she said to me made sense. I wasn't trying to hear all of that noise from any other woman. Hell, I'm a man. Before Holiday my mother was the only woman who could just totally have my attention. For the most part, all I'd meet were the chicken heads and gold diggers anyway. And, who could replace my mother? No one. At least not in my eyes.

Momma passed from diabetes when I was just seven-years-old. Although the counselors kept telling me it wasn't my fault, Dad made sure I knew it was. My mother never suffered from the disease until she became pregnant with me. For several long, agonizing years after my birth, Momma stayed strong and endured the sugar attacks before her body finally succumbed. The only thing I knew to do during that last episode was call for help. When my father made it home, he only had enough time to see the paramedics lift Momma's lifeless body, which had become locked in a fetal position, stiffened by all of her pain. Once the EMTs had placed her onto the gurney, I stepped over to have a peek at her. I couldn't understand she was actually dead. Her face remained in a painstaking frown. The tears she'd shed were dried up, leaving long ashy-brown streams on her cheeks. This is my last memory of Momma because I couldn't bring myself to hover over her coffin at the funeral. Instead, I sat in the pew with my arms folded and chin buried deep in my chest. Even with my eyes squeezed shut, the heap of tears managed to pry through them and soaked onto what I had considered at the time to be my best Sunday shirt and tie.

For years, on the anniversary of Momma's death, I had to listen to my father tell me that if Momma hadn't talked him into having a child, she'd still be alive. He was satisfied with only having my half-sister, Sharonda, in their lives. Dad says he never meant to get Sharonda's mother pregnant—especially since she was someone he could never respect anyway. I'm not sure why. But in spite of those feelings, he did take care of my big sister.

I came to learn that Momma had been envious of the relationship between Dad and Sharonda, so she talked him into allowing her to offer him that same bond with a child she bore for him. The illness started shortly after finding out she was pregnant and never went away. Neither did my father's ill feelings toward my mother's death.

Dad said there would never be another woman to take Momma's place, and he meant it. Every woman he'd bring home was purely for his sexual satisfaction. He'd tell them they meant something to him, but he didn't treat them that way. After I started dating, he made sure he drilled into my head that there wasn't any woman out there like my momma. I figured why waste my time on falling in love with anyone?

Once I got into high school, a brotha was cut in all the right places, had that naturally wavy hair all the girls liked, and kept a good-paying job, too. At lunchtime, girls would surround my table, offering me their lunch money. At first it was cool, but then it got old. I had my own money. I couldn't understand why that didn't register in their minds. All I wanted was to eat my lunch and rap with my homeys for that thirty-minute interval, but those girls made it extremely difficult.

The rest of my life continued to go a little something just like that. Women continued to make me feel like the cream of the crop. Years and years of that kind of shit only convinced me it must be true. Hell, these women took just about anything I'd pull on them, just because I'm a good-looking brotha with some education and a little change in my pocket. The cars I drove and the clothes I wore spoke for my wallet size. Some women can't seem to look past that kind of shit, and for a woman to offer me what I want, how I want it, and when I want it, that's a lot of pressure for a man like me—high natured with a good sex drive.

Getting out of college and landing a serious position at New Vet Life Insurance had no significant effect on my attitude toward life. The women behaved the same as anywhere else I'd worked, and as long as they were giving, I was a willing recipient. I came to expect it from all the ladies, but working with Holiday Simmons presented a different challenge.

Holiday is a classy black lady with all of her priorities in the right order. She was the only woman in the office who didn't seem to have the same attraction for me as the others. I really don't believe it was anything like the fact that I'm not her type, because my boy Lance would get sweated by almost every woman in the office, too. He's the total opposite in height and build with a medium-brown complexion and wore a goatee that the ladies loved, but Holiday wouldn't look at him twice either.

I'd come on to her, and she'd give me that "nigga, please" look, twisting her mouth and tilting her head. Something about that stubbornness kept me coming back, though. Sure, I knew she was a good girl and a classy lady—a whole 'nother breed from what I'd been use to dealing—but deep down, Holiday was the kind of woman with whom I really wished to someday settle. I didn't try to pressure her too much, but I think I used a detrimental approach to gaining her attention by becoming too personal with her. Since we had to work so closely, I would share my experiences about women with her. I told her how I hadn't had any complaints in the bedroom. Then, I told her how I had this woman and that one craving me in the late-night hours and exactly what they'd do for it. She absorbed all of this for a couple of years before finally letting me know she'd never have a man like me. We were in the privacy of her office, but her words still embarrassed me.

"What do you mean you'll never have a man like me?" I had asked, outraged at her thoughts.

"I didn't stutter. Can you understand plain English?" Holiday had said sternly.

"Holiday, I'm a good-looking brotha, highly educated, and it doesn't hurt that I have a little bit of change in my pocket. What's the problem?"

"Am I supposed to be impressed?"

She had clearly scratched my ego—twice. I chose not to answer her because I really didn't know how. She continued, "Yeah, you've got all that going on for you, but I look at how you view women. If a man can't respect a woman like he'd respect his mother—and it's obvious you can't—then he's not in my league."

"Ouch, boo, that hurts."

"Boo? My name is Holiday. Don't you forget it." She had locked eyes with me, and she didn't blink.

"Now see, you'll let my man Lance call you baby girl. What's wrong with me giving you a pet name?"

" 'Cause that's exactly what boo is, a pet name. I'm not a dog or a cat. And coming from a player like you, it never feels like a compliment," she'd said, folding her arms.

Holiday was working on scratching my ego for the third time, so I tried to soften things after she had finished explaining. "I'm sorry, Holiday, but the truth is I only mean it as a compliment when I call you boo."

"Then how about waiting until you do something to give me a newfound respect for you before attempting to call me that again?"

Oh yeah, she done it! She definitely touched my ego for the third time. Except then she didn't just scratch it, she put a big gash in the muthafucker. I couldn't let her know it, though. That would be against all the principles and rules of a playa.

"A'ight, Holiday. No doubt I'll do that. It is okay to call you Holiday, isn't it? Or should I call you Ms. Simmons?"

She'd looked up at me again while continuing to organize the paperwork on her desk and said, "Just Holiday will do fine." Again, she didn't blink.

I didn't know what kind of man Holiday was messing around with at the time, but I really didn't care. All I know is that she had some ways on her that could really blow my mind. I hadn't met anyone like her before, and her attitude was so refreshing.

Holiday had to leave New Vet Life because the company wasn't promoting her. I didn't want to see her go, but the fact that she stood her ground and moved on was just another example of her cleverness and motivation with keeping her priorities straight. It was a big turn-on for me. My best friend, Lance, was equally as impressed with Holiday.

I decided not to tell Lance how much I was attracted to Holiday in the beginning. To Lance, all I've ever been is a playa, which was exactly what I wanted him to think. I've never allowed my homeys to see any other side of me. The soft-hearted men I know come off like punks, but my boys with all the game, I can give them the utmost respect. My father was a playa before and after Momma's death, and people still viewed him as a sharp man. He'd spend a little money on women, but not much. Hell, it's gotta be the reason why he's sittin' on overload in his bank account now, and why he hasn't had his heart broken before. It's because he didn't waste time with relationships and caring too much for women. This was one of the wisest things I've ever observed from my father. Dad always said if I were more like him, I'd be a better man. It doesn't matter now. I'd love Holiday ten-thousand times over again, except now I guess our love will have to wait.

Chapter Two

Every Day Lessons

Holiday shouldn't have denied my love. After our break up, I couldn't deal with not having her by my side anymore. I knew her every move because I'd become obsessed with getting her back. After Holiday moved Lance, a man I once deemed as my best friend, into her home, I became extremely hostile. I set forth with my plan to cause them both harm.

Days had gone by, and then I was there—at Holiday's house to carry out my scheme. Things went far different than I had expected. Lance was more of a fighter than I had originally thought he'd be. Though I came at the two of them blasting gunfire from the start, Lance shot back, nonstop, in order to protect Holiday. The three of us ended up in the hospital with severe injuries, but I came back with a vengeance.

I managed to scheme all the way to the fifth floor of the hospital, where I'd learned Holiday's room was located. As I stood in the doorway, her back was turned to me. I paused a moment to reflect on our happier times and the events that had led us on the brink of death. I could clearly remember the day Holiday went out with Lance and me for the first time and how cozy we all came to be. The memories hit me like flashbacks, except many of the thoughts lingered as if I were watching a long, drawn out movie.

I remembered I had called Holiday to see if she would let Lance and me take her out to celebrate her career enhancement. She had been at the new company for several months by then, but for some reason she kept avoiding my requests to take her out. I missed her, and just because she was working for a new firm didn't mean we couldn't remain close. I couldn't tell what was going through her head, but I just couldn't give up on trying.

After Lance and I finally convinced Holiday to join us for a night out, we hung up the three-way phone conversation and I called Lance back.

"Lance, what's going on, man? Do you think she'll call us back to cancel again?" I asked.

"Naw. I think she's for real on this one. Something's telling me she'll actually go through with her promise this time."

"I wonder what's got her so stubborn. You think she's fucking anybody? Usually when a woman is tough like that, it's because she needs some dick in her life." The fact that Holiday could downplay a couple of good-looking guys like Lance and me made me wonder what was up with her.

"Oh, I wouldn't know if she's seeing anybody right now, but I do know she's been through hell and high water with her past relationships. She even sounds a little bitter at times when we've talked about her experiences."

"Well what she gon' do? Take it out on the rest of us brothas? She needs to let the past be the past. I hate to sound insensitive, but what the last man got to do with me?"

"The last man ain't got jack to do with you or me, Roman,

but of course, I've never come on to her before. She probably only knows I find her attractive, and that's all."

"So would you ever have a woman like Holiday?" I was trying to see what was going through my boy's head.

"Oh yeah. The sista's got it going on, but what you have to
remember is that Holiday knows too much about our personal affairs. We've told all of our business to her for years.
And for that reason, she ain't going there with either one of
us."

"What the fuck you talking 'bout she ain't going there?
Where is she supposed to be going?"

"On a roller-coaster. You know full well like I do that after
knowing what she does about us, she'll never have an interest in either of us."

I wondered who the hell Lance thought he was to tell me
I could never get a woman like Holiday. He must've forgotten for a brief moment who I am. I'm Roman Broxton. I
ain't known a woman unattainable for me. Lance knew this.
We'd been friends for a little more than four years, ever
since coming to the company for training at the same time.
Lance knew me better than my own father. I just couldn't understand how he could forget the fact that I've gotten every
woman I've ever wanted. I didn't stay with any of them for
long, but this was the way I had intended for things to be.
Holiday was a little bit more difficult to reach than other
women I'd come across, but to say she was unattainable only
made me more dogged about getting her.

As for that roller-coaster shit, I never tried to tell any
woman how she should feel. They all knew in advance that
the possibility of being with me for an extended period was
slim. I never hid the fact that I didn't want a relationship. I
made sure I let every one of them know what type of man I
am and whether I was seeing someone else. If they were will-

ing to deal with that, then they could hang with me. If not, then oh well. It was only their loss.

I didn't waste any time going to the barbershop to prepare for my first night out with Holiday. Looking my best was important. She hadn't seen me in several months, and I felt I needed to make a lasting impression on her. After all, I was determined to make her go back on her word of not ever being my lady.

After getting groomed, I sat around the shop and rapped with Lance and some of my old college buddies. Several years before, I had introduced Lance to my barber, Mr. Charles Brown. He is an older and wiser brotha than the rest of us. Mr. Brown had us all sitting around listening to some of his stories of how things use to be when he was growing up. Even once we'd gotten out of his chair, me and my homeys—Carlos Wright, Anthony Stewart, and Lance—remained to listen until the last one of us had been cleaned up.

"Mr. Brown, you tryna tell me that you use to rake *and* bag the leaves from your neighbor's lawns for just twenty-five cents a bag, and I'm supposed to believe that?" Ant asked, frowning in disbelief.

Mr. Brown was in the middle of shaping up Carlos's fade. He cut off his clippers and began to shake and wave them at Ant as he responded, "Son, I was ten years old. Let's see, then the year must've been around 1959. None of you cats were even thought of then, let alone being born. I wonder how you can even make that doubtful face. You ain't ever been on my level to be able to tell me what's really going on, as you cats say."

The barbershop rang like there was an all-male chorus holding out on a whole note, all in unison. We responded,

"Oooooh!" Ant, a six-foot-four, former college basketball player stretched out his legs in the chair he was sitting in then threw his head back and shook it in disagreement. We all sort of chuckled until Anthony could come up with a response.

"Mr. Brown, I respect you and everything, but there's no way you can fairly say I ain't ever been on your level. I have an associate's degree in business and a bachelor's degree in psychology. From what I understand, all you have is a piece of paper that licenses you to cut hair. Sounds like to me you ain't ever been on my level."

The barbershop rang out once again with another tune from our unintentional male chorus, but this time, we couldn't help whispering about the fact that things were getting heated. Mr. Brown took about another five seconds to finish up Carlos's fade then he cut off his clippers. Indefinitely. He asked Carlos to sit in one of the seats in the waiting area then walked around to the front of the barber's chair and sat. He locked eyes with Ant, and then brief whispering began just before Mr. Brown opened his mouth to speak. We knew Mr. Brown was about school us. I shushed everyone, trying to get complete silence because I didn't want to miss a word.

"Son, pay close attention. I'm only gonna teach you this once." Mr. Brown paused, and then spoke up again. "In 1959, the cost of living wasn't even a fraction of what it is today. I had eleven dedicated neighbors who would allow me to service their lawns every week. These yards were approximately twenty-by-fifteen feet, which means I could expect to stuff at least four fifteen-gallon bags for each lawn every time. I hope you listening 'cause I said *every time*—that's once a week, eleven clients, and four bags per lawn at twenty-five cents a bag. Now, I see some of y'all scrambling your brains tryna figure it out, so I'll gone and tell ya that I made a minimum of eleven dollars a week. That's forty-four dollars a month promised to me. My momma's rent was $112 a month for our two-bedroom shotgun house. This meant that four times that year, I could pay the rent for Momma and still have twenty dollars to add to my savings. At the end of the year, I had a total of eighty dollars to do whatever I wanted. Do you have any idea of what eighty dollars could get you in 1959, son? Huh? Do you?"

Anthony just stared at Mr. Brown. The whole room remained silent. Mr. Brown continued on with this life lesson. "Well, I haven't been as fortunate as you to be able to go to college, and as a matter of fact, I know plenty of people who haven't had that same blessing, but in this case, this is when you learn to use what you got. Now, don't stop listening yet 'cause I ain't finished teaching you." This time, no one whispered. Instead, we only drew in closer to Mr. Brown. "Ten years old with eighty dollars, you'd think I'd blow it on junk, but I didn't. I learned that this was what a little hard work could get ya, so I continued with the same path. As the years went by, economy changed, and I was soon able to increase the cost of my labor as well as pick up more paying clients. In 1969, I was twenty years old and still unable to attend college due to lack of funds, and I refused to quit helping my mother out financially. I dipped into my savings and enrolled in a local barber school. After getting my license, I took it over on Jackson Avenue to a white male's house, along with the rest of my savings—$7,369. This man was about forty years old. Said he needed to move to another city by the end of the month. I gave him every penny of my life savings. By the time I left his house, I had the keys and the title to the building you all are sitting in today. So don't tell me that just 'cause you done went and got that piece of paper you like to call a degree that you better than me."

The male chorus rang out once again. Someone even yelled, "Go 'head, Mr. Brown. That's telling 'im."

I have to admit I was pretty proud of the way Mr. Brown had explained things, too. I didn't want to add to my boy's shame, so I just smiled and nodded at Mr. Brown when Ant wasn't looking.

"Well, are you trying to say that a good education doesn't matter since you can make the same salary I do without any degrees?" Anthony questioned.

"No. You doubted the fact that I'd serviced my neighbors' lawns for so little money. I merely tried to show you it did make sense. I wasn't sure what type of education you had before you told me. Had I known, I would've assumed in the time spent getting those two degrees someone would've taught you how to do your math. But, I can see they didn't."

Mr. Brown tore Ant up. I almost felt sorry for my boy. It must've been hard faking embarrassment. He tried to act as though Mr. Brown hadn't said anything, but I caught him in a daze every once in a while until we had left the shop.

I had no words to ease Ant of his shame. I was busy thinking of how I planned to impress Holiday later. The challenge was about to be on.

Chapter Three

Boys Will Be Boys

Lance and I had settled on where to take Holiday for the evening. We'd decided that going to Precious Cargo, a neo-soul spoken word spot, would be great. Although it was an August evening, the nights downtown near the Mississippi River tend to get a little on the chilly side. Lance and I knew to wear pullover sweaters and khakis in order to remain comfortable between the rise and fall of the weather temperature. I wasn't sure of what this place was like, but at least with this type of gear, I knew I wouldn't be dressed too far off from the rest of the crowd. I laid out my black, long-sleeve pullover and my black khaki pants. The sistahs seemed to love it when I showcased my ability to wear a dark color on top of my Nubian black skin and made it look good. I usually wouldn't buy clothes unless they look like they were made exclusively for me. That's how everything I wore managed to be so damn trendy.

Excited about the three of us getting together for the night, I swung by Lance's place to pick him up thirty minutes early. This was fine, though. Lance has always been the type of brotha who wouldn't get stressed out about too much. He has that lackadaisical attitude about things that normally work the best nerves of most people. I don't know how he does it. Kinda made me feel as though I needed some type of stress-management course or something.

Lance was dressed in a cream pullover that flaunted the fact that he routinely works out. The navy khakis he wore were definitely my style. I have to admit, Lance threw together a nice wardrobe. Sometimes he and I would sit around and compare our taste in clothes. Our careers, fashion style, and a love for cars are just a few of the things we have in common. We could sit around and talk about cars all night. We couldn't see eye to eye on how to treat the ladies, but it was our right to differ. Lance is a little too soft with the women if you ask me, where as, I'm bar none.

We made it on time to pick up Holiday for our date. She knew I was driving, and based on past lunch experiences, she was probably expecting me to be late, but I surprised her. She opened the door, and I was flabbergasted. I knew she was fine, but I had no idea she was stacked like that. I looked over at Lance and discovered him wide-eyed and mostly teeth in the face. My man had definitely unmasked his attraction for Holiday with that look. I, on the other hand, played it off by flashing a much simpler and brief smile as I stepped into her house.

Holiday had on a black dress that aroused my wildest imaginations. If only she knew what I was thinking. I don't know why she chose to wear such a sleek little dress, but I was certainly proud to have her join Lance and me for a night out. I found out later that Lance felt the same way. We just didn't have a moment to discuss it then.

Holiday got on stage at Precious Cargo to showcase her talent with the spoken word. The crowd gave her a standing ovation. After that, Lance and I had so much more respect for her. I realized that there was more to the woman inside Holiday Simmons that I should get to know. I yearned to be a part of whatever it was that made her glow. I imagine she thought it was strange, but I called her every day after that night out. During those chats, I learned more of what there is to love about Holiday. I admired the fact that she could teach me about me, even though I often got mad at what she had to say. I remember a conversation starting out descent then suddenly turning ugly as we spoke on the phone.

"Roman, you don't understand. You think that your days should be filled with getting what you want, when you want it, and how you want it, but I say there are certain phases of existence that requires you to live on life's terms. And then, there are aspects that you have to make your own, like demanding respect. If I ask you to give me proper regard, you may, but if I tell you that you will respect me if you plan on hanging around for long, you will. There's the difference."

I huffed deeply into the phone. "Dang, Holiday. You talk like I just set out to pick the heart I'm gonna break each day. I've never hidden who I am to any of these women. They know that at any given moment, I may decide I don't want to be with them anymore. At least I'm honest. Do I get credit for honesty?"

"Maybe with your boys, but not with me. I'm sure they give you props, but in my mind, you're a sad individual."

"Aw come on now. What makes me sad?"

"The fact that you think you don't need to settle with one woman and love her in the manner that she deserves. I don't know the whole story, but I'm certain your behavior is a sign of some deeper issues."

"Okay, Holiday. That's enough. We're through talking about me, 'cause I'm through listening. Last I remembered you were a senior financial analyst for an insurance company, not a psychologist at Riverside Mental Health Center. Stick with analyzing numbers and dollars. That's where your help is most appreciated."

"Well, since you've put it that way, I will. And until you can learn to appreciate constructive criticism from a friend, don't call me. Good-bye."

Holiday hung up the phone in my face. Initially I was pissed, but after a few moments of reflection, I fell across my couch with crazy laughter. I couldn't believe this woman was able to affect my mood in a caring way. I was actually concerned about what she thought of me. These feelings were so strange, and I dared not tell anyone about them. I felt ashamed that I'd allowed myself to be sensitive since I never had been before. I still believe that somehow shielding my vulnerable side is the reason I've been most respected by my peers.

I waited a couple of days before I phoned Holiday back. Although the urge to call her was nagging me every moment before I actually did, I was proud of my ability to hold out. I apologized and let her know that I treasured her criticism. She helped me to see a true reflection of myself. It wasn't cute, but it was me. I discovered the man in the mirror was the result of many years of the same negative behavior and beliefs of how to treat a woman. Changing overnight is practically impossible, but I knew I would have to do something quick if I were to get Holiday attracted to me. That was my ultimate goal.

A few days after the night Lance and I had taken Holiday out, Lance left a note on my desk, which stated we needed to have a man-to-man talk. I offered to buy him lunch, so we went to one of my favorite spots. It was a topless bar, but Lance didn't seem to mind.

"Hold up, man. You mean to tell me this is your everyday lunch spot?" Lance shook his head in amazement.

"Naw. I only come here when I'm having lunch alone."

Half-naked women were everywhere. This place had blessed my eyes with a rainbow of nationalities. A Cuban woman with long, dark-brown hair, wearing a red laced thong and a pair of thigh-high, black patent leather stiletto boots, served our table for two hours. I could tell Lance wasn't use to this type of action 'cause he scoped the entire room while we talked.

"Damn. This place helps me to better understand why you're so fucked up in the head, Roman."

"Hey, what can I say? I got issues. At least that's what Holiday likes to call it."

"What? She really said that to you?" Lance seemed surprised.

"Yeah, but hey, I'm grown. I know how to let Holiday's shit-talking bounce off me," I said laughing. "I'ma put it to you this way: I ain't got no kids, no mortgage payments, and my car is paid for. That leaves more than enough funds to put in a pussy account."

Lance hollered with laughter. "Aw, yeah. Yo' ass got issues. I'm with Holiday on this one."

I was happy to be sharing one of my favorite joints with my best friend. Though this bar wouldn't be his ideal lunch spot, Lance understood me and respected my decisions. After finishing our meal, I was ready to hear whatever he was about to spit at me.

"So what did you need to rap to me about, man? Come on, talk to me."

"Well, it's about the other night when we took Holiday out." Lance paused to sip his soda.

"Okay. I'm listening." I wondered where he was going with this.

"Man, I feel strange saying this, but I'm really diggin' Holiday."

I swallowed real hard and asked Lance what he meant. "Diggin' how?"

"I'm serious, Roman. I can't seem to think about anyone else but Holiday since the other night. I can't believe that I've let all these years of working with her go by without noticing how wonderful she is."

"Really? I've always known Holiday to be da bomb. But you know me. I ain't ever did anything but flirt with her. I never allow myself to think too hard about her, 'cause that would mean I'd have to give up Trina, Debra, and Michelle. And we all know I'd never do that." I chuckled.

"Seriously, Roman. I'm speaking of more than just her looks. Holiday has got poetry in her heart. That means this woman feels deep. I can tell she knows what love is and how to share it, you know? It's just kind of crazy how things happen. Several years of looking for the right woman, and she's been under my nose all along. Man, I know this woman is for me. Without a doubt."

Lance just about had me speechless. He said so much in so few words. His mind was made up about wanting Holiday in his life, but so was mine, and I couldn't let him know it. I refused to share my innermost feelings about Holiday with Lance. I felt he wouldn't understand. He'd seen me at my worst with women, and I felt Lance would never believe that I could be a good man to Holiday. I sat and talked with him a little longer then we headed to work. On the drive, I tried to get into my boy's head.

"So what do you think you're gonna do about these new-found feelings for Holiday?" I asked sarcastically, trying to mask my true concern.

"I don't know yet. I've been thinking that now isn't the time to tell her though. I'd like to take her out a few more times at least before popping it on her."

"I feel ya. Maybe in that time she'll develop feelings for

you, too." I didn't mean those words. I just thought quickly, trying to keep Lance from sniffing me out.

"Oh, I doubt she'll even be thinking about me in that way. You know how Holiday is, man. She's tough as Plexiglas. Unbreakable. She'll probably never speak to me again once I tell her about my feelings."

"Naw, man. She ain't that tough. I mean, you're a good guy, and she knows it. Who knows, someday you may even make her Mrs. Lance Ferrell." It hurt me to even think it, let alone say it.

I realized that I needed to come up with something to deter Lance from being with Holiday. What—I didn't know. I only knew that I would be miserable if I allowed Lance get to my woman first.

Out of all the friends I've ever had, Lance is the coolest. Cool, because we could be so different in a lot of our thought processes, never agree to disagree, and could allow each other to be who we are in the presence of the other. Lance shook his head at my ideal lunch spot, but he didn't shun me either. I never cared for his humbleness with women, but I could see it worked for him. The only thing I'd been sure that we had in common when it came to a woman was not capturing Holiday's attention—until the day Lance decided to spring the news of his admiration for her.

Lance had never come on to Holiday before. After carefully thinking about it, I began to wonder if Holiday would turn Lance down as she had done me in the past. The anxiety was killing me. I knew I had to dampen Lance's plan to be with Holiday immediately.

Chapter Four

If Your Status Ain't Hood

I had a tough time thinking through dealing with the Lance-Holiday situation on my own. I went back to the topless bar and asked my boy, Anthony Stewart, to meet me. Our college clique all liked to call Anthony, Ant. It was our way of teasing him about of his height. We figured Ant would be better than what we use to call him, which was Shorty. Unlike the label Sphinx, which my boys had given me on account of my skin being so dark, Anthony had been spared some embarrassment. I hate to even repeat my nickname. It's sort of degrading when I really think about it, but then again, the sphinxes I've seen represent power. And, at least the guys would only refer to me by that name when just us guys were around.

The bar had just as much excitement going on as it did when Lance and I met there. Ant kept peeling off the ones and five-dollar bills to the dancers as we talked. I shared more of my feelings than I planned to with him. He couldn't believe his ears.

"Come on now, Sphinx. I think you giving me a little bit too much information. Why you didn't choose to share this with Carlos? Huh? You should've taken this to Los, man. I'm not sure I want to help you with this one." I didn't realize Ant wouldn't be too thrilled about me coming to him with my feelings.

"I can't talk to Carlos 'cause you know how he can be. Man, Los will start preaching on me. He'll bring up the Bible by book, chapter, and verse. I ain't tryna hear all that right now. I just want to talk to someone who could possibly feel me."

Ant sighed. "And you thought that someone would be me, huh?"

"Well, if you can't feel me, just try to put yourself in my shoes. Imagine it was you in this predicament. How would you handle it?"

"You know what, Sphinx. Didn't you say that this girl was a good person?"

"Yeah, so and what?"

"Then, you ain't the cat for her. Man, let Lance go for it. That's what's wrong with all our sistahs now. No-good-ass men like you wanna go and fuck with their minds."

"Oh and you ain't one of them no-good-ass men?"

"Hell yeah. But I don't go looking for the good girls. I stay in that other territory with the women who just looking for enjoyment instead of commitment. Them two different kinds of 'ments' right there, boy. One starts with an 'e' and the other with a 'c'. Don't get 'em confused." Ant reached to stick a dollar bill on the side of a dancer's thong once he finished speaking.

The dancer turned to look at me, and I beckoned for her. I gave her a wink and a smile. "Yeah. I guess you're right about that, Ant. Lawd, you gotta be right." I motioned for the woman to turn and bend over then I placed a five-dollar bill between her butt cheeks.

The conversation about Lance and Holiday ended then.

Tryna take my mind off the situation, I focused more on my surroundings: Beautiful women to my left, beautiful women to my right. There were even more gorgeous women to the north and south of me. I ordered another round of bourbon and Coke for both Ant and me. We didn't leave until our pockets were left with only traces of lint. I had a couple of credit cards in my wallet, but this wasn't the type of establishment in which I wanted to use them. I had gotten so drunk that I was leery about driving home, so I asked Ant to drop me off.

Trina, a late-night booty call, came over and spent the night. I liked dealing with Trina because she seemed to want the same thing I did: sex. She didn't ask for more than that, but she was very demanding when it came to satisfying her heat. She kept an attitude of whenever she calls, I better answer. Pleasing her came easy for me, but I never tried to offer her more than the dick. I got Trina to take me to pick up my car the next morning. We said our good-byes, and that was that. Trina was simply an easy fuck, and then she'd go about her way until we met again—usually within a week or two.

Despite my good time with Trina the night before, Holiday weighed heavy on my mind. Ant's advice only made me wish I hadn't told him. The next day at work, the thought of Lance and Holiday being a couple resurfaced, and I was determined not to let it happen. Every time I glanced over at Lance, I wanted to go over and tell him what I was feeling. But pride is a mutherfucker. I just couldn't do it.

Holiday had a friend of many years that she wanted Lance and me to meet, so we took her up on that offer. I was very curious what this woman looked like. It was just my nature. I also had hoped that just perhaps she could take my mind off Holiday a bit. After all, whether Lance could do right by

Holiday or not wasn't questionable. Whether I could remained to be seen.

Holiday's only female associate in Memphis is Erika Peebles. I had no idea that this woman would be so fine. She had everything I liked in a woman's physical appearance. Erika is a very classy and stylish woman, too. She wears the finest rags and could look at anyone and tell what brand name they're wearing and where they had purchased it. Erika even peeped out my Movado watch while standing at a distance. I knew then that this woman had a different frame of mind than Holiday, and she owned all the vain characteristics as the women I've dated in the past. Although Erika is a beautiful woman, something about her didn't draw me in. I think it was the fact that our personalities were so similar. Erika knew she was the shit, and no one could tell me that I didn't have it going on either.

Erika was being flirtatious, and at times it was to the extreme. Usually I'd take a woman up on her passes, but that day, I wasn't in the mood. I did remain polite, as she demanded I talk with her. I even pulled her to the dance floor once we were in Club Raina's.

"Are you gonna dance or watch Holiday and Lance all night?" she asked, turning her backside to me as she began to rump shake.

I grabbed her around her waist and let her booty gyrate against my body. "Girl, what are you talking about? I'm about to make you sweat." I laughed.

"Well, come on. It's about time," she stated.

It had become very obvious to both Lance and me that Erika wanted some attention. I ain't gon' lie. I tried. Damn, I tried hard to be into Erika. But that Holiday Simmons had one of those magical glows on her again, and just seeing my boy Lance trying to woo her made me ill. The whole night felt like a competition type thing between Lance and me. I didn't mean to dis' Erika, but the only thing I had on my mind was not letting Lance have his way with Holiday. I was suspenseful of whether he would tell her about his hopes for her.

Our partying at the club was ruined when some jerk tried to scare Holiday by cussing at her after she asked him to give up the seats we'd left. I walked back to our table just moments after Holiday and Erika, so I didn't hear the entire argument, but I heard enough. I completely lost control.

"What did you say to her?" I asked the man as I approached the table. "Nigga, you done lost yo' mind. I will bust yo' ass. You don't talk to her like that."

The man tried to act bad. "Man, y'all been gone a long time. How you gon' be gone all that time and don't expect somebody to sit here?" he said angrily.

"The same way I expect that this is a mutherfucking restaurant and club and people are going to eat, get up and dance, come back, sit back down for a break, and then get up and dance some more." I was up to my limit with this guy.

"Man, all I'm sayin' is—" he started before I interrupted.

"Man, I'm not getting ready to debate this shit with you. Number one, you wrong 'cause you disrespected my girl. The table is secondary right now. I'm about to get into yo' shit about having the wrong attitude. Fuck the table."

I leaped across the table in a single bound like Superman. The man didn't have time to prepare for what was coming. Once I started punching, there was no stopping. Lance was a brave soul to come between me and the man as I threw blow after blow. I almost wanted to kick Lance's ass for pulling me out of the fight, but I could tell that Lance was equally as upset as me.

"I oughta let him beat the shit out of you for being such an asshole to a lady," Lance said over my shoulder to the man. He was still gripping me under the arms from behind. "If I didn't think we'd go to jail tonight, I'd join in and give you a double dose of whup-ass."

I was furious, and I could tell Lance understood my anger. Security even kept a distance from me as they escorted all of us out of the club. Once we were in the car, I had a notion that the ladies might've been embarrassed at my actions. I begged their pardon.

"Before you crank up, Lance, I need to take this time to apologize for getting so angry and getting us kicked out of the place. I hope you guys understand why I got so upset. Holiday, you're my girl. I got your back on whatever. He disrespected you, and I couldn't handle that. I apologize that everyone had to see such a terrible side of me. Erika, I hope this doesn't shatter your image of me either. I don't have a bad temper or anything. I just couldn't take hearing that asshole talk to Holiday that way. I hope you'll forgive me and still go out with me again."

Erika sort of put on a half grin and replied, "We're all okay, and nobody got hurt. That's the important thing. We all have our limits, and it's unfortunate sometimes when we get pushed in places or among people who we wouldn't want to see that side of us. I totally understand, Roman."

"Thanks, Erika," I said then turned to Holiday. "Boo, do you forgive me, too?" I gave Holiday my playful puppy-dog eyes.

"There's nothing to forgive. You stuck up for me; therefore, I need to say thank you. Thank you, Roman."

That's all I need to hear. I was ready to ride. After discussing it, we all decided to head over to Holiday's for an extended night of fun.

Chapter Five

The Early Bird Catches the Worm

Once over to Holiday's, we fixed drinks then had a wonderful time talking and singing the songs K97 played during late-night backtrack hours. We all had a slight buzz from the alcohol, and it seemed as if everything we said was funny. I kept my eye on Holiday the entire time because she was even more gorgeous when she laughed. When she'd open her mouth to speak, my undivided attention belonged to her.

"Roman, I saw you trying to keep up with Erika on the dance floor. You moved like an old man wearing orthopedic shoes. Every now and then, you'd bring one foot up, and then take it back down real slow." We all wailed with laughter as she continued. "I kept wondering when that foot was gonna catch up to the music."

"Aw, get off me now. Lance wasn't all that on the dance floor either," I said. "You had my man looking like somebody had fast-forward and rewound him while he was still in play mode. His legs and feet were kicking so fast, I thought he was having some kind of attack." I fell to the floor with laugher.

It was a good thing Holiday lived in a house rather than

an apartment because we were so loud that the next day would've surely brought an eviction notice. We all took turns scolding each other and hurting ourselves with crazy laughter. Soon we were tired and began to wrap the night up. Erika let everyone know she was about to leave.

"Y'all, it's been a real good night, but I think I better head home. You know I've got some distance to drive ahead of me," Erika stated.

"Oh, Erika, don't go. Stay here tonight. It's too late for you to leave, and you've been drinking," Holiday warned her.

"Girl, I'm fine now. I had my last drink about two hours ago."

"Erika, are you sure?" Holiday asked, looking concerned.

"Yes. Lance, tell her I had the least to drink between all of us."

"I don't know about that, Erika. I thought I had the least to drink, but I'd be more than willing to follow you home— make certain you're safe," Lance said.

"Are you sure, Lance? I live in the Raleigh area," Erika pointed out.

"That's fine, Erika. It's better to have me trail you than to be sorry later."

"A'ight. I'm ready if you are."

"Come on, Roman. I'll drop you off after we make sure Erika gets home safely," Lance stated.

Holiday butted in with a surprising offer. "No, Lance. That will be too out of the way for you. Just be sure that Erika gets home safely, and Roman, you can stay here 'til morning. I'll take you home as soon as daylight hits."

Lance stood silent, looking as if he wished the offer to stay had been made to him rather than me. I didn't argue. "Well, then it's settled. Lance, be safe. I'll talk to you when I get to my house."

Holiday changed the music and left me in the living room while she showered. I took it upon myself to have a look around. I noticed Holiday's great sense of style. She used exquisite African artwork as her inspiration for the colorscheme in the living room. A picture sitting on the sofa table caught my eye, so I stepped closer to have a look. It was Holiday and a woman I didn't recognize. They looked somewhat alike, but Holiday had never mentioned having any siblings.

I also spotted a picture of Holiday and her little girl, Crystal, who was away with relatives for the weekend. She looked everything like Holiday. Everyone on the job use to tease Crystal by calling her Holiday Jr. Crystal didn't seem to mind it much. She'd smile and look for her mother to say something. Holiday would always reply, "That's right. She's my baby." Crystal would blush every time.

Holiday owned a massive CD collection. She loved just about everything relating to music. Jazz, R&B, rock, classical, you name it, she owned it. In listening to Holiday talk about her love for different types of music, I could tell she understood the language for them all. She even had movie soundtracks. She'd put the *Waiting to Exhale* CD in before going to take a shower.

After Holiday came out of the bathroom, I showered and returned in a pair of her big sweatpants and a t-shirt she'd offered me. Holiday and I decided to sit and talk some more.

"Roman, if you're uncomfortable, I can loan you a pair of my drawers. You'd have to return them before you leave though," she said, laughing.

"Woman, are you crazy? I'm not puttin' no panties on. What would I look like?"

Holiday continued to make fun of me. "You'd probably look cuter than me in 'em."

"Unh-unh, lady. That's enough of those kind of jokes. I ain't puttin' no panties on, and that's final."

"Oh, hush. I wouldn't let your crusty behind put on my undies anyway. I know you can take a joke."

"Not when it's in reference to me wearing your bloomers. No, I can't."

"Uh, for your information, I don't wear bloomers."

"Then what do you wear?"

"Nunya. I'm sure you'd like to know, but I'll never tell."

We continued to enjoy each other's company as Aretha Franklin's "It Hurts Like Hell" began to play. I asked Holiday to dance with me, and she did. It felt so right just holding her close. She began talking softly in my ear. I almost missed what she was saying because my mind had begun to sink into her mesmerizing scent, the smoothness of her silky skin, and the softness of her breasts against my chest.

I decided to share my intimate thoughts of a relationship with her. I knew that Lance would be hurt, but it would pain me more to lose possibly the only woman who could change my life for the better.

"I like the way I'm feeling right now, Holiday," I stated, gazing into her eyes.

"You what?" She seemed confused.

"It feels good to hold you. I love being this close with you. You and I are on a personal level right now, and I'd like very much for us to keep it personal from now on."

"What are you saying, Roman?" Holiday looked stunned.

"I'm saying that I'm very much into you, Holiday. I know you can feel that. I want to be a part of your world. I want to experience a life with you."

"Roman, now I know for sure that you're buzzing. Did I make the career man's drink too strong or something?" Holiday responded, teasing me about my choice drink, bourbon and Coke.

"Holiday, I may be buzzing, but it has nothing to do with the fact that I want some Holiday in my life. This past week, I've grown closer to you, and I feel like I know you on a different level, and I'm really into it. Hell, surprised me, too. But it's a feeling that I can't shake. I only thought I wanted to be a player, but, since we've started having these long, in-depth conversations every day, I've realized that I want something different now. This life policy of yours that we discussed earlier this week, about giving love only to get loved, that's what I want to share with you."

"Roman, I can't. I've just been through too much over the years. I can't commit to a relationship with anyone. I'm just not ready. Although we've been talking every day lately, there's still so much that I feel I don't know about you."

"Shit, that's easy. What do you want to know?"

"You don't talk about your mother. All I ever hear is how much you love your father. Why? Where is your mother?"

"She passed away when I was seven years old. My father never wanted to keep one woman long enough to make her a mother to me. What else you want to know?"

"My life isn't as simple as you think. Besides, how do we know we can trust each other? We don't know that yet, so let's just remain friends for the time being."

"So what happened to your life policy?" I asked.

She allowed me to hold her hands, touch her face, and even caress her back as we talked. She wasn't changing her mind though.

I could've dwelled in that moment forever. Being alone with Holiday, under dim-lighting, slow dancing, and running my fingers through her beautiful hair, made me feel so necessary. Her body language suggested she needed me. She wouldn't stop me from stroking her hair, and for as long as I gazed into her eyes, she was just as attentive to me. She listened to whatever my heart would allow me to say without judging me. I soon slipped her a passionate kiss, and she accepted.

This was my opportunity to show Holiday how much I appreciated her as a woman. I caressed her body, slowly laying her back onto the couch, and sensually spreading her legs apart. I rubbed her gently, then kissed my way to taste the sweet nectar between her thighs. She gasped and moaned at first impact of my tongue. Her body shivered.

"Rome, stop," she said, in the sexiest voice.

Holiday had referred to me as Rome before, and I loved the way she made my name sound.

"No, not Rome, stop. Just Rome. Call me Rome, baby," I said and then buried my face once again.

"Rome. Rome." Holiday moaned.

Holiday said my name just the way I like to hear it over and over. I knew I had her in ecstasy once she screamed, "Oooooh, Roooome," but I still wouldn't let up until she let out an unmistakable sigh that confirmed she had reached the ultimate climax.

"How do you feel? Did you like that? 'Cause that's the way I'd like to hear you call my name every time. Come on, let's go in the bedroom and finish what we've started," Is said once she came down from her high.

"Hold on, Rome. Do you have any condoms?" she asked.

"Of course I do."

"Then, I'm ready if you promise to be gentle. It's been a very long time."

"I promise, Holiday. I'll be as gentle as you need me to be. All I want you to do is remember to say my name how I like it, relax, and enjoy what we're about to share, but wait," I said as she tried to get up. "Don't move. I wanna carry you into the bedroom."

"What? You don't have to do that," Holiday said, looking embarrased.

"I know, but this is about to be more of your night than it is mine."

I picked her up and carried her into the bedroom where I put her down on the bed. This time I took off every stitch of clothing she was wearing and began tasting her juices, which I had caused to flow. This night of passion helped me to better know that Holiday was the woman for me. Too bad for Lance because Holiday was about to be mine.

Chapter Six

A New Roman Holiday

It was Saturday, and Trina, my ex-late-night booty call, had been blowing my cell phone up with calls before daybreak. I had the ringer off so that Holiday and I could share an uninterrupted night. I had also received a few voice mails from Michelle and Donna, more old sexual acquaintances. I expected them to call, so I was one up on all of them when I put my cell on silent mode.

I tried to get dressed and leave quickly but Holiday noticed my phone flashing after Trina called again. I tried desperately to let Holiday know that the call didn't mean anything to me. I brought up the proposal of a relationship once again. I couldn't leave without Holiday understanding that I needed her in my life.

"Holiday, it's not every day when a man meets the woman he feels could possibly be his wife. Yes, I understand that you know my history of playing around and not settling down, but I'm looking you in the eyes now and saying I want you. I'll be good to you, Holiday. I can see you're all I need."

"Rome, I'm just scared. You can't blame me for that, can

you? I know you a little bit too well. I really feel that you
aren't ready to change. Overnight, Rome?"

"Holiday, everything in my heart right now says change.
All the women that I've gone out with lately haven't shown
me anything that said they could've been Mrs. Roman
Broxton. You, on the other hand, have shown me plenty that
says I would be a fool if I let you get away. You're ambitious,
family-oriented, and I just love your inner drive. Give me a
chance, boo. All I want is just one chance. I promise you
won't regret it. You can't know what a love between us can do
if you don't give it a try."

Holiday sighed. "Rome, what are you envisioning when
you think of a life with me?"

"Long-term commitment with you, as well as with Crystal.
Family-oriented activities for the three of us. I see me discovering new and better ways to show you ladies how deeply I
feel for you. I can adhere to all your concerns by doing whatever is necessary to make the situation comfortable for all of
us. Boo, there'll be so much love that it'll result in a lifetime
for us. I just know that I want to share true love with you.
How about that, huh?"

"Rome, it all sounds good, but what about a relationship
with God? Can you see that? Can you see going to church
with me and becoming an active member?"

"Absolutely. I'll start by going this Sunday."

Holiday really threw me off with that going-to-church
stuff, but I answered the way I knew she'd want me to.
Church just wasn't my ideal place for spending time. My
momma use to take me regularly when I was a kid. Even
then, I wasn't into all that clapping and singing, the
preacher hollering every time he tried to make a point, and
listening to people get up and testify about what they say the
Lord has done for them. I felt that if the Lord was all that

good, then why did He allow my momma—a woman who hadn't ever done anything bad to anyone—be so sickly and even die, leaving a seven-year-old child behind? Since my father never took me back to church, I didn't have a desire to learn what people say worship was really all about.

Despite my negative feelings about going to church, I made a pact with Holiday to be the best man she'd ever had, and to love Crystal, too. She finally gave in to my pleas. I went home the happiest man alive, throwing out old hairbrushes that belonged to women and removing pictures of past associates. I wanted to be ready for when Holiday would visit. Finding the belongings of another woman anywhere in my house could definitely ruin things for us. I couldn't let that happen.

My cell began to vibrate on top of the sofa table during my cleaning session. I picked it up, but once I noticed Trina's number, I quickly set it down again and watched as it jolted from one side of the table to the other. I realized the phone was nearing the edge and was about to fall off, but I was stuck in a daze. I thought of how Trina was probably about ready to cuss me out as she had in the past when I didn't answer her call in what she felt like was a timely manner. I continued to stare until my cell paused in a spot just an inch from hitting the floor.

I'd always told Trina she wasn't the one for me. Our bodies became rhythmic and made music every time we lay underneath the covers, but I knew I needed a woman who could stimulate both of my heads rather than just the one in my pants.

I was tempted to answer Trina's call. She really deserved to know things were over between us, but I wasn't in the mood for the attitude I knew she would present. I wanted to be able to tell her we were done with hooking up sexually and make her understand without receiving drama. But, since I knew Trina, ignoring her messages was the best thing to do at the moment.

I turned to walk away but my cell began to pulsate once again. *Trina is not going to give up easily,* I thought. I snatched up my phone before it landed on the floor then answered it without looking at the caller ID.

"Yeah," I screamed.

"Yeah? Yeah? Rome, what's wrong with you? That's no way to answer a call," Holiday said.

"Sorry, boo. I'm in the middle of cleaning, and my phone keeps getting me off track. I had no idea it was you ringing this time."

"Hmmm. I was beginning to think you were trying to say I'm a distraction."

"Never, boo. Please don't feel that way," I responded.

"May I ask who you're straightening up for?"

"You."

"Me?" Holiday sounded shocked.

"Yes, you. Can't have my woman come over to a dirty place, now can I?"

"Well, not if you wanna impress me, but I could've sworn you told me before that you hire a cleaning service from time to time. What happened?"

"Occasionally, I do. But, to be perfectly honest, boo, I'm only throwing out some things."

I decided to be tell Holiday exactly how I felt. I wanted this relationship to be true from day one, so secrets were out of the equation.

"What kind of things, Rome?"

"You're not going to let me beat around the bush, are you?"

"Is there a need to?" she asked.

"No. Actually, I don't mind telling you because I've found

you to be a very understanding lady. I'm throwing away belongings of some friends—women—who mean nothing to
me anymore. Now that I have you, another woman's property has no business in my home."

"Oh, Rome, stop it. I don't know if I should believe you.
Are you serious? Are you really throwing away feminine
products?"

"If you want to put it that way, the answer is yes. Brushes,
combs, pictures . . . none of that stuff belongs here anymore."

"Hey, guess what?" Holiday stated.

"What?"

"I think I'm falling for you, Roman Broxton."

"Holiday Simmons, I fell for you long ago."

After hanging up on such a good note with my boo, I felt
even better and more positive, knowing I was doing the right
thing about ridding myself of old memories. Trina and the
rest of the women in my past had nothing on my boo. All I
wanted was Holiday and the new life we were beginning.
Monogamy was going to be a challenge, but such is life. I
never ran from a challenge, and in my mind, a relationship
with Holiday was a welcomed test. I knew it should be
Holiday and me from then on. I would let nothing stand in
our way.

Chapter Seven

A Day of Discovery

A week passed, and I still hadn't told Lance of my relationship with Holiday. I knew though Holiday wasn't his woman, there would be a problem between us. On the other hand, how could he be angry with me if he had no intimate ties to her? The three of us were good friends, so my closeness with Holiday shouldn't be a shock to anyone, especially Lance. Despite my past, I had every intention on being a good man to Holiday.

Holiday and I invited Lance to have lunch. She didn't know I hadn't told him about us, nor did she know how strongly he felt for her. I wanted badly to tell Lance before the lunch, but I just couldn't fix my mouth to say the words. I feared he'd ruin the closeness Holiday and I had begun to develop by telling her he'd already mentioned his feelings to me. My boo trusted me. Learning that I had ignored Lance's desires for her would definitely change her opinion of me.

We had all began to enjoy our meal. Holiday had that gleam in her eyes that I love so much. It was comforting to know that I had something to do with the reason her eyes danced that day. It had been a few days since I'd last seen her, and we both offered loving eyes glances to each other, until Lance broke the silence.

"Baby girl, what's up?"

"Oh nothing, Lance. Just all work and no play."

"Well, we'll have to see if we can change that, now won't we?" I said, continuing to tease her with my eyes.

"I guess so." She smirked.

"Did something just fly over my head? I *know* I just missed something," Lance pondered.

I cleared my throat. "Oh, Lance, I know we haven't had a whole lot of time to talk, and I've definitely neglected to tell you something. After you left that Friday we all went out, Holiday and I had a lot of time to get personal. A lot of time, if you know what I'm saying."

My man Lance paused and looked stunned. He didn't even speak at first, only stared at me with a look that said he could jack my ass up right then if he wasn't so shocked. Lance set down his glass and coughed as if some water went down the wrong way. After clearing his throat, he paused again before making another move. Finally, Lance glanced at me then Holiday, flashing her a huge smile.

"Of course I know what you mean. Are you guys like a couple now?" Lance asked, sounding as if he was glad to hear the news.

"Yes, we are," Holiday said.

Lance took a few seconds to sip from his glass of water again before responding. "Man, that's great. That is really great. I never would've thought it, but I think it's cool though. Roman, I'm happy for you, man. You've got yourself one hell of a woman. You better be good to her."

"Yes, I know. I have every intention on making her the happiest woman alive."

"Good. I should hope so," Holiday stated, reaching for my hand.

Lance couldn't even look at me anymore. Holiday and I led most of the conversation for the remainder of the lunch. Since we had just shared the news of being a couple, Holiday felt it okay to be cozy in front of him. She slid her chair closer to me and began running her fingers down the back of my neck as we talked. Lance soon got up and excused himself from the table. I knew by the look on his face that he had some shit he wanted to say to me. He did well to hold it back—that is, until I returned to work. Lance pulled me into the conference room to talk.

"Roman, I can't believe you, man. How you gon' go and pull some bullshit like that on me?" Lance's complexion had turned red, and his chest rose and fell as he took in deep breaths trying to calm down.

"Look, man, I know you told me you had a spark for Holiday, but so did I. I mean, what was I supposed to do? Stand back while you got my woman?"

"You were supposed to at least talk about it with me. I'm your boy, right? Since when did you start feeling you couldn't come to me with anything?"

"Come to you for what? I'm a grown-ass man. I don't need your permission to do a damn thing," I yelled.

"What? You mean after all these years of being friends, you never felt the common courtesy or respect to tell me when there's a conflict between us?" Lance asked, stepping closer to me.

"Conflict? There wasn't a conflict about the matter. The only issue was whether the best man would win, and I did," I stated, stepping even closer to Lance.

We stood silently, breathing harder than two bulls after chasing a matador in a bullfight. I waited for Lance to make the first move. His face spoke hatred, and I was sure he'd begin to throw blows within a matter of minutes. I didn't take my eyes off him because I didn't want to be caught off guard. Lance finally spoke up.

"Damn, man. When did you get to be like this? I've always known you not to give a shit about a lot of things, but I never thought it would come to be this way between us."

"It doesn't have to be this way, Lance. We've shared too many great years to let a woman come between us. There's one out there for you. I'm sorry it won't be Holiday, but I'm certain you'll find a woman just as nice."

Lance huffed and shook his head. He then turned and walked away. I felt it safe to let my guard down, so I pulled out a chair and took a seat. Lance looked at me and spat some piercing words in my face.

"So you've made her your woman—for now—but you'll fuck it up. The Roman Broxton I know would never change overnight, not even if his life depended on it. It's too much like going against the rules of a playa," he said sarcastically.

"I'm done with that," I retorted.

"Yeah, right. I really wish you wouldn't do this to Holiday. You'll hurt her for sure. It's a given fact."

"Man, get the hell on out of here. You ain't me. You don't know what I have in my heart. Running around was part of my past. I'm on to a better life now."

"With that said, I'll leave it alone. But once you find a way to mess things up with Holiday, you think back to this moment then come give me an apology."

"Man, for what?"

"'Cause in spite of what you're saying you feel for Holiday, you know full well you'll never be the better man. You're just in the fucking way of what's really meant to be."

"Yeah? Well, check this: what's really meant to be already is. Holiday is my woman. You hear me? No one will come between us."

"Is that what you think?"

"That's what I know, damnit. You can try to act bad if you want to, but Holiday wouldn't want you anyway. You ain't man enough," I yelled pointing at Lance.

I watched Lance pause for a moment, seemingly gritting his teeth. "You wanna play the fucking patronizing game, Roman, we can do that. But when it's all said and done, just remember I said it. You'll never be the better man."

Lance and I locked eyes for a minute, and it bothered me that I couldn't even respond. His words were piercing. In my heart I really felt I could change for Holiday. Lance had fewer flaws than me. He could easily be the man with whom Holiday dreamed of being in love. As for me, I had a lot of work to do in terms of improvement. Regardless of my past issues with women and relationships, Holiday was my woman, so to hell with Lance and what he thought. All I knew is that the muthafucker better had been thinking smart by not trying to stand in my way, or else deal with my wrath.

Chapter Eight

Boys Night Out

My friendship with Lance went untouched. He accepted that Holiday was my woman and we all remained close. There were times when we'd all go out together and even take Crystal along. Crystal seemed to enjoy calling Lance and me Uncle and allowing us to spoil her. Holiday loved to see her daughter so happy. Lance and I began to show up quite frequently to play Scrabble and to take Crystal skating, two of her favorite past-times. Holiday wasn't ready for Crystal to know about the kind of love we shared, so I was careful not to be overly affectionate around her. Lance's company made it easier for me to pretend we were all just good friends. If Crystal felt any differently, she didn't speak of it to either of us.

It was great being able to continue sharing a friendship with Lance. At times, it didn't seem real. Lance was definitely a better man than me. If our circumstances had been reversed, I know I wouldn't have handled the situation well. Given the way I felt about Holiday, somebody would've had to shed blood.

* * *

About three months later, I continued to have a beautiful and loving relationship with Holiday. It was odd not having a different woman call me every day, but it also felt great having Holiday be my one and only. She could make me feel butterflies every time we met each other for a date. It was nothing for me to spoil her. Her wish was my command. I slept, dreamed, ate, drank, breathed, and lived for Holiday Simmons. I made sure I did everything within my power to help her understand my love for her. There was nothing I wouldn't do for her.

I struggled with whether to tell my boys about my boo. I felt they'd feel I was a joke, but on the other hand, I felt they'd understand that I'd turned over a new leaf. Well, everyone except Ant, especially since he made it known that he felt I was the wrong guy to have Holiday. Lance hadn't mentioned anything to any of our clique, so I didn't see a need to update Ant.

Before our fellas' night out, I told Carlos about my relationship with Holiday. After all of his ranting and raving about how messed up the situation was and how Lance and I shouldn't've been caught in such a predicament that could jeopardize our friendship, he soon calmed down and faced the fact that shit happens and that Holiday and I were lovers. I told Carlos why I wasn't ready to tell Ant and made him vow to keep the whole conversation between us.

Another month went by. Holiday and Crystal had their mother-and-daughter night one Friday, while I decided to meet up with the guys to have a few drinks. From time to time, we'd kick it and have our exhaling session, away from jobs, women, and any other stress. This particular night, Lance was late. Carlos was on his third glass of cranberry juice, while Ant and I had thrown back a couple of drinks. We were on the topic of women before Lance showed up.

Ant took a sip of his drink then held up the glass to look under the bottom of it as if he was trying to examine its contents. "Now this is some good stuff," he stated.

We all laughed at the ridiculous frown Ant had on his face. I couldn't resist mocking him. "Ant, what's wrong witcha? You say the drink is good, but you sittin' over there frowning and looking through the glass as if something's wrong. Man, what's up?"

Carlos seconded my comment. "Yeah, what's up? Something that good can't be so bad," he said, laughing.

"It ain't. Ain't bad at all," Ant replied.

"Then whatcha all pruned-faced for, man?" I asked.

Ant took another sip, frowned, and held the glass closer to his eyes, swirling the contents. "Y'all like pussy don't you?"

Carlos and I looked at each other and answered, "Yeah." We were confused as to why Anthony had brought this up.

"Well, if you understand why gettin' some good sex causes you to shrivel and sound like you're in pain, then put it in perspective with this drink. Despite my ugly face, please believe that I'm enjoying every swallow." He took yet another sip and pruned once again.

We all laughed. My boy Ant could be ridiculously funny at times. He made our chillin' times worth it. We knew if we had things on our minds, once we'd get together, Ant would do something funny to make us forget the stress.

Carlos continued to tease Anthony. "That drink couldn't possibly compare to any pussy I've ever had."

"Yeah, and you'd be the one to know with them four babies you and Sonia got, huh?" Anthony cracked on Carlos.

"Okay, but let's not leave out the fact that them four babies got one momma, and she's my wife of ten years."

"Oh yeah. What the hell was I thinking?" Anthony shrugged and laughed loudly.

"Well, all I have to say is, Ant, you're crazy. That drink can't compare to my woman. Hell naw. No way," I said, shaking my head.

"You mean if you had a woman, right?" Anthony asked, laughing at my comment.

"No. You heard right. A drink could never compare to *my* woman."

Anthony quit laughing, set his glass on the table, and stared at me fiercely. His eyebrows dipped toward each other as he began speaking through tight lips. "I know you ain't tryna tell me what I think you are." I didn't responded, so Ant got louder. "Huh?"

"Hol' up. You ain't gotta get all countrified up in here, yellin' like a li'l bitch." We looked at each other, unblinking. "I can answer you. Yeah. Just what you're thinking: Holiday Simmons is my new woman."

"Holiday, huh?" Anthony asked a question, but he was really confirming what he'd heard me say.

"Yeah, Holiday," I stated, nodding and gritting my teeth.

"As in, Lance's Holiday, right?" Anthony questioned, awaiting further confirmation.

"Look. She was never Lance's Holiday. Let me tell you something. Lance and I have already discussed this," I said.

"Oh yeah? Did he kick your ass? Huh? G'on admit you got your ass kicked," Anthony angrily taunted.

"As a matter of fact, he didn't. Now if you'll let me finish what I started . . ."

"Go ahead, brotha man. This ought to be good," Anthony said.

Carlos sat shaking his head. I don't know if he was in disbelief of the argument or frustrated at the whole situation. With Anthony sitting there looking like I had just taken him to the highest level of pisstivity and Carlos looking down at the table, not able to hold his head up to look at me, I didn't want to try to give an explanation.

"Forget it," I said.

"What? Naw, man. You can't leave us hanging like this. Come on. I know you got something good to tell me," Ant replied.

"Look, Lance and I are cool now, so the best thing for the two of you to do is get over any hostility you might be feeling."

Anthony looked at Carlos and sighed. "Hmph. Did you hear that Los, man? You and me should just get over any hostility we might be feeling. This deception ain't involving us, so we just need to get over it. You think you can do that?"

Carlos finally looked up. He never said anything, only sat with his head still, bouncing his eyes from man to man. I couldn't read Carlos, but the fact that he wasn't sticking up for me told me he wasn't feeling everything. Anthony broke the silence.

"A'ight, Sphinx. You got it. We'll get over it. At least now I know to watch my woman around you. Los, I think you better keep an eye on your wife. This nigga just proved to me what I kinda felt all along: our friendship will never be precedent over his own feelings."

"You are a—" I began.

"Shhh. Three o'clock," Carlos snapped.

We all looked to the right. Lance was heading in our direction. He was dressed in an acid-grey denim set, and he'd been freshly tapered up.

"Whazz-up?" Lance asked, extending his hand to me.

I stood just as we slapped hands then folded into a one-armed brotherly hug, patting each other on the back. Lance reached to slap hands with Ant and Los, too.

Los answered Lance's greeting. "Naw, the question should

really be whazz-up with you? Coming in here all late and looking fresh."

"Oh, I had to let Mr. Brown give a brotha the hook-up. For some reason, my fade wants to be gettin' thick a lot sooner these days. Can't wait till our regular barbering day no more. I'm straight now, right?"

"Yeah, you're cool, man. Mr. Brown did a great job," Carlos replied.

"What about the goatee? I'm hooked up, right?" Lance asked, brushing down his chin.

Again, Carlos was the only one to speak. "Yeah, man. You know Mr. Brown don't be slacking on his job. You're straight."

Anthony and I sat in silence as Carlos and Lance continued to chat.

"By the way, Mr. Brown told me to tell y'all to have your raggedy asses up there to the shop on time tomorrow," Lance said, laughing.

Carlos chuckled a bit, but there was no reaction from either Anthony or me. There was no hiding the fact that some type of conflict had just gone on between us.

"Alright, why my boys sittin' up here like somebody died or something? Whatever got y'all uptight, forget about the shit, and let's move on," Lance stated and then flagged for a waitress.

To this day, I believe Lance had a sense we had been discussing the situation between him, Holiday, and me. Lance was just the type of man to want to keep peace. I know I hurt him, and I'm honestly proud of the fact that he would even try to move past what happened between us. Yes, Lance wanted Holiday, too, but my rule of thumb says since I can't make everybody happy, just aim for just pleasing me. That's exactly what I continued to do.

Chapter Nine

A Playa Unlimited

I visited Holiday as often as three times a week. I even took her out and pampered her every weekend. She was definitely spoiled.

The time came for me to volunteer to work on a Saturday in Jackson, Tennessee, which was over an hour drive away. No matter how I tried to debate going, my supervisor wasn't trying to hear it. I had managed to allude working weekends for several months. Since the agents who wouldn't otherwise mind working had something to do, I had no other choice but to drive the extra miles. I didn't know how to break the news to Holiday, so I kept putting it off.

I decided to wait until Saturday morning to mention I had to work in Jackson that day. Holiday took the news just as I had expected. She practically begged me not to leave her. She and her best girlfriend, Erika Peebles, weren't seeing eye-to-eye, and Holiday didn't feel comfortable calling her to hang out. I felt guilty for how I handled the situation by not telling Holiday much sooner, so I called Lance to ask him to take her out. I was on the phone with Holiday when I decided to switch lines to call Lance.

"Okay, how about this. Hold on a second," I said just before clicking to the other line.

"Rome, who are you calling?" Holiday asked, being her feisty self.

"Hold on. You'll see."

"No, don't tell me to hold on. I wanna know. And it better not be Erika, either."

Lance picked up just in time to hear the tail end of what Holiday said. "It's not Erika, baby girl. It's Lance."

"Oh, Lance. I'm sorry. Rome and I just got through talking about Erika, and I thought he had dialed her number."

I huffed. "Holiday, you're trippin'. Where would I have gotten Erika's number?"

"I don't know. You speak to her at church," she exclaimed.

I huffed in the phone because Holiday surprised me with her comment. Since we had been dating, I had kept my promise and attended church with Holiday and Crystal. Erika, who was a member, always made it a point of getting my attention, so I would speak to her. I didn't want Holiday to get any wrong ideas about Erika and me, so I felt obligated to explain. "Un-huh, and you figure that I would get a phone number from her? I don't know what to say about you now. You've completely confused me." Holiday's lack of trust disturbed me.

"I'm sorry, baby. I'm just frustrated," she responded, sounding sweet.

"What's wrong, Holiday?" Lance asked.

"Man, she thinks I'm lying to her about having to go to Jackson today."

"Thanks, Holiday. I didn't know you had changed your name?" Holiday said sarcastically.

"My fault, boo. Go on. Tell 'im what's wrong with you."

"I understand that you have to go take care of business,

baby. I really do. It's just that you've spoiled me. I'm use to having something to do every weekend while Crystal's away with relatives. I guess I'll just have to manage tonight."

"Hey, Lance, man, why don't you take her out for me? She doesn't want to call Erika, and I don't know anything else for her to do."

"Sure. Holiday, do you want to go out with me tonight?"

I kinda wished Holiday would just be a big girl until I returned and stay home alone. But, since I was the main source of her being spoiled and I didn't prepare her to possibly spend the weekend by herself, I offered to pay for Lance to keep her company.

Holiday hadn't met any of my other friends, and my half-sister, Sharonda, just wasn't the kind who liked to hang out. Lance was the only possibility for Holiday to have a good time. After hanging up with them, I wondered what had I done, but I figured I was just being insecure, so I brushed it off. Lance was my boy, and I knew if he really wanted to hurt me in any way, he would've done it long before the weekend I worked in Jackson.

The Jackson office had a full staff on site as if it was a weekday. I arrived pretty close to 11:00 A.M., but suddenly I felt sick to be there. The building was much smaller than the Memphis office, and the storage room, where I had to spend the bulk of my shift pulling old files, was tight and cluttered. I wasn't dressed for climbing shelves. I wore a business suit as I'd always done at the workplace. I missed Holiday, and I became hostile with the other agents.

"This is the sorriest shit I've ever seen," I yelled, strutting to the breakroom for coffee.

"Something wrong, Roman?" Franklin Hubbard, one of the managers, asked.

He followed me as I shouted my frustration through the

hall. I couldn't believe I had given up a day with my boo to work in a hellhole.

"Roman Broxton, I'm talking to you. Is there something wrong?" Franklin asked again, walking right on my heels.

"Yeah, there's something wrong. There's plenty wrong around here. I was told I'd be straightening out insurance policies your staff screwed up. Nobody told me I'd be breaking my back, pulling heavy-ass boxes off shelves in a room small enough to make any man claustrophobic."

"Well, hey, don't take it out on me. Who told you to come in here dressed in your Sunday best? It wasn't me. I thought you knew Saturdays are our casual days."

It was hard, but I managed to disregard Franklin's sarcasm regarding my attire and just kept the conversation on the matter that bugged me the most. "Man, you don't understand. I was made to feel there was a sense of urgency with me getting those policies corrected, but all I've been doing since I arrived is shuffling boxes."

"Oh, don't fret, Roman. You'll get to help with those cases soon enough. We have a few more agents on the way who'll be a part of the team you'll train to correct the policies, but taking those boxes down was a necessity because much of what needs to be rewritten happens to be stored away in them."

"Man, this will take all day and night," I grumbled, turning and noticing the empty coffee pot.

"Maybe. Maybe not. It really depends on how quickly your team picks up on what you teach them today. Besides, everything won't get done. This Saturday workday thing is becoming a ritual at this office. We're approaching our deadline for straightening out the policies of the most specialized accounts in a couple of weeks. If we don't have everything corrected by then, we stand a chance of losing them as clients."

Franklin's medium-brown complexion had begun to turn

flush. He seemed a little nervous that I was thinking of walking out, leaving the office high and dry. I really didn't care to listen to him whine anymore, so I turned my back on him and began opening and slamming cabinet doors and drawers, looking for some coffee. Franklin kept right on talking.

"Hey, man, you don't need to stress. I've been told you're the best at writing policies. I'm sure you'll be able to help the others understand where we went wrong," he said.

"Well, maybe," I replied, opening a new can of coffee.

"Everyone should be here shortly. I see you've found the coffee. Have as many cups as you like, and relax until the others are here." Franklin turned to walk out.

"I can't," I said.

"Excuse me?" Franklin turned to me crumpled and confused.

"I can't. Ain't no damn cups." I sighed, tossing a package of coffee filters on the table then plopping in a chair.

"Hey, hey, now. What did I just say to you? Don't stress. I think I can get Tori on the phone to get some on the way here. Just hang tight," Franklin said, holding one arm in the air, exposing perspiration under his long-sleeve T-shirt.

I nodded. "Yeah, yeah. Whatever, man."

Thirty minutes later, in walked a couple of white guys and a black dude talking all loud and high-fiving one another as they entered the office. I stood at the entry of the break-room and watched as they set up at their desks. Franklin looked over and noticed my blank expression, so he called me over to introduce me.

"Roman, I'd like you to meet the final additions to your team. C'mon over," he said.

"What's up? How y'all doing this afternoon? Which one of you dudes is Tori?" I asked, surprised to see that none had the cups.

"Tori?" one of the men asked.

"Tori's getting out of the car now with a big stack of Styrofoam cups," another one of the men said, looking out of the glass door.

"Good 'cause I really don't think I can make another move without my coffee," I said, anxiously awaiting this dude's arrival.

The agent standing at the door pulled it opened and stepped back to let the individual inside. To my surprise, Tori was a six-foot, light skinned woman with long, dark har. She had keen facial features, and full lips, which she enhanced with a dark shade of red lipstick that matched the red halter she was wearing. I noticed the killer pair of jeans she wore as she headed into the breakroom with her eyes glued to mine. She pushed her sunglasses up on top of her head, causing her to drop her keys as she passed me. When she bent over to pick them up, her backside greeted me as she did a slight twist and wiggle just before straightening to stand tall again. I couldn't help but notice she was a brick house. Her hair was pulled around to one side, exposing a large silver hoop earring in her uncovered ear. My day was beginning to brighten.

I gave Tori a couple of minutes to situate things then I went in to get a cup of coffee. Upon entering the breakroom, I was caught off guard. Tori was bent over, stocking cups in the cabinet underneath the coffeemaker. I cleared my throat to alert her of my presence.

She looked up and smiled. "Hello. My name is Toriana Ponce. Everyone around here calls me Tori. I guess you can, too," she said, extending her hand to greet me.

"Well, Tori, I'm Roman Broxton. Everyone seems to just call me Roman. I'd be delighted if you do, too," I responded, gazing in her eyes and firmly shaking her hand.

"So, are you our instructor for today?" Tori asked.

"I guess you can say that. I'll certainly teach you anything you feel is necessary to get the job done," I replied, still holding her hand.

"Great. I'm looking forward," she said, finally pulling away from me. She placed her hands in her back pockets then swayed to position her weight on one hip.

Tori had already become a distraction for me. Looking at her smooth vanilla skin suddenly gave me a sweet tooth. I began to envision licking her entire body from head to toe as she shook and moaned in pleasure.

"Helloooo. Earth to Roman. Anybody in there," she said facetiously, waving her hand in my face.

I laughed. "I'm sorry. I was noticing your complexion. Are you—" I was cut off.

"Hispanic? Yes. I'm just a little tanner than most of us though." Tori smiled then finished. "I'm also black. Anything wrong with being biracial?"

"No . . . no . . . not at all. I didn't mean to give you that impression if I did," I apologized.

"You didn't. Just wanted to make sure." Tori walked around me, heading into the office. She stopped and smile, then beckoned for me. "You coming?"

I cleared my throat. *Not yet, but I just might real soon,* my sick mind told me. "Umm, yes, as soon as I make this cup of coffee, I'll be right there."

I drank so much coffee it was ridiculous. There was plenty of work to do, and I needed the caffeine to stabilize my nerves. The fellas on my team didn't catch on as quickly as I had hoped. I ended up correcting most of the cases on my own. I called Holiday a couple of times in hopes that hearing her voice would help me refocus on my promise to her to remain faithful. Watching Toriana Ponce sit across from me eating lollipop after lollipop wasn't helping.

Tori disappeared for a while, giving me the opportunity to clear my head. *Roman, man, don't you mess up. You know what you've got at home . . . Nothing is worth jeopardizing your relationship with Holiday,* I told myself. But, the moment Tori returned to her desk, all focus was lost once again.

As the day was nearing an end, Tori walked over to where I sat then raised her thigh to slide her butt on top of my desk. Mesmerized, I was unable to lift my head to look up into her eyes. She ignored my lack of attention and continued to speak to me.

"So how long will you be in town?" she asked.

"Just till morning. I figured I didn't need to head back home tonight, tired and all. Why do you ask?"

"I was hoping I could show you the city, but since you're tired, I won't pester you," Tori said, giving me a wink.

"Show me the city? You mean there's more to Jackson, Tennessee, than just the local Wal-Mart?" I teased.

"Oh, you'd be surprised. C'mon, you'll have a great time. Trust me," she said.

"Well, if you don't mind, I'd like to go to my hotel for a shower and a brief nap. Perhaps we can do something later. Here's my number. Call my cell phone around eight," I said, scribbling my number on the back of my business card.

"Great. I look forward to it." Tori turned to walk away, continuing to look back.

I thought, *Lord, what am I getting myself into?*

Chapter Ten

When You're Hot, You're Hot

Persistence has gotten me everywhere I've wanted to be in life, so I totally understand why Toriana Ponce phoned me soon after me leaving the office. Despite my telling her the best time to call, she decided to hit me up before then. We discussed meeting at my hotel in a few hours. After showering, I took a short nap. And short it was because I was awakened by pounding on my hotel door. I looked through the peephole and couldn't believe my eyes. *She has got to be kiddin' me*, I thought. Before I realized it, I had opened the door wearing my boxers.

"Tori, I thought we were clear you were gonna be here in a few hours," I stated, a little irritated. I was tired, and I contemplated inviting her in.

"I know what we agreed upon, but are you telling me you're not a man of spontaneity? Is everything always planned in your life?" Tori asked just before reaching behind her neck to unleash the knot in her halter dress.

Tori's black dress fell to her feet, revealing her birthday suit. She reminded me of a tall glass of creamy vanilla milkshake. Surprised and embarrassed, I yanked Tori's arm, pulling her into the room, causing her to stumble to the floor with the dress twisted at her ankles. I looked out into the hallway to see if anyone noticed her stunt, but thankfully, no one was out there. I hurriedly closed the door and went to assist Tori off the floor.

"Hey, I'm sorry, but lady, you can't be flashing your business to the world like that," I said, reaching to help untangle her feet.

Tori sighed. "If I didn't know any better, I'd say you were embarrassed just now."

"Who me? Never. I wasn't the one standing in the hallway wearing the same thing I came into this world with. No need for me to be embarrassed," I lied.

"Well, do you mind helping me up? I believe I could better loosen this dress from my ankles that way."

"Oh, sure. I'm sorry for pulling you the way I did."

"I'm okay. Don't worry about it," Tori said as she took off her heels to afford herself more freedom. She glanced at me. "Boxers, huh? Who would've thought."

"Yeah, at times I'm that kind of man. It sort of depends on my mood and what I'm wearing for the day. I mostly sleep in boxers though."

"Oh, that's right. You did mention you were trying to catch a nap. Should I leave and come back?"

Tori was finally free and had put back on her stilettos. She stood seductively with her feet spread apart and her hands behind her back. With one swift flip of her head, her hair swooshed around to one side, adding even more sex appeal to her look. I swallowed hard before I answered.

"No. No. You don't have to leave. I'll be fine," I said, motioning for her to remain where she stood.

"Good." Tori smiled, eyeing me in my underwear.

My cell began ringing as it lay on the nightstand. I turned to look at the caller ID. It was Holiday. Before I could turn to ask Tori to excuse me while I answered the call, she was already standing tight up on me, caressing my chest with her soft breasts.

"Let it ring," she said, tracing my lips with her tongue.

Tori's breath was warm and sweet, kinda like a tropical breeze near a honeysuckle tree. I trembled as I felt my manhood rise. The more Tori licked me, the more I wanted to feel her tongue below my beltline. The phone rang once more. I fought hard to regain control.

"I really need to answer this call, Tori." No matter how I tried, I couldn't talk without panting.

Tori nibbled my chin then my neck as she replied. "If your lady isn't here, but I am, what can she do for you now?" Tori placed my hands on her breasts and began squeezing them.

I heard the beep on my cell, signaling there was a message, but I was frozen in lust. There was nothing I could do to change the way I felt. The moment Tori pushed my face into her breasts, I knew it was on. Her scent was soft like spring and roses. My body was yearning, and it wouldn't let me turn Tori away. Without warning, she dropped to her knees, snatching my boxers down to my ankles in less time than it took to blink. She immediately took me into her mouth. My thoughts of being those lollipops she sucked earlier had come true, and good lawd was I ever grateful.

My cell rang again. Tori began sucking harder and taking me more vigorously into her mouth as if to remind me of her last statement, what can Holiday do for me now? I knew there was nothing Holiday could do for me at the moment, but I also cared enough not to want her to be worried. Unfortunately, it had become more and more difficult to do anything about sparing Holiday's feelings. Every time Tori swallowed me, I heaved and panted in ecstasy. Answering Holiday's call would've been a dead giveaway about what I was doing, so I chose to just let the phone ring.

Another beep signaled a new message had been left. By then, I was having flashes of being at the rodeo because as Tori sat on top of me, I bucked her like a wild bull. As I lay on my back, I straddled her waist and pounded my pelvis into her swift and hard. Tori moaned and kept trying to lean forward to lie on my chest, but I refused to allow her any closer. Not only did I not want that bonding that often comes after having sex, but I wasn't trying to turn this into a love-making occasion. I only wanted to make her take all of me and everything I had to give in our moment. She had arrived ahead of schedule to disturb my sleep for this. If she didn't know that sex was all we could have between us, then she had just been forced into a harsh reality. I made no attempts at even pretending I cared about Tori. I figured if I didn't put my lips on hers, it would be a definite indication I was only in it for the moment.

Tori screamed as I thrust into her one last time, stiffening to allow my climax to drain me. There I lie satisfied and weak. Good thing Tori thought to bring condoms because after all the seducing she did, she was gonna get got with or without one. My plan to not be gentle with Tori worked. I could tell she wasn't pleased with the way I'd just treated her. I turned my back and smiled, thinking at least I knew I wouldn't have to deal with her wanting more. Too bad for Tori, but mad playa points for me.

Two hours later

"Hello. Roman Broxton's phone," I heard Tori say in my dream. I slowly awakened then turned to be certain I was only dreaming. When I saw Tori with my cell up to her ear, I almost shitted on myself. I quickly snatched the phone and yelled, "Hello."

"Hello, Roman? Is this Roman? What's up, man?" Lance sounded confused.

"Yeah, it's me. What's going on? You got my girl with you?" I asked nervously.

"Yeah. I've picked up Holiday. We've been here for about a half hour now. She's been trying to reach you, but I guess you know that, right?"

Before I could say anything, Tori leaned over my shoulder and began talking into the mouthpiece. "Who is it, honey?" she said. "Tell 'im you need to go back to bed."

I was furious, and my nervousness returned. I knew I didn't need to speak to Holiday at that moment because Tori was out of control. Her actions proved she didn't care about making me angry, and she cared even less about my woman's feelings. I decided to plead for Lance's help.

"Look, man, do me a favor. I need you to cover up for me. I'll owe you big time. Just help a brotha out."

"Man, I really think you need to talk to Holiday. Just say something to her," Lance said.

"Shhh. Isn't she nearby? Don't fuck this up for me, man."

"I just got up from the table, so let me ask you something. Was the pussy good?"

"Huh?" I played dumb.

"Roman, man, I hope the shit was good and worth fucking up your relationship with Holiday. Right now I view you as one of the stupidest muthafuckers I've known in my life. Don't you think you could've played your shit off better that this? Huh? I knew you would pull this shit on Holiday."

When I heard Lance's voice on the phone, I was sick. I knew this was a situation that would anger him. I continued to act innocent. "Nothing has happened, Lance. You're jumping to conclusions," I lied in defense.

"Oh yeah? Well explain that bitch answering your phone. You know you were laid out. The only other time I've ever known a woman to answer your cell is when you were hard asleep next to her in bed," Lance stated, obviously reflecting on an incident nearly a year ago when he tried to reach me.

"Say what you wish, Lance, but I'm asking you as a brother and a friend to not disclose anything to Holiday. If you don't do it for me, think of Holiday's feelings. I know she loves me, man, and despite the way things seem, I really love her, too."

Lance sighed. "Shit. This is so fucked up. What do I tell her? She's expecting me back to the table with a response from you. Better yet, I know she wants to talk with you."

I had to think fast. "Tell her I was caught up working too hard in the storage room, and I didn't realize I had missed calls. Make it sound good, though. You can even tell her I've been in a meeting, too."

"Yeah, but what about now? What reason do I give Holiday for you not speaking with her now?"

"Help me, Lance. I know you can think of something. Just be sure you let her know I love her, and I'll see her in the morning for church."

"Yeah, a'ight," Lance exclaimed just before hanging up in my face.

Tori was still laying over my shoulder. I flipped my phone closed then tossed her off me. She jumped quickly out of bed in a daze. I felt my anger raging out of control, and Tori sensed it.

"You conniving whore. You knew that could've been my lady on my cell and you answered it. Who the fuck do you think you're playing with?"

"It's not about games, Roman. I like you. Can you blame me?" she answered sweetly.

"So you try to jeopardize my relationship, thinking it would somehow make me want to be with you?" I asked, looking at her in disgust.

"Ummm, yeah," Tori stated, sounding offended. "To tell you the truth, I figured you'd never go as far as you did with me if you didn't like me."

I couldn't believe my ears. "What? You were sucking my dick, you trifling ass bitch. You think what we just did was lovemaking?" Tori didn't answer, so I continued. "Hell, no. I just banged yo' ass, so don't get it twisted."

Before I saw it coming, Tori threw one of her heels, barely missing my head, but breaking the mirror on the dresser. The room turned crimson red before my eyes as I lunged across the bed at her. I was caught off guard by Tori's will to fight. Just as I landed on top of her, she kicked and scratched with great fury.

I managed to stand, and Tori quickly got up as well. We spat more obscenities at each other then I went to the door to open it.

"Get the fuck out," I yelled.

Tori grabbed her belongings, stepped into her stilettos then began to put on her clothes. "No problem!" she shrieked.

I intercepted her getting dressed. "No, I mean now!" I grabbed her with a force that even surprised me and began shoving her out the door. "You like showing people what you've got anyway, so let me help you." I pushed Tori in the hallway, and experienced a déjà vu, remembering her being out there in the nude a few hours earlier. I slammed the door just before she had time to pitch another shoe at me. It hit the door hard, causing it to rattle.

I hated myself. Everything Lance said to me had come to pass. Tori really wasn't worth the pain I knew Holiday was experiencing. I longed to call her back, but I couldn't gather the right words. Though I was almost certain Lance hadn't told Holiday my secret, I felt ashamed to speak to her. I toyed with the idea of whether to call her, ultimately deciding against it. I figured I needed the time till morning to think. The last thing I wanted was to get tongue-tied when Holiday questioned me. I knew it was going to be tough, but I was going to have to be the smooth operator I'd been for years and put my game face on.

Chapter Eleven

What Goes Around

I returned to Memphis heavy hearted and with much on my mind. For the first time in all my days of being a playa, I felt seriously guilty about having cheated. Lance was right. Holiday didn't deserve to be played, and most of all she didn't deserve me. Still, I had no intention of letting my woman go.

I figured Holiday would be angry, so I prepared myself to be tongue-lashed. I had been with my boo long enough to know she could be fierce with her choice of words. Though reluctant at first, Holiday allowed me to speak with her in her home after we left church. I greeted her with a warm kiss as she opened the door.

"Rome, thank you for such a sweet kiss, but we really need to talk." Holiday seemed disturbed.

"I'm listening, boo." I tried to appear calm, but I truly feared she was about to break up with me.

"While I was out with Lance, I couldn't enjoy myself for thinking of you. You made me feel good at first by trying to confirm for me that you weren't away doing anything deceitful, but then I went to call you back, and I couldn't even reach you . . . You did just what you thought was enough to pacify me—calling me, probably so I wouldn't call you—then you went on to doing your merry little thing."

I kept my composure. "Holiday, boo, where is this coming from? I wasn't expecting this. I really wasn't."

"Oh yeah? Then what were you expecting? Huh?" Holiday stared deeply into my eyes.

For all that it was worth, I refused to loose my boo over the foolish mistake of thinking with the wrong head the night before. I continued to lie. "I don't know, but I wasn't expecting this. Boo, I thought you'd trust me. If I had known this would bother you so much, I would have told management to exclude me from the trip this weekend. I've told you, I can only see a lifetime with you and Crystal. There's no one else out there for me."

"Then, why the hell wouldn't you speak with me when Lance called you? Because, you were with another woman. That's why."

"Boo, no. Please, don't do this to me. Boo, I love you so much. I don't know where you're getting this. Didn't Lance tell you what happened?"

"No. What do you mean?" Holiday seemed surprised by my question.

"We were in the manager's office when he called. We were trying to wrap up a meeting about possibly working next Saturday. Before that, we had spent the bulk of the shift back in the file room. Well, I didn't know it at the moment, but our cell phones couldn't pick up reception back there. I saw that you had been trying to call, but I couldn't talk during the meeting. I knew that you guys were out having a good time, so I told Lance to just let you know that I love you and I would see you this morning for church. Boo, there's no other woman. I wish I had called you last night before I went to bed. Forgive me, please? This is simple. We can get through this."

I held Holiday as I spoke. She stood with her eyes wide and her mouth opened. She began to cry harder than I'd ever seen a woman cry before. Her tears were massive, falling faster and more abundantly as I tried to get her to tell me about her sorrow.

"Boo, what's wrong? Why all the tears?" I was confused.

"Rome, I believe you, but we still can't be together. I'm sorry," she managed to say between sniffling and wiping her face.

I was torn. After all I'd said, she didn't want to accept my apology. I questioned her further. "Help me understand, Holiday. You're hurting me right now. What's going on with you?"

She couldn't even look at me. "We couldn't possibly be together now, even if I wanted to. I've done something terrible. The unthinkable! I can't believe . . ." Holiday didn't finish. She broke down and cried more.

"Holiday, calm down, and tell me what you're trying to say to me." I tried to hold her up by the shoulders as she slumped.

"Roman, I-I-I've already cheated on you," Holiday said, barely looking into my eyes as she trembled.

I couldn't move. I thought, *Maybe I didn't hear her right.* But, as I stood motionless, waiting for her to say something else to relieve my suspicion, she didn't. Instead, Holiday wailed louder and trembled vigorously in my arms. I abruptly let her go then took a seat in the wing chair, attempting to control my emotions. I failed miserably.

My tears were massive and flowing like a raging river. I never knew my heart could accept pain this way. It only took that one sentence from Holiday to pierce me deeply. I knew who she slept with. There was no time for Holiday to be intimate with anyone other than Lance. I made the ultimate mistake of underestimating Lance, so I had paid for it royally. My best friend slept with my woman.

I needed to hear Holiday admit it, so I could release my frustration in one way or another. "It was Lance, wasn't it?"

"How did you know?" She seemed surprised by my question.

"You didn't have time to be with anyone else, Holiday. Something told me to call you back last night. I should've followed my instincts."

"I'm sorry, Rome. I know it's a little too late for that, but I really am."

She was right. Sorry just wasn't cutting it with me. Despite what Lance may have said to her, she was my woman, and she should've at least talked with me before spreading her legs to him. I felt she wanted to lay down with Lance. Holiday wasn't gullible, so she must've wanted to sleep with Lance. Suddenly my hurt turned into anger.

I belittled Holiday right in her own home, calling her names and telling her Lance tricked her into bed. I wanted her to feel low and dumb and to place some of the blame and hurt right back on her because it was too much for me to handle. The thought of my best friend sexually pleasing my woman made me ill.

I couldn't stand to look at Holiday anymore, so I stormed out, leaving her to waddle in her own sorrow. After all of the foul language and harsh words I said to Holiday, walking out was the best thing I could do. I still loved her despite her deceit.

Yes, I had sex with Toriana Ponce the night before, but that had no bearing on how much or how little my heart ached at that moment. Thinking about the night before—Lance and Holiday, and me and Toriana—only made me want to kick myself harder. I should've been at home taking care of the woman I loved instead of falling weak to a slut— something I once promised Holiday I wouldn't do.

Having cried and not knowing how to handle the terrible news from Holiday was even more reason to walk out on her. My next move was to get some answers from Lance. Though he felt I wronged him first, I never would've imagined he could double-cross me the way he did. As I drove from Holiday's house in deep thought, I wondered how Lance would be able to face me. I needed to look him in the eye and let him know I saw him for the punk that he was, rather than the man he wished he could be—me.

Chapter Twelve

Face-off

After arriving at Lance's, we immediately went into a heated argument about his indiscretion with Holiday. I could tell he wasn't prepared for my hostility because he opened the door with no hesitation.

"What's up, man? It's not like you to stop by without calling first," Lance said, inviting me in.

"Yeah, and it's not like you to do some underhanded shit like sleep with my woman," I shot back at him.

Lance was frozen solid. He stared at me in sort of a daze. I don't think he expected Holiday to spill the beans—at least not so soon.

"Snap out of it, mutherfucker. You hear me. You of all people . . . how the fuck did a weak-ass trick like you ever get the nerve to stoop so low?" I demanded a response.

"Wait a minute. Speaking of stooping low, did you forget how you betrayed me in the first place?" Lance yelled.

"Nigga, that ain't got shit to do with shit."

"Hell if it doesn't."

"So, you gon' tell me you fucked my woman to get back at

me? I wouldn't ever have guessed it because I figured you thought more of Holiday than that."

"Hold on. Let's get a few things straight. First, you're wrong to say I fucked Holiday because I didn't. I made love to her. There is a difference. Next, you're right to say I think more of Holiday because I do. I would never have sex with any woman to get back at a man. Last, I made love to your woman because I've got feelings for her that won't go away, and because she wanted me just as much as I wanted her." Lance walked over to the couch then motioned for me to have a seat. "Now are we going to talk about this like gentlemen, or do I need to whup your ass?"

I couldn't believe the coldness coming from Lance as he spoke. I don't know if it was the fact that we were in his home or that he just didn't give a damn what he said to me. I was about to blow a fuse. I couldn't handle his words or his calmness.

"You know what, Lance? I think I'll stand. Whatever is about to happen between you and me is going to happen soon." I refused to move from where I stood.

Lance shrugged. "Alright then, what's up? We gon' talk?"

"I wanna know how you could do it. And, don't bring up that old shit about how you told me of your feelings for Holiday first. I had my own desires, man. I just didn't tell you about them."

"Why not? You never stopped to think that perhaps discussing your feelings with me could help us come to some type of mutual agreement about who would approach Holiday?"

"Lance, let me share something you obviously don't understand," I responded, beating my chest with a closed fist. "Despite my past relationships, I really do love Holiday with every ounce of my being."

Lance spoke up before I could finish. "Well evidently whatever the hell you think you have within you is only an ounce or else you wouldn't have hurt her the way you did last night."

"You don't have faults, Lance? Huh? You standing there acting like you never done dirt in your life. I'll admit I've done some bad things in my time, but I'm trying to change my ways. I didn't mean to do what I did in Jackson."

"Yes, you did, Roman. You haven't been bragging about being the number one playa of the century all these years for nothing. You knew what you were doing when you laid with that woman, and Holiday didn't matter to you then."

"You don't know what the fuck you're talking about. I love Holiday," I shouted, getting even angier. It was frustrating that Lance wouldn't see things my way.

"You don't love anybody or anything but your goddamn self." He continued. "Whatever the fuck you gon' do, Roman, just do it. I'm through talking, and I'm tired of looking at you, man."

"What? What?" I walked up closer to Lance. "I don't believe this shit. You screwed my woman, and now you're acting like I've done you a big injustice."

Lance began pointing his finger as he spoke. "Yeah, that's right. Your sorry-ass ruined the chances of Holiday and me having a beautiful relationship. I vibe with that woman. You, on the other hand, don't know what it is to feel the beauty of a woman's emotions. I love her. You don't."

Shock silenced me. I noticed a large vein appear in Lance's forehead as he turned red and gritted his teeth. Suddenly I felt things had shifted. The blame was now on me, and I was no longer the victim. *Could this be right?* I thought for a moment, never taking my eyes off Lance. His calmness was now lost back in the early stages of our discussion.

I almost felt sympathy for Lance, but I sensed it more necessary to be sorry for myself. No matter what I said or did, I could never prove my genuine love for Holiday to Lance. I realized things were blown when Toriana answered my phone, but I hoped for the best. Now in Lance's eyes, he'd always be the better man.

I still wanted Holiday, and I saw Lance as my enemy. He said she had a strong desire for him, and deep down I didn't doubt it. It was time to play the right card, as my dad had taught me, by keeping my enemies close.

"Look, man, we've both done our dirt in this situation and standing here yelling about it isn't resolving things. I still love you like a brother, but I want my relationship with Holiday. If that means excluding you as a mutual friend then so be it, but I really don't want that. My hope is you'll step back and let her realize what I mean to her. I believe she loves me, whether you want to face it or not."

Lance's temper seemed to cool down a bit. "I still love you like a brother, but now I don't know if things are left in your hands anymore. You'll have to let Holiday decide what she wants. If it's you, then I'll back off."

The scary thing for me was that Lance was right. Holiday had to decide who was the better man. The last thing I remember her telling me was she still loved me, but I didn't acknowledge it. Instead, I walked out on her. She could very easily choose Lance, a man who was known as kind and gentle to the ladies, over me, a stone cold playa.

My best friend and my woman had caused my head to be fucked up, and my heart to know true pain. Still, me loving Holiday didn't change. Though I had to go home to reflect on my resolution, I knew I wanted Lance and me to continue to be cordial and for Holiday and me to remain lovers.

I waited till the next day to call Lance and Holiday. I

needed to make amends before something else happened that would rule me out of her world. After speaking with both of them, we all agreed to meet at Holiday's place to talk.

Holiday began with a question I had hoped wouldn't come. It was a smack in the face. "So, is it true, Lance? Was I just something you were just doing the other night?"

Lance's response was the punch that almost knocked me out. It was just too painful to hear. "Absolutely not. What we shared was very special to me, and if I had my way, it wouldn't have just stopped there. That was your decision. You asked me to go home. I wanted to stay over afterward, but you started feeling guilty, remember? I'm appalled that you would even think such a thing of me," Lance stated sincerely.

"Well, it's not just me. I had a little help in thinking so. Isn't that right, Rome?" Holiday asked.

Anger began to get the best of me. "You're my woman. He's my best friend in the whole fuckin' world, and you fucked him! What kind of shit is that to do to me?"

Holiday and I went back and forth arguing for a moment. She felt I was trying to flip everything around on her. There was nothing to flip. The truth was plain and simple. Lance wanted her, and she agreed. She couldn't take making love to Lance back even if she wanted to.

Lance had his moment with Holiday, but his time was up. I would never see him have Holiday to call his own. What's done was done, but to let the two of them off the hook so they could go and have a happy life, leaving me to suffer, just wasn't going to happen. I ended our little meeting telling Lance off.

"Lance, man, like I told you yesterday, people make mistakes. I still love you like a brother. It hurts like hell, but I can't let this come between us. We've shared too many years of great friendship for me to believe you've never been a friend to me. Holiday is a hell of a woman. I understand why being alone in her presence could be tempting. I'm willing to try to get past this, but I want my relationship with Holiday to work, even if that means you can't hang out with us anymore. In plain terms, man, you're going to have to back the fuck off."

"And like I said, I still love you like a brother, but if you can't be the man that Holiday needs you to be, then you need to back the fuck off," Lance responded adamantly.

Who said words can never harm you? Please let 'im know he lied. I was wounded, but I couldn't let Lance and Holiday know how much. The pride my father instilled in me was stronger than I ever knew.

Chapter Thirteen

Where Do Angry Hearts Go?

Things kept weighing heavy on my mind, so I decided to confide in my boy Ant. I asked him to meet me at Foot Locker in the Southland Mall one Saturday afternoon, so we could talk. I told Ant the whole ordeal about how Holiday and Lance managed to get together, but I left out the part about what I did in Jackson, Tennessee with Tori and the fact I didn't call Holiday that night to explain my whereabouts. I figured leaving my piece of the story out would give me favor over Lance with Ant.

Even Ant couldn't believe that Lance had the balls to betray me. I don't think Ant was taking sides, but he did throw the dirt I'd done in my face.

"This is some crazy shit you're tellin' me, bro. I just never could've guessed Lance would go there," Ant told me. "I thought I knew that guy, but I can see now that I underestimated him."

"Okay. So now you understand why I felt comfortable with Holiday going out with him," I responded. "We were all friends. Lance told me he would respect that Holiday and I were together. Even though he had feelings for her, you'd think he'd understand that certain things were off limits. Taking my woman to bed was just a wrong."

"I still can't believe Lance did it. I mean—I hear what you're saying, but I don't know where he developed the balls. Even I wouldn't have done some shit like that. I understand this woman is supposed to be fine and all, but man, some things a man just shouldn't do. Damn. I'm still trippin'. Can't say you didn't deserve what happened though."

"What? Oh, no. Don't you start that shit with me," I said, bending to place one of the sneakers on my foot. "I know what you're thinking, but the fact of the matter is, Holiday was my woman. Lance had no right to lay her down."

"Um-hmm. No right, but good reason," Ant said, pulling the other sneaker out of the box and glaring at it.

"Man, come on! What are you saying? How can a so-called partner justify sleeping with a woman who's deemed as mine?"

"Lance wanted her first, Roman, and you knew that. You proved your lack of respect for your friendship early in this game by sweeping the woman off her feet before Lance could. I'm sorry, but I think you got the ultimate payback. I ain't condoning Lance's actions, but I know his head was fucked up when you took the woman he wanted. Now your pain had to come around, too."

"Hmph, well, I find it hard to believe Lance admitted to you he was messed up about this situation," I retorted.

"He didn't have to. Sphinx, you forget I'm yo' boy. Same goes for Sir Lance-a-lot and Los. I know when shit ain't right with y'all."

Ant didn't say all the things I wanted to hear, but I appreciated his honesty. I heard what he had said about me getting the ultimate payback, but I didn't care because I knew that the last revenge would be mine. Lance didn't have a woman for me to ruin his beauty of her in bed, but even if he did, sleeping with his woman wouldn't be enough pain to inflict on him. He needed to hurt worse than I did about his indiscretion. I cared about Lance, and I wished we could have our friendship the way it was before all the deceit, but the more I thought about things, I realized he was my enemy, and I needed to either watch my back or take him out.

I took the other shoe from Ant and tried it on. I stood to walk around, testing the fit. Ant looked on as I stomped, tapped, and jogged in place, trying to get a better feel for the shoes. I looked at him, astonished by his frown.

"Ant, whaddup, man? You just gon' sit there scowling with no comments. Let a brotha know whatcha think," I said, shrugging.

"To tell the truth, I'm not use to seeing you in gym wear. The shoes just don't look right on you," he said, still frowning. "C'mon. What's the latest thing happening with you? What's got you in here trying on sneakers?"

"So what, you think I can't decide to do something different now? Can I at least want to enhance my style every now and then?"

"No. Not the Roman I know. Now 'fess up. What's the real reason you're looking at Jordans?"

I laughed then sat next to him as I removed the shoes. "Holiday and I are going to spend more quality time together. She likes to run twice a week, so that's one of her activities I plan to join in on."

Ant gave a deep laugh. "I'm sorry. Did you say you were going to run?" He laughed louder. "Are you serious?"

I didn't see anything funny. "Yeah. I'm dead serious. I really think Holiday is for me, man. I'ma do nothing but right by her from this point on."

Ant looked at me strangely. I could almost feel his stare penetrating my skin as if he was trying to see straight through my soul. If I had to guess, I'd say he was calling me every type of liar known to mankind. Ant was no different than the rest of my boys. He only knew the insensitive me. There was no real reason for him to believe in my decision to be faithful to Holiday, which was fine. The proof wasn't owed to Ant. Just to Holiday. Holiday was about to get a love like no other.

Chapter Fourteen

You're All I Need

Inever realized I could truly feel more than lust for a woman until I became involved with Holiday. I wanted to be on the phone with her every moment I could. I frequently met her for lunch, took her to dinner, and spoiled her with any and everything her heart desired.

Holiday mentioned never having been on a carriage ride, so I took her into downtown Memphis one Saturday evening. I surprised her with her favorite chocolate and caramel Turtles candies then picked up a carriage in front of the grand historic Peabody Hotel. Holiday was carrying a large purse. When I asked her about it, her reason shocked me.

"Did you bring everything but the kitchen sink in that purse, boo?" I asked.

"Ha. You got jokes. No, actually, I'm only carrying this purse because my journal can easily fit in it. I know it's strange to see me with such a huge bag," Holiday explained.

"So you really got your journal in that bag?" I asked, amazed.

"Yeah."

"Why? Please explain this one." I was too curious.

"Just been having a lot on my mind and plenty of things going on with me lately. Every time I'd get the urge to write, my journal wasn't handy. Now it's always available."

"Well, I'll agree with you there. You can carry your journal, a loaf of bread, a blanket—"

"Oh, stop. Here you go with your jokes again. You always find a way to tease me." Holiday laughed.

The breeze was nice until dark began to fall. Once we were closer to the Mississippi River, it became quite chilly. Holiday tried to brave the cold, but I could tell she was uncomfortable. She had become distant and quiet. I wore a T-shirt under my pullover, so I took off the sweater and offered it to her.

"Boo, put this on," I said, pulling the long-sleeved sweater over my head.

"No, baby. I can't let you do that," she responded softly.

I gently kissed her lips. "Really, boo, you need to put this on. I know it's pretty thin, but I believe it'll offer a little more warmth than what you're wearing now."

Holiday's short-sleeve fitted top was attractive, but neither of us had counted on it being so cool after dark. The weather had been tricky that fall with unexpected up and down temperatures. Holiday smiled then returned a loving kiss.

"You are so sweet to me. Definitely different than the Roman Broxton I used to know. I'm still trying to figure out why me? You've been with so many women, Rome. How do you know you truly love me?"

I took a deep breath before phrasing my thoughts. "It's because what I feel for you is unlike anything I've ever felt before. I've stood out on my back porch at night, staring at the stars, thinking of you. Many times the stars seem as if they are winking, and then I think I hear my mother speaking, telling me you're the one. You remind me of her in so many ways it's unreal. I remember my mother being beautiful, strong-willed, yet affectionate. No other woman has come as close to perfection as you. I've never been able to let my guard down to love like this before."

Holiday's eyes were glassy as heap of tears formed. She was clearly moved by my response, and so was I. I followed suit as she lifted her head to look at the stars. *Ma, I see you smiling down on me,* I thought.

"Are you sure you're going to be okay?" Holiday startled me.

"Huh?" I turned away from Holiday, faking a cough to wipe my eyes then answered. "Yes, boo, I'm fine." I gazed into her eyes.

She squinted as if she was trying to read my thoughts. "The sweater, honey. Without your sweater . . . are you sure you'll be alright?"

"Oh, yeah . . . yeah. Boo, you know I'm a tough guy. I promise I'm fine."

I believe we kissed the last twenty minutes of our ride. It felt like nonstop passion—we briefly stopped to catch our breaths then back to kissing. I felt on top of the world. Cars were honking at us, and I could hear happy snickering from people once the carriage stopped. Holiday and I were so involved we hadn't noticed we'd arrived back in front of The Peabody Hotel.

I decided to take my woman to my home. My place was clean and smelled great thanks to The Total Solution, a cleaning service I paid occasionally. I always left a key and a tip under the mat for Shaundra Glaspie, the best housekeeper this city has ever known. Holiday was amazed at the cleanliness.

Crystal was away with family for the weekend, so I asked Holiday to spend the night with me. She seemed a little hesitant at first. I had to question her.

"What's wrong, boo? You don't care to stay with me tonight?" I asked, leading Holiday to the bedroom.

"Oh no, that's not it at all. I'm just a little stunned you would invite me to stay over," she replied.

"Why? Aren't you my woman? Why wouldn't I want you to stay the night?"

"Well, Rome, you know you've had more than your fair share of women. The last thing I want to happen is for me to have to deal with unexpected phone calls, or even worse, an unannounced visit."

I stared at Holiday with disbelief, surprised she'd even go there. "Come on now, boo. This evening has been beautiful. Don't ruin it with talk like that."

"I'm serious, Rome. I love you, baby. I just know having to deal with that type of drama would kill me," Holiday said, stepping closer to place her arms around my waist.

"Okay. Then surely you understand how I feel when I'm at your house and your phone rings. Sometimes I wonder if it's Lance."

She gasped then replied calmly. "Lance doesn't call me, Rome. And, it never crosses my mind to talk to him either. There. Satisfied?"

"Not totally," I responded, kissing her gently on her neck, "But I plan to be before morning."

I lifted her hand then kissed the back of it. Holiday smiled sweetly then puckered, inviting me to her lips. We tongued in what seemed like slow motion. I never tasted anything so delicious in my life. I couldn't get enough of her. I don't remember when or how our clothes got off, but it had to happen in between kisses and catching our breath. I tried to lie Holiday on the bed, but she stopped me.

"Rome, sweety, hold on. Let's take it slower. We've got all night, right?"

"Yeah. What do you suppose we do?" I asked.

"I've never been here before. I was thinking along the lines of christening every room," Holiday replied with a smile brighter than the sun.

"Um-hmm. Where do we begin?"

"The shower," she said, leading me to my bathroom.

Holiday backed underneath the showerhead with her eyes closed, allowing the water to caress her skin. Her breasts stood firm, her large nipples at attention. She looked so damned sexy running her hands through her long, wet hair, massaging her scalp. She opened her eyes, looked at me seductively then smacked her lips at me in a kissing motion. That was my invitation to get closer.

I stepped to Holiday, pulling her body tightly to mine. Her softness along with the heat of the water was sensuous, giving me an unbelievably hard erection. Holiday noticed my excitement. Without looking down, she gripped me, stroking me long and easy. I fought not to erupt in her hands as she took me to another level of ecstasy. I kissed her passionately. She kept stroking me until I began to knead her breasts like dough. My boo trembled, nearly losing her balance.

I turned Holiday away from the water with her back against the wall. As I slid downtown to kiss the tongue between her thighs, she threw her leg over my shoulder. I was pleased she was shaved as she'd always been, making it easier for me to tickle her bare skin. Holiday loved the way I teased her when smacking and pulling on her lips. I didn't stop until she was too weak to stand.

I bent her over, allowing her to grip the built-in soap dish for strength as I took her from behind. She moaned, hissed, and screamed, making it difficult for me to hold back any longer. We exploded together.

We washed each other's backs with what little energy we

had left. Before turning off the water, Holiday let me know my job was well done.

"Baby, promise me something," she said just after sweetly kissing me.

"What's that?"

"Making love to you in the shower was incredible. Promise me you'll never share a moment like this with any other woman."

"Boo, that's easy seeing how you're the only woman for me. Eventually we'll be married and sharing moments like this always, right?" I rubbed her face.

She smiled. "Right."

"Then, I don't have to ask you to make the same promise. From this point on, the shower scene is known as our private joy."

"I love you, Rome."

"I love you more, boo. Now could you turn off the shower? The water's getting cold."

Though Holiday was worried about staying the night with me, she soon got over it and slept like a baby. I looked over her shoulder and whispered her name to be certain she was asleep. When she didn't answer, I knew she was out cold. I turned over to face my dresser, spotting Holiday's purse with her journal peeping out.

I couldn't sleep. I wondered what, if anything, Holiday had written about our future, about her feelings for Lance, or whether she really did love either of us. My curiosity got the best of me. I eased out of bed, swiped the journal then hid it in my closet on the top shelf between several folded sweaters.

Once Holiday awakened to find her bag much lighter, she was upset. It was tough trying to calm her down.

"What the hell do you mean you felt it necessary to hide

my journal. Those are my private and most intimate thoughts. You can't just read it like it's some type of entertainment book."

"Boo, you really should calm down. If there's nothing to hide, then why can't I just read the darn thing then give it back to you at a later date?"

"Rome, you sound like an idiot. You actually know better. Why are you doing this to me? That book is personal. Do you realize what that means?"

"Of course I do. And I'm no idiot. This is why I have your journal in the first place. I'm smart enough to know I should be inside my woman's head, and what better way to do so than to read her secrets?"

"Oh, I can't believe this! Simply amazing, Rome. You're gonna sit up here and try to rationalize doing this to me? Wow. Just when I think I've learned you—"

"Boo, let me help you understand—"

Holiday stormed out of the bedroom before I could finish my thought. I followed her into the living room, where she asked me to take her home. She didn't speak to me the entire ride. Once at her house, she jumped out of my car without saying good-bye, slamming the door behind her. We didn't talk the rest of the weekend.

Chapter Fifteen

Yield Not to Temptation

Monday morning I went to work with plenty on my mind. I strolled to my desk in good fashion. I was wearing my all-black Armani suit with a black silk shirt and tie. I noticed a sticky note on my computer asking me to meet Hilary Smith, my manager, in her office. Hilary was the young woman who was Holiday's assistant before she left. Holiday was right to leave. The company followed through on her suspicions of promoting Hilary over her in the senior manager position. I made my way to tap on the door, but Hilary noticed me as I approached then beckoned me in. To my surprise, a visitor was in her office.

"Hilary, I'm sorry. I didn't realize you had company," I stated, backing out of her office.

Hilary was barely mid-twenties with long dark hair. It was rumored she was the daughter of John Walter Smith, senior manager of compliance reporting. I don't know how it is in most workplaces, but in mine, you had to know somebody to get somewhere.

My manager beckoned me in. "That's not an issue, Roman," she replied.

"Okay then."

"I'd like you to meet Rachel Clark. She's your new trainee for this quarter, and I expect you to teach her everything you know. Think you can handle that?"

I looked at Rachel Clark, a stout, dark-skinned woman with big brown eyes and a winning smile. I nodded graciously toward her as I noticed how well the twists in her hair complemented her face. I reached to shake her hand.

"Hi. It's a pleasure to meet you. I'm sure Hilary has told you that I'm Roman Broxton."

Rachel stood to shake my hand. "Yes, she did, just as she's told you I'm Rachel Clark." We both smiled.

Rachel's dimples caught my attention. I couldn't help noticing how attractive this lady was. Hilary was talking, giving me instructions on where to start the training, but I didn't hear a word she said. I later discovered my lack of focus after Rachel and I sat down to begin.

"Rachel, I'm going to be honest with you. I don't know what I'm supposed to be teaching today."

"I'm not surprised," she said matter-of-factly.

"Oh?" I wasn't expecting her response.

"No. I'm really not surprised. You were busy gazing at me when Hilary was talking. I wonder if she noticed that you weren't paying attention to her."

"You think I was gazing at you, huh?"

"Oh, I know you were. Admit it. You're attracted to me, aren't you?" Rachel smirked.

"Lady, a few minutes ago I thought you were nice. Now, I really don't know."

"Your thoughts haven't deceived you. I am nice. A little upfront and to the point, but all in all, I'm a cool gal." She laughed. "Are you married?"

"No, but I am in a relationship. Why do you ask?"

"Just curious. Wondering what I may be up against." She smiled contented.

"The only thing you're up against is a long road of training on this job. I think you're very beautiful, but I have no intention of cheating on my woman."

"Who said anything about cheating? If I were to have you, you'd be totally mine. Just tell your woman not to let you come out of the house dressed like the Grim Reaper anymore," she said with haughtiness.

I looked at this woman, whose mannerisms reminded me of Holiday for some strange reason, but I didn't say a word. I was adamant about staying faithful to my woman. I smirked then began our day of training. Rachel was fine, but I remembered what happened when I lost total focus the last time. Didn't wanna go there again!

Chapter Sixteen

Love Always

The weekend was approaching, and I still hadn't read Holiday's journal. I wanted to call her, but I wasn't ready to offer her book back. I decided to call anyway. I apologized and promised to return her journal unread by Friday. Holiday fell for it. I was too busy to have read it before seeing her, and I still didn't plan to let the book out of my possession. I knew Holiday would be angry, but she'd just have to get over it.

That Friday, my homey Carlos and his wife, Sonia, were holding a party at their home for their 11th wedding anniversary. All of our mutual friends pitched in financially for the success of the occasion. Every year we took great pleasure in spoiling them with food and gifts.

It was also barbershop day. All my boys, including Lance, were lined up, waiting to sit in Mr. Brown's chair. This day was no different than any other with all the jiving and smack talking. In honor of Los's anniversary, Mr. Brown felt it necessary to school us on marriage and how to hold it together.

"Eleven years, huh? Boy, you done good. Yes, yes, you done good. Ain't a whole lot of youngsters I can give credit to for keeping a marriage together. No, siree. Whatever you doing, son, keep it up. Next thing you know you'll be celebrating thirty-two years like Rhonda and me."

I had to know more. "Mr. Brown, that means you've been married for practically your whole life. How do you keep the fire burning?"

Mr. Brown chuckled then gave me a grin that said my question took his mind to a pleasant place. "See, one thing I don't think you youngsters do very often when the flame begins to burn low, is remember what made you love your woman in the first place. Sure, she'll nag, get lazy when it comes to cooking, might even get sluggish in the bedroom. But, remembering is a key. Was it really any of those things that made you fall for her in the beginning?" The shop was silent. Mr. Brown continued, "Probably not. I don't know a man yet to marry a woman because she nags so good."

"Naw, I don't think I know one either, Mr. Brown," Lance said, shaking his head.

The whole shop laughed and dittoed Lance and Mr. Brown's comments. I couldn't wait to hear what else Mr. Brown had to say. His old school teachings were always right on point with what I needed to know about life.

Mr. Brown continued. "Let go of her negative characteristics and remember all the great things you really love about her. Keep God first in your life, and He'll help you with your memory lapse. The next step is communication."

Carlos spoke up. "Hey, I think you're right, Mr. Brown. Time and time again, Sonia does crazy things to piss me off, but the thing that always leads to our making up is her dedication to me. No matter how angry she gets after an argument, dinner is on the stove when I get home, she greets me at the door with a kiss, and insists we bow our heads together for grace before we eat and at bedtime. Despite her anger, Sonia doesn't take herself out to eat and let me fend on my own. A man can't stay mad at a woman for long when she humbles herself like that."

"Somebody taught Sonia well. She seems to believe in the old saying about a family that prays together stays together," Mr. Brown said.

"Hmm, hadn't thought about it that way, Mr. Brown," Carlos said. "I just admire the fact that even when I disappoint her, she wants to talk things out, and her devotion doesn't change."

"I hear you on that one, son. Do you practice the same?" Mr. Brown questioned. "Do you continue being the man she knew and fell in love with until things smooth over between the two of you? 'Cause if you don't, I'ma letcha know right now, a woman can grow real tired of your egotistical ways."

Carlos defended himself. "I'm not selfish. I understand that a marriage is give and take. We Hammonds got that. We're doing it well I might add."

"Then, I say no more. After all, you're the only one in here, besides me with a relationship that counts. I don't know what the rest of you fellas waiting on. Roman, especially you. It's time to cut out all that womanizing and settle down."

I laughed. "Huh, me? Womanizing? I do no sucha thing."

"Yeah, right. Everybody knows the cards you play, bro," Ant teased.

"Naw, I hear ya, Mr. Brown. I think I might settle down. I just might do that sooner than you think," I responded, staring straight into Lance's eyes.

Just as I looked away, Lance's voice jabbed my ears. "Oh, yeah? That'll be the day all mankind straightens up." His words were like poison.

"Excuse me?" I replied.

"You heard me, doctor," Lance said.

Carlos asked what I wanted to know. "What's up? Why you call the man doctor?"

"'Cause he rightfully earned the title. You got your Ph.D. at the School of Playarism, didn't you, Roman?"

Everyone in the shop sounded like they were in pain as they grunted and moaned after Lance's cheap shot at me. Suddenly, I felt angry. I tried counting to ten, but the volcano in me erupted before I could get to six.

I jumped out of my chair and walked over to Lance, pointing and gritting my teeth as I spoke. "Well, you should've been joining me in getting a Ph.D. in something other than Hateration. At least you wouldn't be sitting here mad now because I got your woman."

The grunting and moaning was accompanied by ooooo's and aaahh's and loud coughing after my response. Lance laughed at me, aggravating me more.

"Roman, why you come standing over me like I'm near deaf? What? You ready to swing on me or something?" Lance laughed harder.

I stared long and hard at Lance until Mr. Brown put a halt to my dangerous thoughts. "Roman Broxton, ain't gon' be no fightin' in here now. You know I don't play that. And, Lance, I'm disappointed in you for even starting this mess."

"I didn't start it, Mr. Brown. Roman did. You just couldn't read between the lines to know it."

"Well, whosonever started it, it doesn't matter. I just know this shop don't tolerate such crap. Now, Roman, go on back over yonder to that chair and take a seat."

Lance laughed more. "Yeah, Roman, go sit yo' ass down. You know Mr. Brown don't play that shit."

Mr. Brown shushed Lance. "Now, Lance, you just hush on up. And respect my no-profanity rule from now on, you hear me?"

"Yes, sir, Mr. Brown. I apologize," Lance responded.

As bad as I wanted to throw a jab at Lance, I respected Mr. Brown enough to let Lance's bullshit walk. Deep down, Lance knew he wouldn't last more than thirty seconds in a fight with me. But, for some reason, he sure didn't mind testing me.

I went back to take a seat. The shop was silent with the exception of Mr. Brown's clippers. Then, he spoke. "What got you fellas so upset anyway? Thought y'all were friends."

Ant stood up for Lance and me. "They're still friends, Mr. Brown. They're just going through something right now."

"Something like what?" Mr. Brown wanted to know. "I don't know but two things that can truly come between friends, and that's money and a woman. Now which one is it?"

"A woman." Ant said, spreading my business to the entire barbershop.

Mr. Brown was shocked. "What? Now nobody could've told me that and made me believe it, but since neither one of you trying to defend yourselves, I'd say what Anthony has said is the truth."

Both Lance and I kept quiet. Mr. Brown continued, "Well, I tell you what. Why don't y'all go on out there on the sidewalk . . . no better yet, the street got more space than in front of my store. Go out there and kill each other since that's where ya heading anyway. Whoever that girl with don't make me no never mind, but I say leave the situation alone when you're here. Better yet, why don't both of ya let her go. If you don't, I guess I'll be reading about one of ya or watching you on the news."

Despite, Mr. Brown's suggestion of stepping outside, neither Lance nor I moved. I chose to sit quietly instead. I felt staring eyes from every angle of the shop. If looks were deadly, Lance would've murdered me in one shot of the double-take he made after my comment of settling down real soon.

I knew the guys thought they could read me, and to say I'd settle down was a bit confusing for some. But, for the first time, my boys knew exactly what I meant. I was playing for keeps with Holiday, and that was final.

Chapter Seventeen

Read Between the Lines

I invited Holiday to the Hammonds' celebration and asked her to tease me by wearing something sexy. Somehow she managed to choose the same black halter dress I'd seen Toriana Ponce wear. Usually I'm full of compliments, but that night all I could say was "You look nice." I could see the disappointment on Holiday's face. She was expecting more from me, but I couldn't fake a better reaction. That dress put me in a bit of a funk. I never wanted to think of Tori and what happened between us in Jackson again, but now the past had revisited.

Ant showed up alone and so did Lance. I watched both Lance and Holiday's actions for a couple of hours. They both seemed to intentionally avoid each other, passing by without making eye contact and never laughing at each other's comments or jokes. I soon relaxed and tried to enjoy the night. If Holiday still had feelings for Lance, there was nothing I could do about it. I took comfort in the fact that she at least tried to ignore him.

Time flew. It was late, but there was at least ten people left in the room including the old Lemoyne Owen College crew. We were just sitting around shooting the shit as the fellas would normally do on a Friday night, except there were women in our presence. We rapped about things from one extreme to another. Somehow we ended up on the subject of sexual relations, and then we progressed to a more sensitive topic of rape. Man, did I learn a lot.

Anthony couldn't help adding salt to a wound. "I got one better for you. I have a partner whose wife accused him of rape." The room filled with sighs of disbelief. He continued. "No. This is true, I'm telling you. I wish a wife of mine would accuse me of sexually assaulting her. Once I got out of jail, I would kill her ass."

Carlos spoke. "Man, I never even thought of anything like that. Can a man really be charged with raping his wife?"

"Hell yeah. I know the dude you're talking about, Ant. He's facing some serious charges," Lance stated.

"I already know, and I can't figure out how a woman can prosecute her husband for something like that anyway," Ant replied.

Holiday had been pretty quiet until this point. When she spoke out, she held nothing back. "There's nothing to contemplate. No means no. If he decided to physically restrain her so he could force penetration after she told him she didn't want to have sex, then it's rape. What's hard to understand about that?"

Carlos came to Ant's defense. "But Holiday, this is his wife we're talking about. Not some stranger off the street. A rape charge can ruin a man's life. Women don't need to be playing around with that kind of accusation."

Holiday wouldn't back down. "And a man shouldn't take a woman's feelings or her body lightly. You can't minimize her telling you she doesn't want to have sex by thinking she actually does. If she doesn't really mean to say no, then let it be her lost. Don't try to decide for her." Holiday looked disturbed.

"I don't mean any harm, but my wife's body is mine," Carlos said.

"Since when?" Holiday retorted. "And, I don't mean any harm either, but Sonia doesn't look like a fool to me."

Sonia raised her glass in the air as if she was looking for cheers. Everyone giggled at her gesture. Well, that is everyone except Holiday. Her look was cold.

Carlos picked the discussion back up. "The Bible says my wife is 'flesh of my flesh, bone of my bone. We are one'."

"Yeah, yeah, yeah, and the Bible also says 'husbands ought to love their wives as their own bodies, nourish it and cherish it, just as the Lord does the church . . . we are all members of His body, of His flesh and of His bones.' You're not going to mistreat or harm yourself, are you?" Holiday didn't wait for a response. "No. So, be just as gracious to your wife."

I had to speak up. "Look, Ant and Los, let me stop you right here, 'cause you ain't gon' win an argument with Ms. Bible Scholar here," I said, nodding toward Holiday.

Holiday frowned. "I ain't trying to win Brownie points, Roman."

Ant lashed at Holiday before I could say anything. "You got that right. You can't sit up here quoting Bible verses like you some type of angel when everybody in the room knows you fucking Sphinx and done fucked Lance at least once."

The room was immediately filled with loud gasps from both the men and women. Sonia cupped her mouth and mumbled, "Oh my God." We all appeared shocked that Ant would take the debate to a malicious level. I was more ashamed of his comments than Holiday. Anger seemed to have a hold of her. I looked at Holiday with a pleading face of apology. Her eyebrows grew closer together as she squinted and filled with tears.

Resentment and humiliation shielded Holiday's once pleasant face. She jumped to grab her jacket, but I caught her before she was able to leave. Ant's liquor must've taken control of his mouth because he wouldn't be quiet.

"Naw. Let her leave, man. She can't handle the truth."

Holiday retorted fiercely, pointing and yelling. "Naw! You're the mutherfucker who can't handle the truth. Evidently you're guilty of rape or else you wouldn't be so defensive. I wasn't the first to bring the Bible into this, but since your ignorant ass is obviously intimidated by my knowledge, then I'll be the first to apologize for thinking I could make a stupid mutherfucker like you understand."

Holiday was right, but she also embarrassed me. The more I tried to shush her, the more she kept talking and pulling away from me. I snapped before I knew it.

"Now wait a minute, goddamnit." After total silence fell on the room, I spoke again. "That's enough from both of you. Holiday, you're out of line, and Ant, you're out of line. Holiday, sit down, and we're all going to get along."

Either Holiday wasn't hearing well that night or the wine she'd been drinking made her comprehension level low because she jerked from me one last time, then headed out the door. I stood more confounded as everyone waited for my reaction. It didn't take me long to decide to follow my woman. I found her at the end of the driveway putting on her jacket.

"Boo, where are you going?"

"Away from here," she said with her tears on the verge dropping.

"I understand you're upset, but Ant and Los really are good men—"

"I don't wanna hear it," she exclaimed, placing her palm in my face. "If you won't take me home, just say so. I'll walk."

Lance came out of the house. I turned to see him standing on the porch round-mouthed as if he had something to say.

"Man, what do you want? Do you mind if I have a *private* discussion with my woman?" I asked angrily.

Holiday interrupted before Lance could say anything. "Speaking of the word private, I'll take back my journal now." She stood with her hands on her hips, tapping her foot.

I took a pause for the cause, ogling her from head to toe as she began to repeatedly shift her weight from side to side. I had told her I would bring the journal with me. "I-I don't have it with me," I finally said.

Her eyes spoke a terrible sadness. "So, you lied to me?" Her voice trembled softly. "You never intended to bring it back to me, did you?" One blink brought the tears down her cheeks.

I turned to notice Lance still gazing from the porch. I opened my mouth to cuss him, but was distracted when I felt Holiday break and run from me. I yelled for her to return, but she was running nonstop.

Everyone heard me yelling, so they stepped outside to see what was going on. I darted for the house to grab my car keys. Frustrated and upset, I had trouble locating them. I hurriedly threw the couch pillows onto the floor as I searched. Ant and Los entered the house with more distraction.

"Look, Sphinx, I think you should know something," Los said out of breath.

Since talking and gasping was a problem, Ant summarized the rest of Carlos's thought. "Lance just jumped into his truck and sped away from here looking like Captain Save-a-Hoe."

"I tried to stop him," Los said, panting.

Just then, I noticed my keys on the mantel. I grabbed them then headed for the door. Los grabbed my arm, slowing my haste. "Don't do anything stupid, man," he pleaded.

I yanked from him without a word then rushed to my car. It took me nearly ten minutes to catch up, and when I did, I was hurt to see Holiday sitting in Lance's vehicle. I parked where they couldn't see me watching them in front of her home.

Half an hour went by. Did they not think I'd follow them? Did they believe I wouldn't show up at Holiday's house? I couldn't understand why they'd be so foolish to sit out in front of Holiday's home, kissing. Maybe Holiday was never certain of whom she was fucking with, but Lance definitely knew my temper. He was obviously trying me. Payback for this kind of shit in most niggas' minds warranted blood. I hadn't thought of taking it there, but the consequences would definitely be a bitch.

Chapter Eighteen

Make Me Break You

After seeing Holiday kiss Lance in front of her home, I waited to see if he would follow her into the house. To my relief he didn't. After watching him drive away, I drove to a nearby payphone to make a call I believed necessary. I needed to show Lance that he shouldn't test pissing me off.

"Hello?" a tired feminine voice answered.

"Look to find your son floating in the river before long," I said in the deepest menacing voice I could mimic.

"Hello? Who are you? Hello?" Lance's mother continued to yell. She was clearly upset.

The next day, Saturday morning, I staked out near Lance's condo. I was pretty sure he'd gotten the word from his mother of the threatening call. I wanted to follow him a bit to see what his first move would be for the day. He came out of his place early as I had suspected. He talked on his cell as he got into his SUV.

As I trailed Lance, I remained several cars behind so he wouldn't spot me. Confident he didn't know I was watching, I sat patiently as he entered a gun shop. I laughed at the fact that Lance obviously felt unsafe. I knew he already owned a

357 Magnum, so I wondered if he was out of bullets since he was at the gun shop so early. Little did he know I was about to put more fear in his heart. After about twenty minutes, I decided to go into the store. Lance's back was to me as I entered.

"Take your time with that, sir. I'll be back with you in just a minute," the male clerk helping Lance stated.

Lance never looked up. He was peering through a nine-millimeter chamber as I stood next to him. Once the clerk returned, Lance passed the weapon to him. "Yep. This is it right here. I'll take it," he said, sliding a box to the clerk.

"Good," the man replied. "You won't be sorry for the trade-in, sir."

I was quite surprised. I couldn't keep silent any longer. "Damn, Lance, you trading in the 357 Magnum, man?"

Lance looked a bit startled by my presence. He didn't respond immediately. He had the scared face I expected on him. I wanted him to be shaken by me popping up on the scene, and apparently he was. I was about to break the ice since he was frozen, but he finally managed to open his mouth.

"What if I am? Last I checked, a man's property is his to do what he wants. You don't agree?"

"Man, you were crazy about that gun. I never thought I'd hear of a day you'd let it go." I smiled.

Lance wouldn't break a grin. "Who says I'm letting it go?"

"Well, I guess you haven't mentioned it. I just kinda took for granted that when the clerk took your box and said you wouldn't be sorry for the trade-in, that that's what you're doing. Goes to show a man should never assume anything, huh?" I liked being cynical with Lance.

Lance went silent and began digging in his pocket. He pulled out his wallet and ID. I kept smiling because I could sense he was nervous. He had to know by my expression that

I was having fun with the moment. He fidgeted as he tried to take his driver's license out for the clerk. I roamed about the store until the transaction was complete. I wasn't going anywhere until I had the opportunity to walk Lance to his truck.

Lance was clearly annoyed. He fidgeted, scratched his head, and huffed repeatedly. He spoke short and snappish to me as he headed to his truck. "Roman, what can I do for you? Why are you here on my heels, man? Don't you know the law considers what you're doing as stalking?"

"Aw shit, man, looks like you and me had the same idea this morning. I woke up thinking about getting me a new gun, too. When I pulled into the parking lot, I glanced over at this truck, but heck I've seen far too many silver Cadillac Escalades in Memphis to be assuming one is yours. But, tell me something. What got you gun shopping this morning?"

Lance looked at me for a second and got into his truck. After rolling down his window, he responded, "I tell you what. You really don't wanna know, but keep fucking with me and you just might find out." He started his SUV then drove away.

I walked back into the store. The same clerk who assisted Lance asked if I needed any help. "Yes, please. I'd like to purchase a gun like the one my friend just bought. Do you have one available, and if not, how long will it be before I can get it?"

After the many years of working alongside Lance and being friends with him, I had just realized he still didn't know who he was fucking with. I deemed it my job to show him.

Chapter Nineteen

If Only for One Night

A month went by without me speaking to Holiday. I had called her several times after Carlos's party, but she wouldn't respond. I finally decided to hold out to give her space and time to cool off. Lance popped in to work every day, speaking as if he didn't care what I thought of him.

One Monday morning, I dragged in to work late, frustrated about not having spoken to Holiday. Lance was already seated with several files in front of him on his desk. I nodded, giving him the whaddup gesture. After that, I couldn't look at him any longer.

Rachel, my new trainee, pranced over to my desk ready for a productive day. I wasn't in the best of moods, but Rachel wasn't making it easy for me to stay in a slump. For some reason, she insisted on rubbing some of her bubbling spirit off on me.

"I don't know what's on your mind, but you're not gonna sit here and take it out on me. Do you hear me, Mr. Broxton?" I don't know how, but Rachel managed to fuss with a smile.

"Nothing's on my mind," I lied. Lance was sitting nearby. I couldn't have said more if I'd wanted to.

"Sure there is. But you know what? I'm going to put a happy face on you in just a minute."

"Really? How so?" I couldn't imagine what this woman was thinking.

"After we finish on the Cornerstone policies, I'm going with you out into the fields."

"Do what? Excuse me?" I just knew I hadn't heard her say she was riding with me.

"You heard me. You get to escort me on your assignments today," she said, flashing her pearly whites.

A thought came to me that Holiday had been the only woman to ride in my precious Lexus, Black Onyx, since we began dating. I felt guilty at the idea of Rachel sitting in my car, even though it was work related. When the phone on Lance's desk began to ring, I looked over at him, straining to hear the conversation. Once he noticed me staring, I turned away, then agreed to Rachel tagging along for the day.

"I suppose having you accompany me wouldn't be so bad," I teased.

"Trust me, it won't be bad at all," she stated with confidence. We packed and left immediately.

Half the day had gone by and all our outfield tasks were complete. Rachel recognized we were near Dr. Martin Luther King Jr. Park and suggested we go there.

"Rachel, I don't wanna be in a park this time of day, dressed in my business suit," I protested.

"C'mon. I haven't been over there in years. We don't have to get out of the car. I'd just like to ride through for a glance, maybe reminisce on my youth."

I sighed. "Alright. Since you tryna find your childhood, I

guess we can stop for a minute," I said, turning into the park.

Rachel smacked me across the shoulder. "Don't mock me like that."

"Ouch! Damn, you women take some things too seriously," I replied, rubbing my shoulder.

"What women? Who are you talking about?"

"Well, Holiday, my woman, I mean she's sort of my woman . . . well, never mind." I couldn't help stumbling over my words.

Rachel removed my hand then began rubbing my shoulder for me. "Hey, pull over if you don't mind. I can sense you need to talk."

I found a nice secluded place to park. "What do you wanna talk about?"

"You. What's going on? Just the other day you were confident about this woman. Now you don't sound so sure. What's wrong?"

"I love her, Rachel. I'm just not so sure she feels the same for me. I saw her making out with another man recently, but she doesn't know I saw her."

"Whoa, that's awful. You haven't spoken with her about it?"

"No. I don't know if I can. It's a little more complicated than I can explain. I'm just hoping time will fix everything. You know what I'm saying?"

"Yes. But, Roman, you've got to know you are too damn fine to be waiting on a woman to love you back. Do you realize how many women would die to have a man like you? Brother, you've got it goin' on. And, you've got so much goin' for you. Stop wasting your time on that lady. You've already admitted she doesn't make you feel loved. What is the wait really about?"

Rachel sounded as if she cared for me. Instead of answering her question, I dove for her mouth. Rachel's tongue happily greeted mine. Her lips were soft and moist, just what I needed. I knew we should've been getting back to work, but Rachel made me feel that time and nothing else mattered. Besides Holiday, Rachel was the one other woman who made me drunk with her reasoning.

I slid my fingers under Rachel's blouse then unsnapped her bra. When she didn't protest, I slowly moved my hand around to one of her breasts and began massaging it. She moaned but never stopped kissing me. I wanted her to belong to me, be mine, forever and always. I unlocked our lips momentarily to lick her neck. Rachel heaved from the sensual touch. She stroked her neck against my tongue as if she wanted me to not only have it, but to have all of her. Before long, I accepted her invitation.

I knew I was wrong for raw-dawgin' it with Rachel, but I didn't have condoms. I needed to bond with her in the worst way. The more I thought not to do it, the hotter I became. I laid Rachel back in the passenger side of my car and climbed on top of her.

"Let me inside you, Rachel," I whispered, grinding fiercely.

"You sure you want to?" she asked softly.

"I don't have a condom, but please don't turn me away. I need you," I panted.

Without hesitation, Rachel raised her skirt, slid off her panties, and spread her legs as much as the space would allow. I glimpsed the wetness between her thighs before eagerly taking her to another level. I sexed Rachel with nothing but fire and desire. For all the moments we were into each other, she belonged to me.

* * *

Rachel and I arrived back at the office an hour before quitting time. She decided to leave early since we'd been sloppy at making love and her skirt was damp. She left the office almost immediately upon our return.

I checked my voice mail, email, and cell phone for any indication Holiday had tried to reach me, but she hadn't. My disappointment began to put me back in a slump, so I focused on the awesome time I'd shared with Rachel just hours earlier. My mood picked up in a hurry. I could still taste her wet kisses, smell her moisture on my fingers, and could vividly envision her breasts bouncing as I penetrated her deeply. The ringing phone on Lance's desk interrupted my daydream. It rang three times before I decided to go answer it. Before I made it close enough to glance at the caller ID, Lance intercepted me.

"I appreciate that, bruh, but I can get it," he said, stepping in front of me, placing his hand on my chest.

Lance made a slight turn to answer the call, but he never pulled away his hand. Angered I couldn't confirm my suspicion that Holiday was on the other end, I slapped Lance's hand away.

Lance looked stunned. He begged the caller pardon. "Excuse me a second. I'll be right with you," he said, placing the party on hold. He then turned to yell at me. "Man, are you okay? What's up with you?"

"Shit. What's up with you? You're the one playing traffic cop."

Lance looked me up and down as if he was ready to leap on me. I braced myself just in case. After a brief moment, he returned to his phone conversation. Still, I couldn't hear anything. I snatched my keys and headed home, ready to run over the first driver or pedestrian to get in my way.

Perhaps I need to make a few more disturbing phone calls to Lance's mother, I thought. *Surely his mother's worry would give him enough reason to back off. If not, then I'd just have to make good on my threats to do him harm. Nothing can come between me and Holiday. Nothing.*

Chapter Twenty

A Dear Journal

Once I arrived home, I popped a TV dinner in the oven then jumped in the shower, trying to ease my tension. I sat in front of the big screen wearing nothing but boxers, eating my food. By 8:00 P.M., I was in bed, but I couldn't sleep. I wondered if I could forget Holiday and just love Rachel. I decided to give Rachel a call.

"Hey, sweetness," I said just after she answered her phone.

"Hey there. I must've really put it on you because I'm surprised to be hearing from you so soon," she responded.

"Oh, you definitely put something on me. You can pat yourself on the back for that one."

"Well there's more where that came from. If you don't believe me, all you got to do is say the word, and then I'm over there."

"Is that all I have to do?" I asked, excitedly.

"That's all."

"Give me your address. I'm on my way over."

Rachel gave me directions to her home, and I spent the rest of the night with her. I even turned my phone off, so I could totally be into her. Holiday was the only other woman

I had done that for. I really liked Rachel. After a pleasurable night of getting to know each other mentally and sexually, I began to think there was a possibility that I could let Holiday go.

It was hard for me to hold back my feelings for Rachel while at work, but I did my best to remain professional. I didn't want Lance to get the clue that I had more than a work relationship with her. Rachel and I had only been sleeping together for about a week, and I still had love for Holiday. I couldn't help anticipating her call.

One night, I couldn't sleep because I began to feel a little anxiety about whether Holiday was seeing Lance. She wasn't calling me or responding to my messages. Though I liked Rachel, my feelings for Holiday weren't going anywhere. As I lay in deep in thought, I suddenly remembered I had Holiday's journal. I sprang out of bed and into my closet to retrieve it.

I opened it to the first page where it read: THESE ARE THE PRIVATE THOUGHTS OF ONE HOLIDAY SIMMONS. PLEASE DO NOT READ. I briefly thought, *Great penmanship.* Her plea failed to stop me.

After reading several notations and poetry, I decided to turn toward the middle of the book. One title sparked my interest. Holiday called it "Without a Breath".

A breath of fresh air meant everything to me
When you entered my world, joy was all I could see
You were the oxygen of my soul, fulfilling as could be
So, why am I now scarred and feeling no longer free?

It's because of the time you held me a little too tight,
Making me your prisoner during the entire night

You stole my energy though I put up a good fight,
But nothing could prepare me for all of your might.

I remember thinking, *This can't be happening, could this be a
    dream?*
Would this man I know and trust wholeheartedly be so mean?
I got my answer as you abruptly pulled my hair,
Snapping me into reality though I didn't wish to be there.

I knew I wasn't dreaming, I just didn't want to believe
That you'd leave me devastated and all alone to grieve.
My heart now aches for sovereignty, the unleashing of sor-
    row's chains.
Ever since you robbed my purity, the gross memory is the
    same.

You were everything I wanted when our love first began,
But I'd rather die a lonely death than to trust you again.
What you did was unruly, an unpleasant astonishment.
It should be deemed as cruelty and inhumane punish-
    ment.

How do you live with yourself daily, or even hour by hour?
No, I don't want your apology, your candy, or your flow-
    ers.
Instead, I prefer the times when it was easy to catch a
    breath.
But you can't give me that now, not even with news of your
    death.

I'm fighting suffocation 'cause I'm afraid to inhale.
I fear being tainted by the next air to avail.

I pray to one day lose this mental scar that rules every part
   of me.
For I know it's the only way I'll see heaven and once again
   be free.

Holiday's words hit me like a ton of bricks—heavy and
hard. It was then that I realized the reason she was so upset
over the discussion of date rape at Carlos's house. She'd told
me of past relationship experiences, but rape was something
I didn't know until I read it in her journal. *Who did this to her?*
I wondered. *Why hadn't she shared this aspect of her life with me?*
I reached for the phone.

"Please pick up the phone, Holiday," I said after listening
to it ring more than three times.

I hung up then dialed her home two more times. Then, I
rang her cell. My calls went unanswered. I jumped into a pair
of jeans and a T-shirt then headed for Holiday's house.
When I made it over there, she wasn't home. I wanted to wait
for her, but I decided against it. Holiday and I hadn't been
on the best of terms, so I didn't want to rattle her more with
my unannounced presence.

After I left, I couldn't help thinking about that poem.
When I talked to Holiday, *how would I explain reading her journal against her wishes?* I realized I needed a few days to get
myself together. Justifying my actions to Holiday would be
tough.

Chapter Twenty-one

I Need You

Another week went by without me hearing from Holiday. Either she wasn't thinking about me, or she was still pissed off. Though Rachel and I were still sleeping together off and on, I kept trying to remind myself that I was a better man than I was before Holiday came into the picture. After giving my life some thought, I felt I could be more patient for Holiday's sake, but the silence between us was killing me. I finally gave calling her another try. I was at a backyard barbecue given by an old college friend when I dialed Holiday's number. The noise level made it extremely difficult to hear her pick up.

"Hello," she yelled.

"Hey, boo. What's going on?"

"Roman, either go someplace private or call me after you're finished having fun. I only yelled about five times before you finally responded," Holiday snapped.

"What? What are you talking about?"

"The noise, Roman. I can hardly hear you, and you can barely hear me."

"Oh, boo, I'm heading inside the house now," I replied just before walking through the back door. "See, it's much quieter. So, whatcha up to?"

"Nothing."

"Nothing? What's that supposed to mean? Come on. I know you've gotta be doing something."

"Well, believe it. I'm down on the riverwalk enjoying the sun and the breeze . . . alone," Holiday said solemnly.

"Where's Crystal?"

"It's Saturday, Roman. She's away at cheerleading camp."

Holiday didn't sound thrilled to hear from me. It was obvious that I was annoying her because she kept calling me Roman instead of Rome. I felt bad that I hadn't invited her to the barbecue. I had hoped she would cheer up and accept my request to join me. "I'm at a friend's backyard party. Wanna join me?"

"Nope. You go on have your little fun. If you had truly wanted me with you, you would've invited me before now. What's wrong? The women there aren't pretty enough? Huh? What's the real reason you're calling me, Roman?"

Holiday sounded so sad. It was torture on my heart listening to her voice. And, knowing what I'd been doing with Rachel behind Holiday's back began to weigh heavy on me. I swallowed hard before responding.

"Because, boo, ever since you got mad at me, I've had nothing or nobody except you on my mind. I wanted to call you this morning, but I felt you needed more time. I couldn't stand holding back any longer. Tell me how you do it. How could you go so long without contacting me? I'm still your man, right?"

"I don't know," she spoke softly.

"What do you mean you don't know?"

"Roman, I'm still hurting. You've betrayed me . . . not once, not twice, but three times, damnit."

"Boo, the only thing I might have done wrong was not call you while I was in Jackson."

"That was the first time," she huffed.

"And, the only other thing I believe I did wrong was not returning your journal when I said I would."

"That was the third time. Do you pick and choose what's considered deceitful? I guess actually stealing the journal in the first place isn't wrong in your eyes, huh?"

"Boo, let me come see you. We need to discuss this face-to-face. What area of the riverwalk are you?"

"Please don't come. I really don't want company. Just stay where you are. Have fun. I'm content being alone."

"Boo—" Holiday didn't let me finish before she hung up.

I was determined to see her. I mentioned to a few people that I had to step out, but I would be returning, then I headed downtown. After parking on one end of the river-walk, I got out to look for Holiday. About halfway down the park, I spied her sitting on a blanket reading. She was breathtaking. Though her back was to me, she looked like an angel wearing a white, off-the-shoulder sundress. Her long dark hair blew freely in the wind. .

"You look beautiful," I complimented, sneaking up be-hind her.

I had thought my voice would startle her, but she never lifted her head out of the book. I gave her a few moments of silence then I spoke again. "Boo, please. I've been missing you all week. The silent treatment is growing old. Can't we talk?"

Without turning to look at me, Holiday spoke out. "Why should we?"

I stepped around in front of her. "Because I love you, and I have something for you."

Holiday finally looked up. She tilted her head, trying to get a glimpse of what I had behind my back.

"I don't want your candy or flowers or whatever gift you—" she began.

I dropped to my knees, shushing her and staring deeply into her eyes. Then I whipped out my surprise. "Boo, this is already yours," I stated, handing her journal back. "I had no right to take it, and even less right to read it, but I did, and I'm sorry."

Holiday had tears in her eyes as she whispered, "You read my journal? How could you?" She tried to get up to leave, but I held her arms. "No, let me go, Roman."

"Boo, wait. Just listen." We wrestled as I tried to keep her there on the blanket with me. "Please. I need to explain. I know I hurt you, but you've gotta hear my side of things."

"I don't give a damn about what you wanna say right now. That book has my private thoughts in it, and you shouldn't've ever touched it, let alone read it."

We continued to wrestle as she tried to free herself. "Holiday, hold on. I was wrong to read your journal, but aren't you the one who taught me that everything happens for a reason?"

Holiday stopped struggling. "Say what? Roman, please don't try your little game of flipping things around on me."

"I'm not, boo. I swear. I'm just saying that reading your journal has helped me to better understand you. I know why you snapped at Los's anniversary party, and I know why you kissed Lance that same night."

Holiday was silent. She seemed a bit surprised to hear me say I knew she kissed Lance, but I couldn't see her remorse. I felt her relax, so I let her arms go. She sat speechless, staring at the blanket we'd rumpled during our fight. After more silence, she began to look even sadder than she sounded on the phone. I wanted to console her, but I feared rejection. As I sat quietly with her, I pondered her thoughts. Finally, I decided to move closer to her. I stroked her face then asked her to share her sorrow.

"Holiday, Lance was more understanding. And, he happened to be the man there to comfort you. I forgive the kiss, but I'm having a hard time forgiving myself for not being in tune with my woman that night. You feel like talking?" I reached to rub her shoulder.

Holiday shrugged. "I guess."

"I'd like to know about the man who raped you. Who is he?"

"I can't. It's been nearly twenty years, and yet, I can't bring myself to talk about it without crying," she said, turning away from me.

I stroked the side of her face then tilted it so she'd look into my eyes. "Who says you have to speak without crying. I have an extra shoulder. It's yours if you want it."

The tears came immediately. "I was only fourteen that summer. My mother lied about my age in order for me to work at a fast food restaurant. She didn't like me working late, but I pleaded with her to do it. I figured it would be nice to pay for my own school clothes for a change." Holiday sniffed, shedding more tears.

She continued. "One night, I was scheduled to work until midnight. My father was out of town with our only car, so I planned to walk home. Momma knew I would be walking, so I expected her to be up waiting for me.

"Phillip, my hairdresser, came into the restaurant just before quitting time. I was excited to see him. He was a tall and sexy, twenty-six-year-old man. I loved his hair. Back then, he had one of those Prince-looking hair cuts with the low sides, and a Gucci tail in the back." She gave a dry laugh then continued. "His skin was golden-brown, and he had eyes that sort of reminded me of the singer, Prince. They were large and spoke a silent language. I could never tell what he was thinking, but his glare drew me to him and kept me curious.

"Phillip could tell I wanted attention, so he used it to his advantage. Now that I look back on things, I know Phillip knew I liked him from day one. I was so naïve. I just admired his maturity and the fact that he would chat with me from time to time. He asked if I needed a ride home the night he came into the restaurant, and I nodded. He hung around until I cleaned up, then we left."

Holiday took a deep breath, then continued. "I didn't live far from my job, and I began to panic when Phillip drove past my street. I told him he was going the wrong way, but he shook his head and kept driving. When we got to his house, I told him to go in and do whatever he needed to do, then to take me home. I knew my mother was worried sick. He kept walking as if I hadn't said a word."

"Phillip opened my car door and reached for my hand. Confused, I allowed him to lead me into his home. What little light I noticed came from a room just ahead. Once we were in the room, I noticed it was his bedroom. I didn't want to be there and I let him know it.

"I fussed and tried to pull away, but all of my protesting didn't work. Phillip managed to get me inside the room anyway. He closed the door and my heart began to pound. I looked at Phillip. This time his eyes weren't so silent. They spoke louder than the words he said as he grabbed me and threw me onto the bed. He began French kissing me. I couldn't stand his tongue in my mouth, but I tried to kiss him back, hoping he would let me go." Holiday let out a deep sigh before she continued.

"Once I realized Phillip wasn't going to stop, I pleaded with him. The more I begged, the more he snatched at my clothes."

Holiday began to cry more. I wondered if I should let her continue. Before I could ask if she was going to be okay, she started talking again.

"I told him I was a virgin, but that didn't stop him." She sobbed even more, then continued. "I told him he would get me pregnant, but that didn't stop him either. He promised not to hurt me if I calmed down and just let him have his way, so I did. He entered me, and it hurt like hell. I kept telling him he would get me pregnant, but he pulled my hair, told me to shut up, and that he wouldn't get me pregnant. He finally ejaculated on my stomach. He repeatedly raped me until daylight then dropped me off so I could catch the bus."

"My mother was at the kitchen table when I walked in. Her head was buried in her arms like a small child taking a nap on her desk. When she heard my voice, she lifted her head, but I didn't recognize her. In all of the years of cruelty my father dished to my mother, I'd never seen her as sad as she was this day."

"She didn't move. She stared blankly as if I was a ghost. Just as I was about to step to her, I felt a hammering thud in my back. My father was home from his trip before I had returned. He beat me with a vengeance . . . as if this was something he'd longed to do for years. My mother screamed until she fainted. I thought the beating would last a lifetime."

I interrupted Holiday. "Boo, what finally made him stop?"

"I was fresh out of tears after so long. I began to flinch at every lick, but my face was dry. Anger had set in, and my breath was short and hard. My father stopped, and we stared at each other unblinkingly. He lifted his hand in a motion to swing and hit me, but that time I didn't flinch. My eyes remained on his, and my breaths became quicker. We continued to stare at each other, and I could tell by the tears in his eyes that he knew I'd had enough. I'd never seen my father moved by anything. He put his hand down by his side then turned to walk out of the kitchen."

I felt horrible for Holiday. I held her tight. She wept like a hungry newborn, except her hunger wasn't for food. Holiday was starving for true affection. I gave her time to calm down before I spoke. "Boo, did you ever press charges against the rapist?"

Holiday couldn't lift her head to look at me. "No. I was too naïve to realize it wasn't my fault. I felt I had caused the rape. I was ashamed of getting into the car with an older man. Though I knew who he was, I felt I had let my mother down. She'd raised me better. I shouldn't've taken that ride from him. I've allowed my parents to think the worst of me all these years. Look at how my father reacted not even knowing the story. I probably had another beating coming if I had admitted to getting into the car with a grown man. I decided to lose my parents' complete trust rather than let them know I wasn't just out being the bad girl they thought I was."

Holiday chuckled a little. "You know the craziest part about what happened to me? I continued to allow Phillip to do my hair. I didn't want my folks to be suspicious of anything. I continued to believe for years that what Phillip did to me was solely my fault."

I cradled Holiday and kissed her forehead. "Give me another chance, boo. I've done my dirt, but I know now I only want to love you. You deserve my full heart. I can't take back what's done, but I can damn sure be your everything from now on." I wiped her tears then planted my lips on every inch of her face, one soft peck at a time.

I sat a bit longer trying to get Holiday to agree to go back to the barbecue with me. As we were talking, I noticed a woman in the distance with binoculars. I wasn't sure if she was looking in our direction, but she soon confirmed she was staring at us when she put the binoculars down, slid on a pair of sunglasses, then waved good-bye before getting into a black SUV. Something about the woman looked familiar, but I didn't recall knowing a white woman with short blonde hair. She drove away, and I focused back on Holiday. I meant every word about giving her all of my love. I was ready to let Rachel know we were a done deal.

Chapter Twenty-two

Test Me Not

I was beginning to feel that Holiday was destined to be a part of my life. No woman had ever moved me the way she did. I loved everything she represented—beauty, brains, affection, the total package. Holiday was for me. It was only too bad that Rachel Clark was now gonna have to forget everything that happened between us. Rachel came close to being what I thought I wanted, but the truth of the matter was she just wasn't Holiday—nor would she ever be.

I began to reflect back on how rough the last twelve months had been. Lance and I were no longer close, and Holiday and I seemed to have had so many obstacles in the way of our love. After the tragedy of the terrorist strike on September 11th, my relationship with Holiday kicked up a notch. I realized that life is too short. All I wanted was to give Holiday the affection she deserved, and the 911 incident made me feel I needed to seize every opportunity to show her how much she meant to me.

I decided to take Holiday to meet my father. He'd had a

bit much to drink, so I asked to speak to him alone. Once in his bedroom, his words were unkind.

"Whaddaya want?" he slurred, staggering to the bed. "Whatcha pull me back here fo'?"

"Because, Dad. We needed to speak in private," I responded.

He turned and began swinging his arms and legs as he spoke. "Private? I'm in my own goddamn house. All these walls is mine. Anybody don't wanna here what I gots to say can just get the hell on out!" he said as his feet slipped. Thank goodness his bottom landed on the bed.

I sighed out of frustration. I knew talking sensibly with my father was going to be tough. I watched him sway as he sat, mumbling to himself. I decided to try beginning the chat from another angle.

"I dreamed about Momma the other day. How about you? Anymore good dreams lately?" I asked.

"Yup. Oh, and yo' momma says to tell ya you're being stupid. Says ya oughta leave that so-called woman alone," he responded coldly.

"Dad. If Momma could see me right now, she wouldn't say anything bad. Those harsh words are your thoughts."

"Son, I've seen her kind before. She's a doll. I'll give her that, but I done told you ain't a woman alive as loving as your mother. All these little winches today looking for is somebody to pay bills for 'em. I bet that gal standing in my living room don't know shit about keeping a man happy."

"Dad, c'mon now. You don't know what the deal is with Holiday."

"Oh yeah? I betcha she got a kid, ain't she?"

"Yes, and, so? What's your point? You think I'm just supposed to be single all my life?" I became more frustrated.

"Son, the more I teach you, the dumber you get."

"Forget it, Dad. I don't wanna hear any more you have to say. You've got me messed up enough as it is already. I will thank you for one thing though." My father stood drunk and silent as I continued. "Had you not fed me all that garbage about falling in love not being worth crap, I might've chosen the wrong woman and never met a good one like Holiday."

Dad staggered past me then turned back to comment, "Like I said . . . the dumber you get. Leave my house, Roman, and take that tramp with you."

I stared coldly at my father. I had no more words for him. I went back into the room with Holiday. She seemed surprised we were leaving so soon, but thank goodness she never questioned it. Dad stood in the doorway and watched as I backed out of the driveway.

Three more months passed, and it was Christmas time. I spent almost every day of the holiday season with my boo and her daughter, Crystal. We visited The Enchanted Forest out at Shelby Farms, and we attended The Nutcracker at the Orpheum Theatre. I hadn't experienced such happier times since my mother and father use to create them. Crystal seemed somewhat distant, but I knew that loving Holiday meant Crystal was part of the package.

Just after the New Year, I was asked to work more weekends and to take frequent trips out to the Jackson office. I was reluctant at first. Holiday and I were on a beautiful track with our relationship. I feared causing friction by not spending our usual quality time together. After talking it over, Holiday assured me she would be able to cope with me working extra hours.

The first trip to Jackson made me nervous. The entire drive there, I dreaded seeing Toriana Ponce again. After I had been at the office for two hours, I hadn't seen signs of Tori. I finally asked someone and found out she had transferred to Nashville. Hearing this news made my day go much smoother.

I called Holiday early one Saturday morning, before going in to work, to confirm we'd go see a movie when I got off. She agreed and wished me a good working day. I thought about how I wanted to wine and dine her, take her to the movies, and then return to my home for some hot and steamy sex. Crystal would be away with relatives for the weekend, so my plans were bound to be on. I couldn't focus on my job for thinking of my boo. I found myself doing everything except the tasks at hand. I searched the Internet for popular romantic spots in Memphis then printed them out. I jotted possible dates in my calendar when we'd take advantage of each place. I wanted to spoil Holiday for a lifetime.

Half-finished with my duties, I got off the Internet to do some work. When my desk phone began to ring, I got excited. I hoped it was Holiday. The caller ID revealed an unavailable listing.

"Hello, Roman Broxton. Long time, no hear," the woman said after I picked up.

"Trina. What's going on?" My response was dry, definitely lacking enthusiasm.

"You, baby boy. I miss you. You don't try to hook up with a sista no more. Did I do something wrong?"

"No. I've just changed some things about how I want to live my life. My list of priorities don't include doing you anymore. Sorry."

"You sure have a way of being nice to a lady. I just wanted to see you, no strings attached."

A thought came to mind of how fine Trina is and how much I loved getting into bed with her, but I shook it off. "Trina, I have a lady with whom I'm very much serious now. I love her. She's the only one I think of these days."

"Daaaggg. When did you get to be a one-woman man? I

put up with your bullshit for years. Whoever this woman is I sort of feel sorry for her."

"Oh yeah? Then what the fuck is yo' ass doing calling me?" I asked pissed.

"Don't get me wrong, Roman. I miss the sex, but you ain't shit to be declared as a man. If that bitch of yours truly knows you, then she understands you can't be claimed as someone to call her own."

"Fuck you, Trina! Dial my number again and see what happens to your ass." I slammed the phone down then looked around to see if I was still the only one in my area of the building. Luckily I was.

The phone rang again. I snatched the receiver to my ear and began yelling. "You must think I'm playing with you, bitch! I will rock your world and make you wish you hadn't met a muthafucker like me. You hear me?"

"Roman, this is Sharonda! What's gotten into you?" my half-sister said on the other end.

I slapped my forehead out of frustration. I could've lost my job had that been one of my superiors on the line. I took a deep breath and tried to sound calm as I responded to Sharonda. "Sis, what's going on? I'm sorry. I thought you were someone else."

"Apparently. Who is this woman who's got you so uptight?"

"Nobody, Sharonda. Can we not talk about it? What makes you call your younger brother today?"

"Aw, you make it seem like I never call you. Every time we speak, it's because I was the one who did the reaching out. I just wanted to see how you were doing. Oh, and I spoke with Dad, and he told me you should be working."

"Yeah, well how does he know?"

"He says you left a weekly planner over to his house the last time you were there."

"Oh. Well the least he could've done was informed me. I looked all over for that planner. I had to get a new one."

"He'd like to talk with you, Roman. He just doesn't know how. Dad and I stay at odds more than the two of you. Your mother was his life, Roman. He's never tried living without her. The drinking is an illness. It's captivated him. Don't fault him. Just try to understand him."

"He doesn't want me to be in love. That's crazy. He was in love once."

"Roman, Dad just has a way of thinking that nobody will ever understand. He's still your father. Go see him."

"That's what this call from you to my workplace is about, isn't it?"

"It's not the only reason. I love you, li'l bro." Sharonda sounded as if she was smiling.

My heart smiled back. "Thanks, sis. And, in case you're wondering, the woman I was yelling at when you called is not the one I love."

"Cool. I assumed that much. I wasn't gonna dig too deep. Just wanna make sure you're okay."

"I'm straight. Thanks," I replied before hanging up.

It was good hearing from my sister. Sharonda and I were the only two siblings. Though we didn't share mothers, she was more determined than me to remain as close as if we came from the same womb. I resemble our father, but Sharonda looks so much more like him than me. She's what I call the female version of Dad with her full lips, mahogany complexion, and almond-shaped eyes.

Sharonda's call was the start of my day getting back on track—until I was misled by yet another unidentifiable call. I picked up the phone and teased. "Yeah, Sharonda . . . what did you forget to tell me this time, sis?"

An unfamiliar, raspy, yet feminine voice responded. "This

isn't Sharonda, mutherfucker. Time for playing games is almost up. Are you ready? I am."

The caller immediately hung up. My blood began to boil all over again. Trina had gone way too far. I wondered why the hell she wouldn't just leave well enough alone. Trina knew from past experience that I ain't the one to play with, so her threat was totally out of character for her.

I thought long and hard, but the more I meditated, I realized the voice over the phone didn't sound very much like Trina at all. As a matter of fact, it didn't sound like anyone I knew. I sat a while longer in deep thought then refocused on my work. Remembering I had a love sitting at home waiting on me was enough motivation to set all bullshit aside, but I would definitely deal with the harasser later.

Chapter Twenty-three

Oh No . . . Not Again

I finished all of my assignments and left the office singing. On the way home, I decided to detour by Holiday's place. I wanted to see if she wouldn't mind getting ready for our date at my house. I pulled up to an unpleasant surprise: Lance's truck was parked out front, which could only mean one thing. He was inside with my woman, probably screwing her brains out.

I stood in front of the door, contemplating if I should knock or go back to my car and wait. Before I could make up my mind, the door pulled open. Holiday was shocked to see me. I couldn't speak because I was so furious.

"Rome! Rome, baby, it's not what it looks like," Holiday said.

I made my way past her into the house. Holiday's hair wasn't combed, which really struck me as odd. She never did that way, not even sitting around the house. Plus, she had company. Holiday would never let Lance or anyone else inside her home without combing her hair. I looked around the living room for any piece of evidence to back my suspicion that she and Lance had been fooling around. Lance stood silent, seemingly unfazed. After scanning the area, my eyes met with Holiday's. I began to yell at her.

"What the fuck is he doing here?" I huffed, pointing at Lance.

"I came to—" Lance began until I cut him off.

"I wasn't talking to you. I'm talking to my woman right now. Answer the question, Holiday."

"Rome, baby, Lance just came over to pick up his sunglasses. He was just leaving."

"Do you have 'em?" I asked. Lance's hands were empty. If he couldn't do some type of magic to produce those sunglasses, his ass was about to be mine.

Lance was silent. Considering the circumstances, he seemed pretty calm. Holiday was in a severe panic. Her gaze looked as if she was scrambling for something to say. She came to Lance's rescue when she turned to pick up the shades over on the couch.

"Oh, here, Lance, you're about to forget them again. They're going to get broken if you keep leaving them over here," Holiday said, half smiling, and looking semi-relieved.

"Thanks, Holiday. Take care," Lance said just before leaving.

I looked around the place some more. For what I didn't know. I just had to find something to confirm my instinct. I knew they had to be having sex, but gut was warning me to chill before I found the evidence, which I wouldn't be able to handle. I decided to continue with my search.

I found Holiday's bathroom heated from a recent steamy shower. The air was filled with fresh soap, the carpet was soaked, and two damp towels were on top of the clothes hamper. Not only had she been naked with Lance again, but she had just experienced a moment in the shower, which we both declared as our private joy. She made me vow to never share intimacy in the shower with anyone but her.

I stormed out of the bathroom to confront Holiday. She looked nervous as I opened my mouth to speak. Before I could say anything, I was caught off guard by another revelation. Holiday's bed was a mess. When I'd spoken to her earlier that morning, she was in the process of placing clean sheets on it. This bed was so far from being neat that it looked like mad dogs had trampled on it.

I sat on the edge of the bed, speechless. *Not, my woman. No, no, no . . . she didn't do this to me again. I must be dreaming this,* I thought. I looked up into her eyes hoping to see a sign to confirm I'd overreacted, but instead, her face spoke guilt in a thousand languages. She couldn't have faked a smile even if I had told her she'd just won a million dollars. Suddenly, it dawned on me that I'd just sat on the bed where she had just screwed my ex-best friend. I jumped up, startling Holiday as I hurriedly brushed past her. Holiday tried to apologize before I left, but I wasn't trying to hear it.

As days went by, I could slowly feel myself losing it. My mind told me I should harm both Holiday and Lance and be done with the past, but the more I thought about being without Holiday, the more my heart ached. I just wasn't used to being hurt by a woman. I was confused about how to handle it, so I chose to hold everything in. I hung out with my boys on the weekends, and I worked alongside of Lance as if he wasn't a factor of my concerns.

It was tough seeing Lance every day without kicking his ass, but I had other plans that would make him wish he'd thought twice about fooling around with Holiday again. I began to wonder if Lance had been with Holiday more times than they had admitted. My hurt turned into urges for revenge. I didn't deserve this betrayal, but because of my feelings for Holiday, I dismissed thoughts of doing her harm. Lance, however, would soon meet the Roman Broxton he never wanted to know.

Chapter Twenty-four

A Little Love is All it Takes

It was March, two months since Holiday and I talked. I was still filled with anger and hurt. She left me with memories of a wonderful holiday season, including bringing in the New Year at a popular restaurant seventy-five stories in the air in Atlanta, Georgia called The Sun Dial. After discovering her deceit with Lance, I gave her space because I was beginning to wonder if salvaging a relationship with her was worth the time. It didn't seem fair that we didn't get to share Valentine's Day, and I thought about her the whole day. My love for her hadn't faded. I had only lost the desire to chase her. I figured if given enough time, she'd come to her senses and realize she missed me.

I turned to Rachel for comfort. She had initially accepted me not dealing with her outside of work, but as soon as I told her that Holiday and I were having problems, she opened up and welcomed me back into her life. I spent many nights in Rachel's arms. I wanted to love her, but I just couldn't get Holiday out of my system. I made sure Rachel understood that I felt my separation from Holiday was temporary. The last thing I needed was more drama in my life.

By June, I'd been given a promotion on my job. Lance and I were up for the same position in compliance reporting. To be honest, I was surprised I was promoted over him. Lance's attendance history was better than mine—so was his work performance. I had only met a few of the company's goals in the last year, whereas Lance met goals almost every quarter. Lance seemed to have a problem because a few of the company's most important cases somehow came up missing while in his care. His troubles with the cases started shortly after he and I began having our issues with each other, and then again just before we were interviewed for the promotion. I gladly accepted the position and moved into my new office, which I shared with another manager.

Rachel Clark hounded me to spend more time with her, but I had come to realize I didn't want to continue our bond. I knew I wanted to be with Holiday months before Rachel began putting pressure on me, but I didn't bother to discuss it with Rachel again because I feared hurting her. I began avoiding Rachel because I wanted to get Holiday back.

I dodged Rachel as much as possible by sneaking out into the field while she was in the ladies' room or when she stepped away from her desk. I soon began to run out of excuses when she'd call me at home or on my cell. It wasn't until a week after my promotion that I was cornered by Rachel in my office.

"Come in," I responded to the knock on the door.

Rachel walked in looking sexy as ever in a fitted red top and a tight black skirt that rose just above her knees. She closed the door behind her. "We need to talk," she said, placing her hand on her hip.

Donnell Stokes, the co-manager in my department slid his chair back in an effort to leave the room, but I held up my hand and nodded for him to stay. Since I had been ignoring Rachel for a couple of weeks, I felt it safer to have someone in the office. I looked Rachel in the eyes then motioned toward the chair in front of my desk.

"Okay, Rachel. Please have a seat," I said.

"So, where're we headed in the fields today?" she asked, sitting posed with her back straight and legs crossed.

I cleared my throat. "Excuse me? We?" I played dumb in order to keep the conversation friendly.

Rachel did a double-take then twisted her lips. "Wait a minute. Let me start over. Am I right to accuse you of dodging me?" I sat quietly, staring at her. She continued. "I mean . . . I've been doing everything possible to give you space, Roman, because I understand that's how you are. But what about what I want?"

I glanced over at Donnell, who was ferociously pecking away on his keyboard, pretending not to be into our conversation. I responded to Rachel in a way that pretty much dared her to try to go there with me. "I don't know. Try sharing your thoughts with me, Rachel." I remained calm.

She looked over at Donnell then back at me and went where I thought she wouldn't with the conversation. "I wanna be closer to you. I want you to want me. Don't get me wrong. I knew you weren't over your woman, but I hoped as time went by, what you felt for me would change. I felt we had begun a different kind of friendship."

The sigh that left my body was intense. I tried to respond to Rachel in a whisper. "Well let me ask you this, did you think I would forget about my woman for you?"

Rachel shook her head then leaned in to me, lowering her voice as well. "No . . . no . . . no. I'm just saying, I could tell you were at your end with her, and to be honest, what we had felt kinda nice. Kinda like something I want to share with you on a more permanent basis." She smiled then reached across my desk to stroke my hand.

I continued to speak softly. "Rachel, it was nice. You were everything I needed for a while, but I've given my life some more thought, and I've come to the conclusion that I still want my woman."

Rachel sat back and shrugged. "And . . . so, what about us?"

I scratched my head and answered. "What about us?"

I've never seen tears flood someone's face so rapidly. Though Rachel's tears fell like Niagra Falls, her anger would not go unseen. Donnell looked up and stopped typing because Rachel went ballistic.

"Oh . . . oh . . . Hell naw! I've been patient, Roman, waiting for you to realize I'm better for you." I stood when Rachel began beating her fist on my desk. "I opened my legs for you time and time again. I've been there for you in every sense that a woman should for a man. How dare you sit there and be so nonchalant."

"L-L-Look, Rachel, y-y-you need to calm down or else leave," I stuttered.

"Leave? Leave? Oh . . . now you gon' put me out of your office, too? Man, life just doesn't get any funnier than this. Let me tell you something, Mr. Roman Broxton. I may leave this office, but I won't be leaving your life because I happen to be carrying your seed inside me." Rachel paused to wipe her tears. My face went white as I did nothing to mask being stunned. She looked me in the eyes as she continued. "That's right. I'm pregnant with your baby."

It was time for some privacy. "Donnell, I'm sorry about all of this, and I wish I didn't have to interrupt you while you're busy, but do you mind if Ms. Clark and I have a private moment?"

Donnell hesitated for a moment. "No, I don't mind, but are you sure you're gonna be okay?" he asked.

"I'll be fine," I responded.

"Yes, he'll be fine. I won't kill 'im. After all, he is my baby's daddy," Rachel taunted.

Donnell's eyes never left Rachel as he passed to exit the office.

Once again, I pleaded with Rachel to take a seat. She was a little stubborn at first, but sorrow got the best of her. She broke and cried some more. Her beautiful chestnut-colored eyes were red and swollen. I sat quietly, collecting my thoughts as I listened to her whimper. Rachel spoke out before I was ready.

"Don't you have something to say, Roman? Anything at all?"

"Yes," I whispered then cleared my throat.

Rachel lifted her head, peering at me, waiting for more response. I had to swallow hard before I could talk. "I'm sorry."

"Hmph. Not as half as sorry as I am, Roman. You don't have a clue, do you? The reason you have this position is because of me."

"Say what? Just what do you mean by that?" I was totally puzzled.

"Roman, you know Lance should've gotten the promotion. You feared he would get the job, and other agents were talking about how they could see there was no contest between the two of you, especially since Lance is well up on his skills compared to you. I didn't want to see you hurt, so I conveniently made a few major cases disappear in the system as well as from hard files."

I couldn't believe my ears. "You did what?" I paused, hoping she'd retract her story. Silent tears continued to roll down her face. "Rachel, please tell me I didn't hear you correctly."

"I know I was wrong. I don't apologize for being immoral, but I'm beginning to be remorseful about caring so much for you," she said sarcastically.

There are no words in any language that could adequately explain how stunned I was to hear this news from Rachel. I had wondered what was going on with Lance. Mishandling his cases just didn't seem like of him. Never did it cross my mind that someone had sabotaged him. This was a lot of information for me to absorb in one sitting.

"Whoa. Rachel, I'm speechless. Except, you're right, I had no idea you cared enough to take drastic measures for me. Seriously, I'm sorry, but I can't condone what you did to Lance."

"And, I'm not asking you to. At least acknowledge my pain."

"I didn't mean to hurt you. I shouldn't have carried on an intimate relationship with you knowing I was still in love with Holiday."

"Oh, so I finally get to hear a name. She's not just 'my woman' anymore, she's 'Holiday.' Cute. Real cute," Rachel said, sniffling.

"Rachel, you must know I'm blown away right now."

"Why, Roman? I thought you knew that pregnancy is what happens when two consenting adults get together and fuck without condoms. You never had the talk about the birds and the bees with your parents?" Rachel was being sarcastic, but I didn't quite appreciate it.

"Look, this is a bit much for me to handle at the moment. How about we discuss things later this evening?"

"No, how about you let me ride along on your runs today? We can talk more then. Plus, the reason I asked to tag along is because I need a lift to the doctor's office at three-thirty."

"Oh. Well, I really don't have runs to complete today. Do

you think you'll be able to drive my car okay? I've got so much to catch up on here at the office," I lied. I was too dazed to deal with Rachel's pregnancy at the moment.

"You want me to drive Black Onyx?"

"Sure. Why not? And, I promise we can talk later this evening. Right now, I need to get some work done." I began shuffling things around on my desk.

Rachel looked surprised, but she accepted my offer. "Alright. I'll be back around three o'clock for your keys."

"See you then." I tried to smile, but I think all I managed to do was curve one side of my mouth upward.

As soon as Rachel closed the door behind her, I began calling clients to cancel my afternoon meetings. There was no way I could focus after the bitter pills Rachel gave me to chew. I felt like having some really strong alcohol. My regular "career man's" drink, bourbon and Coke, wouldn't have helped me much. Something like Tequila would've numbed me good, but I'd already promised Rachel my car. Leaving the office for the day was out of the question.

If Rachel was really pregnant, my shit was about to hit the fan at work and in my personal life. Donnell had already heard the news, and I figured he probably ran into the conference room with other members of management to blab my business. I stayed hemmed up at my desk just about all day. I didn't break for anything but to use the restroom because I was afraid someone would stop me to ask about the incident in my office.

As I headed to the men's room, Lance's phone rang. He was out of the area at the time, so since Donnell was near, he reached to answer it. Donnell placed the call on hold then asked me if I knew where Lance had gone. I answered that I didn't and offered to take a message for him. My heart raced when I saw Holiday's number on the ID. I answered the line, but she hung up. I tried to dial her back, but she wouldn't pick up her phone. I stood puzzled for a moment. Donnell asked if I was alright. I told him I was, so he left it at that. I was glad he did. I couldn't answer my own questions, let alone somebody else's.

To say I was disturbed about the possibility that Holiday was dating Lance is an understatement. Being fucked up in the head was more like it. How could I not see that coming? Of course if I wasn't going to have anything to do with Holiday, Lance was gonna be there to be her knight. Me being out of the picture was all Lance needed. I couldn't figure out exactly why Holiday constantly fell so weak for him. I knew she loved me, and there shouldn't have been a mistake about whether I loved her. Somehow, I needed to figure out a way to make my love for her be enough. I went back to my office, deep in thought, plotting my next move.

Chapter Twenty-five

On and On It Goes

It was close to evening when I realized my whole day was a waste. Rachel had driven away with my car an hour before, and I was left at work unable to focus. Donnell left on an assignment with another associate, so our office was quiet, but I had far too many problems affecting me mentally to get anything done. I decided to visit the other departments for a while to get my drama-filled life off my mind. I froze at the sight of a new ornament in the office. Standing not even six feet away from me was Holiday Simmons, the most beautiful decorative piece New Vet Life had seen in a long time.

Holiday was in the middle of a conversation with an analyst when she looked up and noticed me. She returned my stare unblinkingly as she finished her discussion. Holiday slow strolled over to me. My heart skipped a beat, and for some strange reason, I felt nervous to face her.

"Hello, Holiday. I see you couldn't even be a big enough woman to ask me if you could speak to your man. You didn't have to hang up in my face. I wouldn't have had any problem letting Lance know there was a call waiting."

Holiday was quick to respond. "Well, first of all, congratulations on your new position. And second of all, I didn't realize you were aware I was still seeing Lance. I didn't want to cause any trouble."

"I didn't know you were still seeing him, but I do now. When Lance was called to the phone, I decided to take a message for him since he was out of the office. I happened to glance at the caller ID before picking it up and discovered your number. Tripped me out."

After the revelation of Rachel sabotaging Lance, I felt it necessary to be totally honest about how I came to answer Lance's phone. I didn't want Lance to think I was the one trying to hurt his career.

We continued our conversation as I stood in the doorway of my office, too shocked to invite her in. "So, where's your car? I didn't see it outside," she asked.

"When I realized that I wouldn't have to be in the field, I let a coworker take it to the shop for me. I'm getting some more tint put on the windows, and with all the work I have to do around here this evening, I knew I wouldn't have time to wait for it."

"Well, who is this privileged coworker? You didn't even let me drive Black Onyx."

"You didn't ask," I replied, knowing full well I never meant to let anyone drive my car. I finally got the courage to ask Holiday inside. "Look, do you have a minute to step in my office? I want to ask you something."

Holiday took the lead as we entered the room. I knew she'd probably come to see Lance, so to keep her at ease about being alone in the office with me, I left the door opened.

"Go ahead, I'm listening." Holiday turned toward me.

I spilled my guts to her, letting her know how in love with her I still was. I needed to know if she felt the same for me. As we talked I got the confirmation for which I hoped, but it came along with excess baggage. Holiday wounded me by telling me she was also in love with Lance and had no intention of giving him up.

Before I was ready to let her go, Lance appeared in the doorway. "You ready to go, baby girl?" He spoke to Holiday softly, but his face hardened when he looked at me.

My guess is that Lance probably overheard some of my discussion with Holiday, which didn't matter. All I hoped was that I'd said something to Holiday to move her heart more toward me.

This game of life was gonna have to change for me somehow. I wasn't totally giving up on Holiday, especially since her revelation she and Lance were continuing to see each other. Holiday was mine, and I was determined to keep things that way. My passion for her was driving me crazy. Not even the fact of possibly having a child with another woman could steer me from thoughts of being with Holiday forever. I knew I would get her back, and it didn't matter whose heart got hurt.

Chapter Twenty-six

Red-Hot Desires

I had to know if Holiday still loved me. I called to ask if I could see her. When she agreed, I felt I would soon own her heart. I didn't quite have a plan for winning her over. I decided to do the simple thing instead, taking things one day at a time.

I knew Holiday was still seeing Lance, but he didn't have a clue I was back in the picture. I looked at Lance daily at work, grinning to myself because he thought he was reigning over Holiday's heart. As long as Holiday allowed me to have a part of her world, I was fine, and I felt Lance wasn't a threat. I figured once Holiday realized she was ready to completely dedicate herself to me, I'd get more satisfaction from her being the one to hurt Lance's pride.

I decided to call my boo one Saturday to see if we could hook up. Usually, Crystal would be away with relatives for the weekend, so I wasn't worried that Holiday wouldn't have time for me. She answered the phone sweetly.

"Hey, baby. What's on your mind?" she asked after picking up the phone.

"You, boo. What kind of question is that? Not a moment goes by when you're not on my mind."

"Oh, aren't you sweet? Glad to know somebody's thinking about me."

"Always, boo. Always. Why don't you let me spoil you tonight?"

"Hmm. Whatcha got in mind?"

"I want to see you layered in red. If you don't have anything in the closet, go buy something, and I'll reimburse you."

"Red, huh? Roman, you know I don't do that color."

"Why not, boo? A woman as sexy as you can wear every color in the rainbow at the same time and still be a stunner."

Holiday laughed. "Roman, you can be so silly. Well, just so you'll know in advance, I'm going shopping. I don't have crimson colors in my closet, but even if I did, I'd still go buy something new, simply because you offered."

"Cool. I don't have an issue with that. You know you my boo. You got it like that. By the way, be sure to visit Victoria's Secret for the underwear. When I say I want to see you layered in red, I mean the total package."

"Oh, baby, I can tell you've got a wild imagination for tonight. I'll be sure to do all I can to create your fantasy."

"Well, as long as you're doing all you can, I'm sure you'll have no problem. Love you."

"Back at you," Holiday responded before hanging up.

My intention was dinner and a movie at my place. After a little casual entertainment, the formal activities were to go on in the bedroom. Holiday didn't seem surprised. I don't think anything I've ever done has been really astonishing to her. If so, she sure is great with playing off her emotions. Well, except in the bedroom. Holiday couldn't act hard even if she wanted because I put the smack down on her time and time again. I know because Holiday can be extremely vocal during sex.

I was in the mood for Italian, so I purchased samplings of everything on the menu from the Olive Garden. We decided to order a thriller on Pay-Per-View, but we never had the chance to see it all the way through.

As we were sitting on the couch, I reached underneath Holiday's dress and discovered a mesh of softness. Though firm, Holiday's ass felt smooth as I ran my hand over her lace boy-cut panty. I picked up the remote and turned off the TV immediately. I asked Holiday to stand, spin around, and then lift up her dress. I saw just what I expected. Holiday's butt cheeks were well rounded with a silk, chocolate glow. She bent over and touched her toes, causing those red panties to creep, creating a misdemeanor as they formed a heart-shape over her ass. I was about ready to take a bite out of crime.

I slid the panties aside as I began to lick her from behind with slow, luscious strokes. Holiday gripped her ankles as I buried my tongue deep into her canal. Once she began to tremble, I knew it was time to assist her with standing up. Holiday placed her hands flat on the floor for more support, then I took a nosedive in for the finish. I could barely catch all of her succulent nectar as it rapidly flowed, coating my face.

Although weak and out of breath, Holiday muscled the strength to return the oral favor. We made love off and on the entire night. There were intervals in which I'd wake her up, and then at other times, she'd wake me up with her soft lips and her wet, warm tongue.

Somewhere around three-thirty in the morning, I was awakened by a knock on the door. Holiday was out cold from our last episode of smack down. I left her snoring sweetly while I got up to see who could be visiting at such an ungodly hour. I peered through the peephole, but no one was in view. Even after asking who was outside my door, there was no response and neither did anyone appear within sight.

The knocks kept coming and getting louder with every beat. I went to retrieve the gun I had purchased after seeing the one Lance got. Ready and loaded, I began unlatching the locks. I could hear footsteps running away. They sounded like a pair of women's heels clacking on cement. I released each lock as quickly as I could. I was determined to catch this intruder.

I flung the door open and was only able to dart one foot onto the porch before I heard a poof and felt a smack in the face. My eyes were burning beyond control, and I feared opening them. I could hear the sound of a car cranking, so I force my eyes open and caught a glimpse of what looked like the same SUV truck I'd seen down on the riverwalk. I couldn't tell who was inside because the person skidded away.

I went inside, closed the door, and staggered into the bathroom in the hallway. I flushed my eyes with cold water for nearly half an hour before I felt enough ease to open them. It was good that Holiday never heard a thing. I scampered about the office in my house, searching desk drawers for my insurance cards. My eyes were red and swollen, and it was going to be tough trying to explain things to Holiday. I was sure if I told her the truth, she'd never spend time with me at my place again. My mind was made up. She couldn't know what really happened to me.

After finding the insurance card, I sat at my desk, wondering. *Who is this mystery person?* Trina is a sista. The lady I saw at the river, driving a truck like the one that sped away from my house was a short-haired blonde, and Caucasian. I never fooled around outside my race. Maybe Trina had hired someone. She did have several friends of other ethnic groups. It wouldn't surprise me if one of her white friends would be willing to clown on her behave.

Then again, Rachel Clark wasn't all that happy with me either. I wondered if perhaps she had put someone up to following, threatening, and attacking me to teach me a lesson.

I became nervous after hearing Holiday call for me. "Rome, sweetheart, where are you?"

I jumped up from the desk then headed into the hallway. "I'm about to go into the restroom, boo. I didn't want to disturb your sleep by using the one in the bedroom."

"That's okay, baby. You can use this one," she yelled.

I went and stood in the doorway, looking everywhere except straight at Holiday. It was dark enough to get away with her not seeing the redness in my eyes, but the swelling was a different story. I didn't want to chance her noticing the awkwardness. "Naw, boo. I'm gon' be a minute. That Italian food was good, but now it's got my stomach hurting."

"Okay, love. Hope you feel better," she responded.

I closed the bedroom door then headed to check out my front porch. It was full of black ashes and pieces of something that looked like a grenade. Suddenly it dawned on me how lucky I'd been. The intruder had thrown some kind of smoke bomb in my face. *This person is out to kill me,* is what came to mind. *I've got to get to the bottom of this.*

I went into the kitchen to retrieve the broom and some cleaning materials. I couldn't let Holiday see the mess lying there.

I never went back to sleep that night. I sat up on my couch thinking until daylight broke then I decided to awaken Holiday with the smell of hotcakes and bacon. The ploy to lure her out of bed worked. My back was to her as she entered the kitchen, but I knew she was there because she began to sigh with sounds of a hungry woman.

"Good morning, boo," I said as I removed the bacon strips from the George Foreman.

"Morning, baby. Mmm-mmm. This is a pleasant surprise. You're gonna make me sleep over more often if you keep spoiling me like this," she said, gripping my waist from behind.

"Really? If I'da known this was all I had to do, you'da been moved in," I said just before turning to face her.

Holiday jumped back and screamed. "Rome, what happened to your face? Dayum."

"Oh, boo, do I look that bad?" I didn't let her respond. "It's allergies. I tasted all the Italian dishes last night, knowing full well what shrimp does to me. I just got carried away because the seafood pasta was so good. Now I'm paying for it."

I worried that Holiday didn't believe me. Her face was scrunched as if she was looking at a monster. I continued to lie and explain things, hoping she'd give in and let the conversation go. I really felt I didn't look so terrible. My eyes looked bad, but I managed to come out of the situation without burn marks or any other permanent damage. I was sure my doctor was gonna tell me my eyes would return to normal.

No matter how much I talked, Holiday's expression wasn't changing. After smelling something burning, she finally opened up a new topic of discussion. Thank goodness for the scorching intervention.

"Wow, those hotcakes are sticking to the pan, Rome," Holiday said, peering around me at the stove.

"Oh, sorry. I've got more batter. It won't take me long to whip up some. How many cakes can you eat?"

"I'm starving. Fix me three hefty ones."

I headed to the refrigerator. "Certainly, ma'am. Will you

be having orange juice, milk, or water with your meal this morning?"

"Orange juice is fine, but I'd like a cup of coffee as well if you don't mind."

"I don't mind at all, boo. Coming right up."

Just as I was beginning to think I'd shook the conversation about my face, Holiday brought the subject back up. I could've screamed bloody murder because I'd had enough of trying to convince her I would be okay.

"Rome, are you planning to see a doctor, today? I really think you should have a physician check you out."

"Yes, boo, I'm planning to go to the minor emergency room if I can find one open on Sundays."

"Good because I'm worried. I've never seen you have this type of allergic reaction."

"That's probably because in the past I've been more careful about what I ate. Last night was special, and I got careless. That's all, boo. You don't have to worry, okay?" I stroked her chin as she nodded then I continued. "Now go have a seat at the breakfast bar. I'll be over in a minute with your food."

"Does that include you on a plate?" She smiled.

"I'll see if I can make that happen," I responded, giving her a seductive wink.

Holiday's cell began ringing. "Must be yo boy, Lance. Tell 'im you a'ight. You're with me," I teased sarcastically.

Holiday looked puzzled as she glanced at the caller ID. "Hello?" she answered. "Heelloo? *Hello?*"

"Boo, who is that?"

"I don't know, Rome. Somebody on the other line is just breathing all hard into the phone. Pervert. People just don't have anything better to do, I guess."

I immediately became suspicious the harasser had phoned Holiday. I tried not to show worry, so I responded with cool. "Yeah. There're some weird folks in the world, boo," I said.

Then my cell rang. "Hmmm . . . imagine that. Maybe they're calling me now," I mocked.

As funny as it seemed, the truth was the same person must've dialed me, too. I didn't want to alarm Holiday, so I faked a conversation. "Hello?" I paused when I heard the heavy breathing. "Good morning to you, too, Ant. Whatcha got up for the day?" Holiday looked on as I continued my make-believe conversation. "That's cool. I'll be sure to holla back atcha then," I said just before hanging up.

"That was Ant?" Holiday asked.

"Yeah, but why are you looking surprised?"

"I never imagined a chat with Ant to be so friendly." Holiday frowned as she spoke.

"C'mon, boo. I know you got issues with Ant, but he's my friend, you know?"

"I know, but that doesn't mean I have to like him. I'll keep my distance because otherwise I might slap some sense into him." Holiday laughed, and I joined in.

Later I found a clinic that would see me. I was right. My eyes suffered minor irritation and would be back to normal within days. I was prescribed drops to prevent further burning or pain and to help clear the discoloration.

My eyes felt better, but my mind was weary. I needed to find out the identity of the woman who showed up at my house to do me harm. I knew I had to watch over my shoulder from then on, but I would stop at nothing to find this lady and cause her some well-deserved pain.

Chapter Twenty-seven

Drama-fied

My boys, Ant and Carlos, were pretty much clueless regarding all the hype in my life. After the scene between Holiday and Ant at Carlos's anniversary party, I figured it was a good idea to keep my girl away from my friends and to do all I could to prevent her from wanting to be with Lance. Though Lance managed to remain in the picture, I was certain he'd kept quiet regarding all the problems between him and me. The fellas never asked me anything else regarding my three-way situation with Lance and Holiday after the party.

My life was becoming more and more complicated. I had begun to feel the lost of self-control. The least little thing someone did or said that I didn't like, I lost my temper, especially when it came to Rachel Clark.

Suspicious that Rachel could've been responsible for making the harassing calls to me and Holiday, I tried to keep things kosher as much as possible. Rachel made it extremely difficult to keep my cool. I understand that pregnant women are moody, but Rachel was a demon compared to most I've seen. She began to have tantrums. One day when I didn't go with her to the doctor when she wanted, she got vicious. There was an altercation which began between us in my office, after everyone left for the day.

"I didn't lie down and get pregnant by myself, Roman. The least you could do is support me by going to my doctor visits. This is your child, too," Rachel said, almost spurting fire as she spoke.

"Excuse me? Umm, I don't think it's been proven I'm the father yet, Rachel."

"Uhn-uhn. Don't you go starting that shit. You can reject me, but I won't let you slight our baby."

"Rachel, if that kid is proven mine, you don't have to worry about me taking care of my responsibilities."

I could see pain in Rachel's eyes, but I could do nothing to alleviate it. I still didn't know whether I was truly the father of her unborn child. Noticing how I wasn't moved by her haughtiness, Rachel walked up in my face as if she could intimidate me. "Do you deny sleeping with me?" she asked.

I huffed. "No, and why the hell are you questioning me?"

"Do you deny not using a condom?"

I was losing patience. "I was there, Rachel. I realize we didn't use protection. Again, what the hell are you trying to get out of me?"

Rachel blew a fuse as well. "Wait a minute, damnit!" She was now closer than I wanted her to be. I could feel the heat of her breath as she huffed just inches in front of my face. "I hear you saying you're not in denial, so your actions need to reflect that you can deal with the facts."

"Or, maybe it's you who needs to learn how to deal with facts, Rachel. How many times have you opened your legs every time the nearest man stroked you on the thigh?"

Rachel's slap landed harder than a man's closed fist. I tried my best to refocus while dazed and throbbing with pain. I held my jaw and glared at Rachel, seriously contemplating hitting her back.

"C'mon. What? What else you got to say?" she taunted.

"Get the fuck out of here before I do something bad to you, Rachel."

"If you so bad, nigga, I suggest you do what you gon' do."

I could feel my blood boiling. I grabbed Rachel by her throat. "Trick, you about to make me go to jail. I really don't want to hurt you. Now get out," I said, pushing Rachel away from me.

Though she was still angry, I could see in her face that she'd gotten my point. She rolled her eyes as she walked away. I had just about let my guard down, turning my back on her as well when I heard a loud scream. I looked around to see Rachel charging at me. I lifted my arms, prepared to block another one of her vicious blows, but instead I received a fast-flowing glob of wet saliva in my face. Oh, it was about to be on.

"Is everything alright in here?" I heard a male voice say.

I put my arms down and noticed Donnell Stokes standing in the doorway of our office. I didn't know the reason for Donnell's return, but I think his appearance was the best thing to happen for Rachel. I was so mad I could hardly breathe, let alone speak. I ignored Donnell for a moment, then went over to my desk to retrieve a napkin. Rachel stood silent and stone-faced. Donnell spoke up again. "Roman, are you okay, man?" He walked over to me handing me extra napkins.

"Yeah, man, I'm straight." I looked at Rachel then addressed her. "Am I gonna have to tell you again to leave?"

Rachel elected not to respond aloud. She folded her arms then moved in closer to whisper in my face. "This ain't over."

"Bet," I retorted.

Donnell and I stood, watching Rachel until she had exited the building and was far out of sight. It was a bit too late to be embarrassed, so I sparked up a decent conversation with Donnell as if everything was on the up and up. "What are you doing back here so late?" I asked, trying to cool down.

Donnell went over toward his desk. "I left the keys to my storage room. I've got some moving to do this evening. I figured I better come back to the office because there's no telling when my wife will be home with the extra set."

"Yeah, I hear ya. Do women ever come straight home from anywhere?"

"Not mine, but it looks like I did the right thing by returning here. All hell broke loose, man."

"Man, that girl is going to be a trip. I can see that now," I responded.

"Is she really carrying your baby?"

"Honestly, I don't know. There's a slim possibility, and I say that because she admitted to sleeping with some other guy in between the times we weren't fooling around. I could beat my own ass for not using protection. You feel what I'm saying?"

"Naw. Not me, man. Before I got married I stayed strapped with a condom. All I can say is I wish there was a way for you to get out of this mess. If life doesn't kick your ass straight up and down its path, that Rachel Clark certainly will."

"You said a mouthful, and I can believe that." I shook my head as I slapped hands with Donnell.

"The months ahead are going to be tough, but I suggest you do what you can to get along with her."

"I hear ya. I'll give her time to cool off then I'll call her," I said, frowning.

"Well judging by the look on your face, phoning her would be the best option. Just don't go try to meet her anywhere. We might have to put out a missing persons report to look for you," Donnell teased.

Donnell and I had idle chitchat then he left. After thirty-minutes of solitude, I decided to go home. I locked up everything then headed to the parking lot, fastening my carrying case along the way. When I raised my head, I almost lost it. Someone had keyed Black Onyx, and there was no doubt in my mind that the culprit was Rachel. My comments as I got closer to my car ran together as one thought, "Fuck . . . sonofabitch . . . you crazy-ass heifer you, Rachel Clark."

Rachel had expressed to me that our issues weren't resolved. Since she wanted to start war, and I was about to finish it. Plain and simple.

Chapter Twenty-eight

She Ain't the One

I got my car repainted then let a few days go by, plotting the perfect payback for Rachel. I knew I had to do something to shut her mouth, and to let her know that I ain't the one to be messed with. I was now thinking Rachel was responsible for the prank calls and just maybe even for the recent injury to my eyes. Donnell was right. It was going to be pure hell dealing with this woman for eighteen years or more.

The fact that she was pregnant made my planning more difficult. Consciously, I couldn't hurt a child, unborn or otherwise. So, I had to practice patience until I could come up with the right scheme to suit the situation.

I was sitting at home one Saturday, thinking I should be out enjoying myself with my boo. The old Roman Broxton could never pinpoint who to chill with for the evening. There would've been far too many options. That crazy-ass Trina had blown her chances of ever getting with me again. That chick was totally out of the equation for good. Rachel made nice company, but she'd become a psycho, too. I thought, *Man, I'm good, but I never figured I'd see days when I could drive women totally crazy.*

I phoned Holiday in hopes we could hang out. She didn't answer at home, so I tried her cell. After getting the voice mail on that line, I hung up. I wasn't giving up so easily though. I desperately wanted to see Holiday. I tried to reach her once again on her cell, and this time I was successful. When I heard a lot of noise in the background, I instantly knew Lance had gotten to her first.

"Hello," Holiday answered sweetly.

"Hey, boo. Are you with Lance?"

"Mm-hmm," she responded.

"Is he looking in your face at this moment?"

"Yeah."

"Then just respond to this: I want to see you later tonight."

"Okay," Holiday said.

"I need to know when you'll be home."

"Then I'll just call you later."

"Okay, boo. Bye."

Excited, I started thinking of how to make this occasion special for Holiday and me. Yeah, I knew she'd been hanging out with Lance, but the fact that I was going to be the one she spent the night with was all that mattered to me. She gave me her word we'd hook up, so the little dinner or whatever Lance was doing with her was crumbs compared to the feast of activities I was planning.

I showered and packed my overnight bag. It had been a long time since I had stayed over at Holiday's place. I began to have flashes of our first intimate episode on her couch. I had to go fix myself a drink. Thoughts of our first night got me more and more excited.

After throwing on a pair of chocolate slacks and a chocolate silk shirt, I jumped into my car to take a ride, awaiting Holiday's call. I took a stroll to see what Beale Street had going on. There were people everywhere. Holiday is not big on tight crowds, so I knew I wasn't going to invite her down-town. I decided to park and take a walk until I got the okay from Holiday to come by.

Memphis has a reputation for the most beautiful women in the South. Still, I couldn't bring myself to lust over anyone but Holiday. Even when a fine, honey-colored sista walked up to me just after I picked up a drink from a street vendor, I couldn't bring myself to enjoy her presence. This woman had at least a 38 cup size, and she accented them with a low-cut, coral-colored halter top. Usually, I'd fall weak at this type of invite for attention, but that night I just didn't have it in me.

I looked the woman up and down then spoke. Before I could give the street vendor my ten-dollar bill, the woman handed the man a twenty and told him to keep the change. Although she didn't flatter me, I felt the least I could do was make small talk.

"Thank you," I said.

"You're welcome, handsome," she responded.

"So, what's your name? Ms. Big Money?" I threw her a friendly smile.

The woman laughed. "You're funny, but no. My name is Ginger Tarver. What's yours?"

"Roman Broxton. Nice to meet you, Ginger," I stated, reaching for her hand.

She gave me a firm handshake and asked if I'd like to stroll down Beale Street with her. I reluctantly agreed. We had more idle conversation with Ginger leading most of the chat.

"I kinda had my eye on you since you parked your car. I noticed you were alone when you got out, so I watched as you crossed the street then headed up Beale. Are you waiting on someone?" she asked.

"Sorta. I'm stalling time until I receive a call from my girlfriend. We're going to meet up pretty soon," I replied with no hesitation.

"Oh, I see. Well, lucky her because I was just about to move in for the kill. You're a very hot and sexy man, and I know what I want when I see it."

I smiled. "Hmm, you might want to keep that attitude. It'll get you far in most cases. The problem with me is that I happen to be in love, so at this point I can only concentrate on one woman." I looked at my watch. It was getting late. "As a matter of fact, Ginger, excuse me while I make this call."

Ginger smiled back. "Hmph. I ain't mad atcha. You're what I say a real man is, and you're good-looking, too."

I briefly stepped away from Ginger to give Holiday a call. I couldn't reach her, so I left her a voice mail. I walked back over to continue chatting with Ginger.

"I was just thinking," she said. "I should give you my card just in case you change your mind."

Ginger reached into her purse to give me her card, but after she held it out for me to take it, I took her hand and closed the card into her palm. "Sorry, Ginger, but I won't be needing this."

Ginger's mouth flew open. For a minute, I thought she was speechless. "Well, this is a first."

"I'm sorry you seem so surprised."

"Yeah, to say the least, I'm definitely shocked. Let me ask you something personal."

"Go for it," I stated.

"Are you on the DL? You know . . . down low?"

I laughed. "Far from it. I suppose you think because a brotha openly states he wants to be with one woman that he must be either gay or bisexual, huh?"

"Well, not meaning to sound vain, but look at me." Ginger brushed her hand over her body from head to toe then she continued, "I'm all that and then some. Who wouldn't want me?" Ginger struck a seductive pose, placing her hand on her hip just after swerving to reveal more of her backside.

"Who wouldn't want you? Me! Sorry, but that's just the way it is." I pulled a twenty-dollar bill from my wallet then placed it into Ginger's hand. "Thanks for the drink, but if you couldn't tell by the black Lexus you saw me park, I make my own money. Have a nice evening."

I turned and walked away, leaving Ginger even more dumbfounded. I didn't intend on looking back, but the shrilling sound of my name being called force me to spin around. Ginger wasn't responsible for the unwanted yelp. It was the familiar voice of Rachel Clark. *This can't be happening,* I thought.

"Roman Broxton, I know you heard me the first time," Rachel stated, marching toward me like an angry Sophia in the movie The Color Purple.

Though her face was hard with anger, and her body language spoke war, Rachel sparked me as a beautiful image of an African queen with child. Her twists were neatly styled in an updo with just a few locks hanging down on the sides. She was wearing an off-the-shoulder, long-sleeve denim jumpsuit that cupped her breasts, but bloused over her stomach. I never knew maternity wear could be so fashionable.

Immediate shame came over me as I spied Ginger looking on. "What's up, Rachel? Why are you out here among this crowd and cigarette smoke?"

"Do you really give a damn, Roman? Are you playing concerned all of a sudden?"

Ginger walked closer. "Is this her, Roman? Is this the woman who has you wrapped up?" she asked.

Rachel looked Ginger up and down. I tried to grab Rachel's arm to pull her away, but I almost lost my balance as she jerked from me. Rachel stepped into Ginger's face, and I knew it was about to be on.

"Who are you?" Rachel asked, rhythmically rolling her neck with every syllable.

Ginger stretched her hand in an attempt to receive a friendly shake from Rachel. "I'm Ginger Tarver. I was just making small talk with Roman. Nothing else."

Rachel refused to take Ginger's hand. Instead, she stood ogling her as if she was a ghastly sight. Again, I tried to take Rachel by the arm, but I was rejected once more.

"I'm gonna tell you something, Ginger. I hear you saying 'nothing else,' but if I find your number in my man's pockets or even in his cell phone, I'm going to look for you. And believe this as a promise."

Ginger took a step back, looking at Rachel as if she was trying to figure her out. Just then two women, a part of Rachel's crew walked up, huffing because they were out of breath.

"Rachel, what's up, girl? Why did you take off from us like that?" one of the women asked.

"Is everything okay?" the other one asked.

Rachel never took her eyes off Ginger as she responded. "Yeah, I'm cool."

I tried a different tactic I hoped would get Rachel away. I slid my arm around her waist as I whispered in her ear. "Rachel, c'mon."

Rachel seemed to melt like butter. She followed me as I took the lead, and her road dawgs tagged along. I needed another drink—fast. I went back to the street vendor and ordered a double Hurricane. The regular alcohol blend wasn't going to be enough to settle my nerves. I took a few gulps then turned to ask Rachel a few questions.

"I know you were the one to fuck up my car, Rachel. I hope you feel better after doing that shit."

She just stood looking at me with her arms folded. She really did have a sexy glow, but I refused to tell her so. I didn't want to give any more mixed signals than I already had by putting my arm around her earlier. I looked at my watch. It was later than I expected. I suppose my gasp and the frown on my face was what finally forced Rachel to speak up.

"You gotta be somewhere?" she asked with much attitude.

"Umm . . . yeah . . . I do. Let's pick up this conversation tomorrow, alright?"

"Excuse me? You just gon' leave me like this?"

I looked over at Rachel's friends. "Take care of her, and keep her out of trouble," I said then turned to Rachel. "I'm sorry, Rachel. I've got to take care of something really important."

I gulped the rest of my drink and darted off to my car. I called Holiday, and after failing to reach her again, I left her a voice mail expressing my concern. My next aim was to drive over to her place to make certain my suspicion that she was still spending time with Lance wasn't true. I arrived in Holiday's neighborhood, and I found the info I needed. Lance's truck was parked outside Holiday's house. It was time for an all out war.

Chapter Twenty-nine

The Broken Heart of a Playa

I pulled up to Holiday's place and noticed Lance's SUV. My stomach was ill. I contemplated creating a distraction by blowing the horn, or by doing something to force his vehicle alarm to blare. Holiday said she would spend time with me that night. *Why did she lie to me?* I thought. I had plans for us. I needed her. I knew she loved Lance, but my feelings should've mattered more to her. We were together first. We shared some pretty good times, and besides, she'd told me many of her deepest secrets. I felt betrayed as I sat parked alongside Lance's Escalade.

As if I hadn't had enough to drink already, I left to go to the liquor store. Once I made the U-turn in the street, I noticed Rachel driving past me. We made eye contact, and she looked at me with disgust. I kept driving, expecting her to follow me, but once I pulled into the store parking lot, I looked in the rearview mirror, and she was nowhere in sight. I figured once I returned to my car, she would appear, but I was wrong. I had no idea where Rachel decided to go.

I sat in my car, drinking Vodka—straight. Suddenly depression began to set in. I picked up the phone to call

Holiday a few more times. I left messages, but my responses became far less calm. I was tired of being patient with Holiday. Besides it hurt to see my ex-best friend having his way with her. Thoughts of her being touched by him and loving it were driving me crazy. I went against my first mind and decided to drive back over to Holiday's house.

I was ready to make my presence known. As I approached Lance's truck, I spotted Rachel having her way with a can of spray paint. Lance's vehicle was completely defaced. I pulled over and got out of my car to confront Rachel.

"Yo' what the fuck are you doing?" I asked, trying to keep my voice down.

It was twelve-thirty in the morning. The last thing I needed was to awaken Holiday's neighbors to see me and Rachel standing outside of Lance's Escalade. I took a quick glimpse at the graffiti, and it became quite apparent she was setting me up. She knew that was Lance's truck, and her message read as though it came from me.

"You trying to fucking set me up or what?" I asked angrily.

"I'm trying to set you up and what, muthafucker."

"Bitch, you're sick, but not as half as sick as you're gonna be when I get through with you. You obviously think you can keep playing games with me."

"That's right because you're a fucking toy. A muthafucking yo-yo is what you are. You never bothered to tell me Lance was the man your girl was cheating with. Why not?"

"That's not—," I was cut off by her hand in my face.

"Because you like being a yo-yo for this woman. You'd rather let her play between you and Lance than to allow a good woman like me to love you. You oughta want to care for me on that strength alone, not to mention the fact that I'm carrying your child." Rachel had tears in her eyes.

"Rachel, you don't know the whole story. Holiday loves me, and I love her."

"Yeah, that's why she's laying up with Lance right now, thinking of you I guess."

I locked eyes with Rachel. Her comments were adding fuel to my fire. I was getting angrier by the minute. Nothing I said would make Rachel leave. Finally, one of Holiday's neighbors turned on a porch light. Rachel and I parted ways, jumped into our cars and drove away before the person could open the door to see us.

I didn't get any sleep. I drove around all night drinking, hoping it would drown my sorrows. I realized I was turning into my father, and it was a scary notion. I was becoming angrier about women, about love, and about life. I thought, *What if Rachel's baby is mine? Will I become my father and teach the child to be bitter toward the world?* Then I realized that I didn't want that to happen. I became more determined to make Holiday love me, so that I could prove my father's negative thoughts about life to be wrong.

I thought about Rachel as I drove. Even in my drunken stage, I realized I had caused much of her pain. Rachel was a descent woman, but bitterness is what happens when good women fool around with bad boys like me. As angry I as was at Rachel for having possibly keyed my car and setting me up to look like I had damaged Lance's truck, I had to calm down and take the blame for all the hell she had in her. I dismissed thoughts of getting revenge.

Once daylight hit, I parked not from Holiday's house so I could see their reaction of the vandalism to Lance's truck. Holiday was the first to come out on the porch. Then, I witnessed Lance stomping around the SUV, frowning and talking to himself. I saw Holiday standing on the porch crying, cupping her mouth, and shaking her head. Lance walked up to her and put his arms around her. The closeness the two shared made me ill. I continued to peer at Holiday's door as she and Lance re-entered the house.

The police came, but all I saw was what seemed like meaningless chitchat between the officers and Lance. I could see the policeman writing as Lance talked, but Lance still appeared angry after the conversation was over.

Holiday reached to hug Lance then he kissed her before driving off. I cranked up my car, and Holiday turned to notice me as I made a U-turn to speed away. I figured she wouldn't confront me about it, so I tried not to let it stress me. I needed to figure out a way to convince Lance that I wasn't involved with the destruction of his truck, but with Holiday having seen me on the scene, it was gonna be tough.

Chapter Thirty

Still Mo' Drama

The atmosphere was strange the next day at work. Lance and I weren't speaking, and Rachel and I were walking by as if we didn't know each other. She rolled her eyes whenever we mistakenly made eye contact, but I didn't let that get the best of me. I made up my mind to stay in my office as much as possible. Besides, I had plenty of things on the day's agenda to keep me busy.

As I tried to focus on work, Holiday repeatedly came to mind. I phoned Carlos to ask for his advice. I knew Ant wouldn't be objective after telling him all the latest happenings between me, Lance, Holiday, and the issue with Rachel, so I called the man I knew would listen.

"Carlos, man, I need you to make time for yo' boy," I said after he answered.

"Whoa. You sound like things have really gotten bad, man," Carlos responded.

"Yeah, man."

"Okay. Then if it's like that, why don't we meet for lunch?"

"Naw, dude. You don't understand. I mean we need to

talk now. Shit is really out of hand. I'm feeling myself going crazy. Literally," I stated.

"Oh, well . . . you wanna speak over the phone, or should we meet somewhere."

"I guess I can share a bit now. It might do me some good."

"I'm all ears. Take your time, bro," Carlos replied.

I spilled my guts to Carlos even though I knew he would throw God and the Bible up to me—the last thing I wanted to hear. I respect that the man had a Christian heart, but I didn't want him trying to force it on me. After we got past the religion stage, he offered me some very comforting advice.

"Given everything you've told me about Holiday, I believe she loves you. She is confused, and she's in no position to make a decision between you and Lance. You fail to realize that with you and Lance adding to the charade, Holiday will never be in a position to choose. Both of y'all need to let go long enough for her to decide who, if either one of you, she misses and wants to be with."

"Now if I let go, but Lance doesn't, then how will that help me?"

"Have you even tried to talk to Lance from the angle of the two of you giving the woman a break?"

"Naw, man. Holding a friendly conversation with Lance is more difficult than you can imagine right now."

"Get over that pride, man."

"Yeah, I hear ya," I responded matter-of-factly.

"No, bro. Don't just hear me. Feel me."

"A'ight, dude. I gotta let you go. Thanks for rapping with me. I can always count on you to come through for yo' boy."

"And you know this, man. One love," Carlos stated.

"One love," I responded just before hanging up.

I spent a couple of more hours hemmed up in my office then I walked out to get a change of scenery. Lance was on his phone, smiling as he talked, and I could faintly hear what he was saying. From the sound of things, he was speaking to a woman. My heart began to thump rapidly against my chest. I feared he was chatting with Holiday.

I headed back into my office to call her, but before I could reach the doorway, I was stopped by Tim Johnson, the agent who sits at my old desk, telling me I had a call. I wondered who it could be. Without looking at the caller ID, I took the line off hold and answered. To my surprise, it was Holiday.

"Roman, we need to talk," she stated.

"Hey, boo. How are you? To what do I owe this call?" I said just after picking up.

"Don't 'hey, boo' me, Roman. You know exactly why I'm calling." Holiday was a little feisty.

"No, boo. Really. I don't know, but from the sound of your voice, I'm sure you're going inform me."

"Let's meet for lunch," she stated rather shortly.

"Wow. Are you serious, boo? You wanna meet with me?"

"Yes. I see I need to set you straight once and for all," Holiday said, damn near barking at me.

"Hmph. Cool. Just tell me where, and I'm there."

Lance was still on his call, but he was staring in my face after I hung up with Holiday. I aggravated him by walking away and whistling, "My Girl" by the Temptations. After walking into my office, all my concentration was lost. I was going to see Holiday, and I knew this was my chance to spill my heart to her.

I pulled up to the restaurant parking lot and noticed Holiday outside pacing. She looked as if she needed to smoke a cigarette, but since she doesn't smoke, I decided to take her inside to buy her a drink. I walked up to her and she stuck her hand out for a shake. Immediately, I lost it. I grabbed her in a tight bear hug.

I spoke through clenched teeth. "I'm sick of you treating

me like some type of stranger. When is the last time you've seen me, huh? Huh?" I could see in her face that I had startled her. She kept silent as I continued. "That's what I'm talking about. You can't remember. So where do you get the nerve to offer me a handshake?" Still, Holiday didn't respond. "Don't ever do that to me again."

I was sure I had frightened Holiday, so I made a conscious effort to calm down. I reached to open the restaurant door for her then motioned for her to go inside. Once we were seated, we began small talk then Holiday was ready to speak her mind.

"You know what, I'm just gonna cut right down to it. Spray-painting Lance's Escalade was very immature. Help me understand how a thirty-four-year-old man could still be interested in playing games like that."

"Whoa, whoa, whoa. What are you trippin' on?" I asked.

"Here we go again, Roman. I've told you not to try and play me stupid. You could've gotten your ass locked up doing some mess like that."

"Holiday, all I did was try to reach you through a few phone calls while you were laid up with him. I don't have time to be out doing crazy stuff like vandalism."

"So you do admit that it was crazy, huh?"

"Absolutely. I mean I'm pissed off at your boy, but I wouldn't play with him like that."

I could tell Holiday didn't believe me. As a matter of fact, her expression showed very little faith in me period. I continued to try to plead my case, covering for Rachel, in hopes that I wouldn't have to tell Holiday the truth—that my pregnant coworker, a woman with whom I cheated on her, set me up. The more I defended myself, the more difficult things got for me.

I told Holiday how much I loved her and the only way she

knew how to respond was to let me know she wasn't gonna choose. I felt helpless begging for her love.

"I haven't seen Lance's Escalade," I stated to Holiday.

Holiday and I were shocked when Lance spoke out. "And you expect for me to believe you? That you didn't even bother to take a drive down Elmhurst Road looking for my truck in front of Holiday's house last Saturday?" Lance said as he approached our table.

"Lance, how did you know we were here?" Holiday asked.

I spoke up before Lance could answer Holiday. "Like I told Holiday, I did make a few phone calls to try and reach her. There was no need for me to drive down her street if she wasn't gonna answer my phone calls."

"So, now I'm Boo-Boo the Fool, huh? You think I don't have sense enough to know you're lying, Roman? After all the years of knowing you, man, I've never known you to be this selfish. You knew I wanted Holiday, yet you still made a move on her first. She doesn't deserve a lowlife like you, Roman. Give it up."

That was it. I let him have a piece of my mind. "Well, I really don't even know why you're here right now. This was supposed to be a private lunch. Ain't that right, Holiday?"

"Holiday didn't invite me. I invited myself. I pulled one of those old Roman Broxton routines by looking on the caller ID at work. When I found out it was Holiday I heard you discussing lunch with, I followed you. Pretty smart, huh? I learned from the best. You taught me well, man."

Holiday started to leave, but Lance stopped her. "Holiday, wait. I still have some time on my lunch. If you have any time left, please, let's just go somewhere and talk for a minute. We really need to talk."

This nigga pissed me off something fierce. He knew I was trying to place my rap on thick with Holiday, yet he continued to try to block. I knew within seconds it was about to be on.

"Oh, we can go. We can go outside." I slid my chair back and jumped into Lance's face.

Holiday made the terrible mistake of standing between Lance and me. Before she could get out of the way, blows were thrown. Holiday ended up tangled in the middle. I felt awful for not controlling my temper once I saw her bloody face. The restaurant managers pulled Holiday from in between Lance and me. Lance and I stopped fighting shortly after we could hear Holiday's cries. Lance seemed just as surprised as I was to see her bleeding. Although she was badly hurt and bruised, Holiday showed more compassion for us than we had to her by advising us to get away from the restaurant before the police came. Lance and I ran out of there in a hurry.

I hated the fight had to end so soon. I wasn't finished with trying to stomp a hole in Lance's ass. His ass-whupping had been a long time coming, but I didn't get a chance to do him real harm. As I jumped into my car, I looked over at Lance, giving him an evil eye. I wanted him to know that the shit was far from being over.

Chapter Thirty-one

Never Satisfied

I returned to work after the fight with Lance. Neither one of us had visible bruises, so all we had to do was take a deep breath then walk into the office as if nothing happened. After about an hour and a half, I noticed Lance hadn't returned. My blood began to boil again because I knew he was somewhere trying to be in Holiday's face. I worked as hard as I could to finish my projects so I could get out of there.

As I packed up to leave, Rachel walked into my office. She closed the door behind her. "Still mad at me?" she asked.

"Rachel, today ain't the day to start shit with me," I responded, wishing Donnell was sitting at his desk to help cut the slack.

"I didn't come in here to start anything, Roman. I just wanna know if you're still mad at me."

"Yeah . . . try pissed, and I'm about to be irate if you don't stroll your ass on out of here the same way you came in."

"What if I tell you I'm sorry?" Rachel asked, batting her eyes innocently.

"Sorry? Sorry? You set me up to go to jail then I end up in a boxing match with Lance because of it, and you ask me what if you tell me you're sorry? Here's your answer: take your sorry and shove it. Don't fuck with me today, Rachel, I mean it."

She stood silently looking at me as if she couldn't believe her ears. I continued to pack my belongings and ignored her. When my desk phone began to ring, I answered it in a hurry.

"Yeah, Roman Broxton here," I stated loudly into the receiver.

At first I didn't hear a sound then I heard heavy breathing. My face almost went white as I realized that Rachel wasn't on the other end of the line because she was standing right before me. I thought I had figured out the culprit harassing me and Holiday. I put the phone down, staring blankly at Rachel.

"What? Why are you staring at me like that? I haven't said a word to you. I'm just standing here looking," she said.

I grabbed my things and walked from behind my desk. "Out," I said to Rachel, gesturing to the door. "Out!"

"Don't get mad at me because Lance took your woman," Rachel stated, obviously thinking she could hurt me with those words.

I wasn't hurt, but she did strike a nerve. I chose to fight back with fire. "He didn't take my woman. I loaned her to his punk-ass, but it looks like I let him borrow the wrong one considering how you and he have more in common since you're a punk, too."

Rachel tried to land another one of those heavy slaps to my face, but my reflexes were up on their game this time. I grabbed her arm before it came close to me. I squeezed her wrist hard enough to break it then spoke. "I've told you before. I don't wanna hurt you, Rachel, but you're coming real close to making me renege on that statement. Don't keep testing me."

I released her, and she immediately grabbed her hurt wrist. She looked up at me, but I didn't even blink. I stared her square in the face as she spoke. "I hope Lance beat the tar off your black ass because you need it." Rachel opened the office door and headed out.

"Yeah, well I don't think he's the man to do it, so you better come up with somebody else to fulfill that dream," I stated as she continued to walk away.

I locked the office then headed straight for Holiday's house. I pondered what I would do if I saw Lance's truck parked outside. I tried not to think too long and hard because even I feared the consequences. Once I drove down Holiday's street, I could tell there were no cars in the driveway, or parked on the street. I was a bit relieved except Holiday's Mercedes wasn't even there. I drove around a bit more trying to get my head together then my cell distracted me as it rang.

"Hello," I answered.

"You got life so fucked up, Mr. Broxton. Your ass is grass," a harsh voice said.

"Who is this?"

No one responded. After a few heavy breaths the phone line went dead. I thought about how I had once terrorized Lance's mother with harassing phone calls. *Perhaps Lance is responsible for the messages,* I thought. *He must know I'm the one who placed those menacing calls to his mother, and now he's paying me back.*

I decided to drive over to Ant's house. As tall as Ant is, I was surprised to see him with a four-nine, eighty-pound soaking-wet Asian lady. He shrugged when I looked him up and down as she headed to the bedroom so he and I could rap.

"Man, whatcha gon' do with that besides put her on your hip and sing lullabies to her?" I asked jokingly.

Ant laughed. "Man, that woman's fine. I don't know what you're talking about."

"Hey, I didn't say she wasn't fine. I'm merely trying to point out the fact that you're six-six and weigh at least 240 pounds. You gon' break that woman in half." I laughed as I continued to tease Ant.

Anthony couldn't help but laugh, too. "She's a lot tougher than she looks. That's all I can tell you, man."

"Hmph. I hear ya, but look . . . I was just dropping through. I didn't know you had company. I'm gon' let you get back to that, and I'ma holla atcha this Friday." I reached to slap the black man shake on Ant then I left.

I lied to Ant about just dropping through. My mind was really made up to talk to him about the fight between Lance and me since I'd already gone against Carlos's advice of a friendly chat. I left Ant's house and headed back to see if Holiday was home.

This time Holiday's car was in the driveway as I expected it to be given that it was after nine. Confident Lance wasn't with her, I made a U-turn to leave the area. I looked in my rearview mirror and spotted Lance pulling in front of Holiday's house. I drove farther up the street then turned around in someone's driveway. By the time I made it back to Holiday's house, I witnessed Lance entering her home with a huge arrangement of roses. I have to admit, those were some beautiful flowers. I was positive Holiday would forgive Lance once she had a chance to take a good look at her gift.

I drove around for a bit contemplating knocking on her door. I decided against it because I knew her daughter, Crystal, was home. Holiday would never forgive me for causing a scene in front of Crystal. I decided to call Holiday instead of showing up unannounced.

"Um, I don't mean to interrupt your little late night cap, but I was hoping to be able to talk to you for a minute. Will you ask your boyfriend to step into another room and let us talk? That is, if I'm not already interrupting something important," I stated sarcastically.

"Roman, are you outside my house?"

I became a bit disturbed by her remark. "Holiday, I don't want to come in. Tell him I'm through fighting, but that's not gonna make me stop seeing you though."

I could hear Lance ranting and raving about popping a cap in me and kicking my ass and so on. He almost made me laugh because I knew he really thought he could put fear in my heart. I blew into the phone then told Holiday to calm Lance down. "I told you to tell 'im I'm through with that nonsense. All I'm asking is for my share of time in this relationship with you. I'm your friend, too, remember? That's all. Lance doesn't even matter anymore. You're what's important to me. I ain't trying to lose what little involvement we do have over trippin' with his ass. By the way, tell Lance I said the roses are a nice gesture, but I'm the one you love."

Holiday didn't bother repeating everything I said to Lance, but my real aim was to get her to understand that I still loved and needed her. I drove away with a strong feeling that Holiday had forgiven me, too.

Chapter Thirty-two

Friends and Enemies

Lance and I continued to see Holiday, but we stayed out of each other's way. I tried to be as cordial as possible without giving him signals that I felt it was okay for him to see my girl. I only wanted to hold out long enough to let Holiday realize it was me who she loved.

In the meantime, winter rolled around. Rachel was six months pregnant, but she looked as if she was due any day. I had to be creative with ways of keeping her out of my face and making her happy at the same time, so I told her Holiday and I were done dealing with each other. Rachel seemed happy with the idea I wasn't sleeping with Holiday, and her contentment simplified my life.

The harassing calls never stopped. Holiday constantly complained to me about the verbal threats, and she refused to believe it was Lance. Even my boys, Ant and Los, didn't feel Lance was responsible for the calls. I still wondered if it was Trina. I wasn't afraid as much as I was angry. I just wanted the nonsense drama to stop.

One Friday evening, Los and Ant met me at Mr. Brown's shop. The place was packed as normal, but as usual, we didn't mind hanging around, chatting and listening to Mr. Brown's stories. Besides, it was cold outside, and there wasn't much going on in Memphis that night. Had it not been for the Christmas party New Vet Life was giving the next day, I might've stayed at home for the evening. I couldn't go to the Christmas party without tightening up the do, and apparently Lance felt the same way about his hair because he walked into the shop about thirty minutes after the rest of us.

Lance slapped hands with Los and Ant then he threw up the peace sign my way before he opened his mouth. "What's up, Roman?" he asked.

"I can't call it. You tell me what's up," I responded.

"Naw, I don't know the happenings, man. Haven't you heard the rumors?"

"What rumors?" I asked.

"That I'm just a squirrel in this world, trying to get a nut." Everyone laughed in the shop except Lance and me. Lance kept his eyes on mine as he continued. "They tell me you're eating up all the crackers, but I'm just licking up the crumbs."

Many ooos and ahhhs filled the shop. I wasn't sure if Lance was picking at me or trying to find out something. I responded to him carefully because I didn't want to create trouble in Mr. Brown's place of business.

"Well haven't you heard that you should only believe it when it comes straight from the horse's mouth?"

"Yeah, but when you go to the horse and all he's doing is barking like a dog, what next?"

I heard men in the background throwing uh-ohs and ooos around. I wasn't going to give them any more of a show than Lance had already, so I remained calm.

"Look, Lance, I don't know what's on your mind, but I ain't tryin' to have beef with you up in Mr. Brown's shop. As a matter of fact, I don't want beef period. Whatever somebody told you, just believe half of what was said and none of what you heard."

Mr. Brown spoke up. "Believe half of who and none of what? That's not what the saying is. It's believe all of what you see and none of what you hear. Son, you all messed up."

Everyone laughed, even Lance. Suddenly we were all in a debate about what the old saying was.

The atmosphere turned out okay for the evening. Mr. Brown kept us laughing, and so did Ant as he was his normal, humorous self. I had gotten over the cold weather and convinced the guys to go to a strip joint with me. I stood and was the first one heading out the barbershop when my cell rang.

"Hello?" I answered.

"You're a bitch, you know that?" a deep, cold, rugged voice stated.

"Say what?" I asked. I turned to notice Lance laughing and shaking hands with Mr. Brown—obviously not on the other line of my cell.

"Look, stop playing games and make yourself known," I stated.

Carlos was behind me as I pushed the door open to step out. "Roman, who is that on the phone, man?"

"I don't know," I replied.

I saw a dark SUV double-parked next to my Lexus. It was the same truck I'd seen on the riverwalk and speeding from my house. I picked up my pace as I headed to my car. I was only about six feet away from the truck when the person inside smashed a beer bottle on top of my hood then sped off.

I jumped into my car and tried to catch up, but the driver was too quick for me. I was lost by the time I reached a three-way intersection. I had no idea which street the SUV had jetted down. I slowed my roll then answered my ringing cell.

"Roman, what's going on, man?" Carlos questioned after I clicked on the line.

"Man, whoever the hell is in that truck has been harassing me. I'm not sure who it is, but when I find out, the mutha-fucker is gon' be sorry."

"So, where are you now?"

"I'm heading to the club. Tell Ant and Lance y'all can meet me over there."

"Alright. I'll pass the word. You just be careful. You never can be too cautious, ya know?"

"Yeah, I know. I'm cool. I'll see you in a minute," I responded.

I met the fellas at the strip club, and then I had to go into this little spiel about who, what, and why regarding the incident when I was leaving the barbershop. I heard Mr. Brown was extremely concerned, especially since he tried to keep his customers' vehicles secure while parked outside the shop. The incident happened while the outside security guard was on a restroom break.

I tried to enjoy the remainder of the evening at my favorite hangout. I downed a few drinks and pulled a few g-strings, but my mind stayed on the earlier incident with the stalker. Though the voice on the phone was malicious and harsh, my instincts told me it was a female. Besides, the person I saw near the river was a short-haired, blonde, white woman.

Ant interrupted my thoughts. "Roman? Roman, can you please come to the joint where the rest of us are," he stated, cupping his hand over his mouth as if he was speaking into a walkie-talkie.

"Yo', man, I'm here," I responded.

"Sho don't seem like it to me, bro," Ant replied. "I'm looking at a man whose mind is a million miles away."

"I can't lie. I'm still trying to figure out this mystery person. I've got to get to the bottom of this shit. This same wacko almost put my eyes out recently."

"What happened?" Carlos asked.

"Well, me and . . . well," I paused. I almost said Holiday's name, but then I noticed Lance listening intently. I figured there was no need in heightening my drama-filled night, so I paused to retract my thoughts. I took a sip of my drink then started again. "Someone knocked on my door early one morning. Finally, I unlocked the door, and as soon as I was about to step onto the porch, an explosion cracked my face."

"Oh crap," Carlos stated.

"You can say that again. My eyes were burning like somebody had thrown salt in them."

I finished telling them the story of what the doctor said, and why I chose not to let them in on the stalker situation before. They all understood, but they were also concerned. Even Lance offered me advice on making sure I protected myself.

That evening, Lance and I got along fine. I have to admit that not arguing with him was kinda nice, and I was forced to remember the old days when there was no beef between us. It could've been the alcohol, but I started thinking of taking Carlos's suggestion of talking to Lance. The music was a bit loud, so I decided our conversation could wait. In the meantime, I was at the club for other reasons—to drink and enjoy the ladies.

Chapter Thirty-three

A Surprised Holiday

Every time I thought I was making progress with Holiday, something would push me back. Although Lance and I had a cordial evening that Friday, he went and proved once again that he could be dirty when he wanted to be. I didn't want Holiday to find out the date of New Vet Life's Christmas party, but Lance saw things another way. He showed up with Holiday on his arm.

When I saw Holiday, I almost pissed on myself. The only way I'd been able to keep Rachel calm was to promise her a little time every once in a while, even though we weren't sexual. I didn't invite Holiday to the party because that night was supposed to be when Rachel and I would to begin our mending process. It was Rachel's idea, and I didn't argue with her on that because I actually agreed that there couldn't be a better time for us to work on being cordial. The Christmas party was an open environment, and I planned to make Rachel feel wanted in front of her friends and coworkers, so she'd cut me some slack. I would've succeeded with my scheme had it not been for Lance.

I kept doing a disappearing act between the two ladies,

trying hard to keep peace with Rachel and to keep Holiday from recognizing Rachel's pregnancy. But, despite my efforts, my shit hit the fan as I tried to sneak in a small chat with Holiday once I thought Rachel wasn't looking. Rachel walked up to me with an attitude out of this world.

"Roman, aren't you going to introduce me?" Rachel asked.

Aggravated, I answered her rather shortly. "Later," I coughed out.

Both Rachel and Holiday looked confused by my response. Holiday immediately demanded an explanation. "I don't understand," she said.

I tried to get Holiday to excuse me while I speak privately with Rachel. "Holiday, where's Lance?" I asked.

"He's over at our table," she stated, pointing in Lance's direction.

"Good. Do me a favor and go chill with him for a minute. I'll be over there shortly."

After Holiday walked away, looking back, frowning in confusion, I began pleading with Rachel not to start acting out or doing something to embarrass both of us.

"Rachel, I'm sorry that I didn't introduce you, but you know you have a way of overreacting. That lady is a friend of Lance's, and I was just about to dance with her."

"I thought this was our night, Roman. Why are you ducking and dodging me, and to top it all off, now you're telling me you were about dance with someone else when you haven't even asked me yet."

I tried to kill her with kindness. "Rachel, sweetie, I'll take you on the floor in just a minute. Lance and I have been getting along much better, and I'd like to show a little courtesy to him and his friend for a moment. I won't be long. I promise."

"I guess Lance finally forgave you for the scribbling on his truck, huh?"

"Don't go there, Rachel. Please don't take me there. I'm trying not to think of how you set me up, or any other negative things that went on between us. I just want us to get along. Can you work on being nice tonight?"

Certain Holiday couldn't see me because my back was turned, I began stroking Rachel's chin. She seemed to be melting a bit, so I grabbed her hand and gave her puppy-dog eyes. I knew my actions would get the best of her.

"Well, I'm feeling hot, so I'm going to catch a breath of fresh air. I'll see you in a minute, and I do mean in a minute."

We locked eyes for a while then Rachel walked away from me. I hurriedly headed to Lance and Holiday's table. I didn't see Lance there, and I wondered where he had gone.

"Where's Lance?" I asked.

"As I was heading back over here, I saw him walking in the direction of the restroom—with my purse." She laughed.

"Huh? With your purse?" I began to laugh also. "What're you talking about?"

"I had asked him to watch my belongings before I got up to speak to you. I guess he didn't see me as I was on my way back to the table, so he took my purse with him."

Holiday and I chatted some more, but I wasn't sitting there long before she asked me to dance. Considering how Rachel had already been acting up, I was feeling uneasy. I felt trapped into saying yes because "It Hurts Like Hell", me and Holiday's song was playing.

I can't explain how great it felt to hold Holiday once again. At first when she began playing in my hair, I was nervous about Rachel seeing me. Then, I chose to relax and enjoy the moment. I soon discovered I made the wrong decision once I felt a thump on my shoulder and Rachel's voice piercing my ear.

"Excuse me, Roman. Roman," Rachel screamed.

"What?" I answered in a harsh tone.

"You want to tell me who this is—and this time, tell me the truth 'cause I know damn well this is not Lance's woman. She's dancing this close to you, rubbing all in your hair like that. Come on talk to me, baby."

"Rachel, this is Holiday. Holiday, this is Rachel." I closed my eyes, awaiting the next piercing remark from Rachel's mouth.

"No, tell it right. It's Rachel E. Clark, if she just has to know, and you ain't told me jack. So, Holiday, do you mind telling me who you are and what you're doing with my man?"

Rachel knew damn well who Holiday was once she heard the name, but she wanted to continue to be difficult, and to my surprise so did Holiday. She wasn't backing down from Rachel by any means.

"Actually, Rachel, I kinda thought this was my man. As a matter of fact, we've been together off and on for a couple of years now. How he got to be your man, I don't know."

"Oh, so Roman, this is the one you told me about several months ago? You told me you weren't with her anymore. You said you wouldn't take her back 'cause she cheated on you." Rachel kept adding fuel to the fire. "Oh, so now I know why you've been so sneaky tonight. And, why did you swear to me this was Lance's woman?"

"Wait a minute. Roman told you that?" Holiday asked.

"He sure did," Rachel answered, taking great pleasure in bursting Holiday's bubble.

Holiday gawked at Rachel's belly. "I don't mean to be rude, but I just have to know. Are you pregnant, Rachel?"

"Yes, I am. I'm exactly six months today. You didn't bother to tell her you had another woman pregnant, Roman?"

Holiday didn't want to hear anything else. The way she took off from the scene told me she'd heard far too much—the last thing I wanted to happen. I ran behind Holiday because she had been known to run away in the dark, and considering the weather, I didn't want her to dart off in the cold rain. I caught Holiday at the door of the hotel. She was crying like someone had stolen her last family heirloom. Nothing either Lance or I said made her feel better. As a matter of fact, she screamed obscenities at us both and expressed how she never wanted to see either of us again then she ran off as I expected.

It was time for the old Roman to play dirty again. I tried to suppress my bad side for too long. Lance only thought he had one up on me, but he ended up hurting himself in the process because Holiday was determined not to see either of us. I wasn't going to stand for it. The old me was back, and I knew I was going to have Holiday at any cost.

Chapter Thirty-four

Once Again, It's On

No matter what I did, I knew I should remain close to Holiday despite her anger about Rachel's pregnancy. I sent Holiday flowers, and I slipped in a few pieces of poetry I found in the library and on the Internet. I think it was the poetry that won her over more than the bouquets because I had a little trouble locating the roses Lance once bought. Holiday expressed to me how much she adored those particular flowers more than any others she'd ever received.

Once I pulled Holiday back into being nice to me, I was pleased. I just couldn't see leaving Holiday with enough space to allow Lance to fully step into the picture.

I'd been trying to get Holiday to let me come over ever since the scene at my job's Christmas party, but she kept saying she wasn't ready for company. One night I got a surprising invitation to visit her, but it wasn't because she missed me. It was because she received another one of those harassing phone calls that set her nerves on edge.

"Roman, I'm scared," she said after explaining the rudeness of the prankster.

"You don't need to be afraid, boo. Whoever this person is, they're obviously punks. Don't you recall how long this has been going on? If they wanted to do something harmful to either one of us, I think it would've been done by now."

"Yeah, but didn't you recently tell me about someone breaking glass over the top of your car?"

"Yes, boo, but that was to my vehicle, not me. I don't believe the harasser's intent is bodily harm. You understand what I'm saying?"

"Well, I guess. If you say so. I think I better let Crystal stay over to her cousin's house a little while longer. I just have a weird feeling about that last phone call."

"What did the person say this time?" I asked.

"Well, to put it plan and simple, somebody wants to hurt you, Rome, but I'm wondering why me too. I don't have anything to do with your bullshit. I shouldn't have to feel threatened."

"You know what, Holiday, I think the calls are being made by Rachel," I lied. I knew Rachel wasn't at fault, but I couldn't figure anything else to say.

"Roman, please. Even you know better than that. Those calls began far too long ago. Rachel didn't meet me until a week or so ago."

"Yeah, but she knew about you, boo. She admitted that to your face, remember? She claims she thought we'd broken up."

"I guess she could be the one getting on my nerves, but how do you suppose she keeps finding my numbers after I've changed them over and over?"

"I can't answer that, boo. Sorry."

"Will you come over and stay the night with me?"

"Now that I can answer—yes," I responded.

"What time will you be leaving?"

"Is immediately too soon?"

"You are so silly," Holiday said, laughing. "C'mon. I'll see you when you get here."

We hung up, and then I went to take a bath and pack my bag. I danced and sang about the house as I prepared for my evening with Holiday. I put on a Christmas CD my coworker Donnell had made for me. He'd taken songs from various albums and placed them on one disk. After inserting the music, the first track to play was *Silent Night* by the Temptations. I popped my fingers, turned up the volume, and headed to the bathroom. I left the door open so I could hear my favorite Christmas song.

As the warm shower rained on me, I felt my body relaxing, then soon I began having flashes of Holiday being in there with me. Reminiscing was nice. At least at first I loved thinking of the time Holiday and I shared in my shower, but then my smile was replaced by a frown once I began to have flashes of Holiday and Lance under the water together. I became angry because I remembered she'd promised me to never make love so sensuously to anyone but me. I hit the wall in frustration.

I quickly finished my bath and headed over to Holiday's. I took the CD with me to listen to in the car. I was hoping the music would place me in better spirits than I had been when I left the house. Thinking of Lance and Holiday was getting the best of me, but by the time I reached Holiday's place, I felt great.

Holiday opened the door in a pair of sexy, tight jeans, and a fitted v-neck, cream-colored sweater. Her hair was up in a bun, but she let a spiral curl fall down on each side of her face. I dropped my bag on the floor as soon as I stepped inside and kissed off all of her lip gloss before she could speak. She seemed pleasantly surprised.

"Dang, Rome, you act like you miss me or something," she stated, giggling as I held her.

"Umm, might be something like that, but I don't know. What do you think?"

"I think you miss me, but I'll let you show me how much later."

"Promise?" I asked pleadingly.

"Promise."

"Great," I responded.

My cell began to ring to the tune of *Jingle Bells*. I looked at the caller ID, but it stated PRIVATE. "I wonder who could be calling me with an unidentified number," I said, thinking aloud.

"Don't answer it, Rome. It's probably the prankster."

"I hope so because I've got something to say," I said just before pressing the button to talk. "Hello?"

"What's up, man?" the voice on the other line asked.

"Nothing, but who is this?"

"It's Los. You mean to tell me you don't recognize my voice?"

"Oh, what's going on, Los?" I stated, nodding to let Holiday know everything was alright.

Holiday pulled out of my arms and walked over to the Christmas tree. My manhood began to rise as I watched her fine frame sashay to the other side of the room. I could barely focus on what Carlos was saying.

"So did you hear me, man?" Carlos asked.

"Uh, naw, man. I've got other things going on here. What did you say?"

"I said can you believe Sonia let me out of the house and it's not even our regular boys' night?"

"Whaaat? Naw, man, I ain't believing that. No wonder you're calling me from a private listing. Are you at a pay phone or something?"

"Yeah. I came down to your spot, man. The honeys are looking hot tonight. They're wearing Santa suits and some more ole kinky stuff?"

"Man, Sonia gon' kick your ass. Oooo, you better not let her find out where you are," I mocked.

"Who's going to tell her? I know you're not the strip-club police." Los laughed.

"Naw, not me, but considering how you can't ever get out other than Friday nights, I think something is up. Sonia probably followed you just to see what you'd be up to."

"Man, don't say that. Please don't say that. If she did, I'ma tell her something like I only came in here to preach the Word to some of these married sinners."

"You're so fake, it's a trip. And you know Sonia won't believe mess like that." I laughed.

"Maybe not, but I won't own up to being in here for pure satisfaction."

"I hear ya," I responded.

"You gon' come join me or what?"

"I told you I've got other things in the making right now. I'm over to my boo's house. Besides, it's cold out, and my boo got all I need to keep me warm," I said, winking at Holiday.

"Well, I won't interrupt that, bro. Just holla at me tomorrow."

"Alright. One love," I said before closing the flip on the phone.

I walked over to Holiday, eyeing her up and down. She was the best sight I'd seen all day. I could care less about what Los was seeing down at the club. Holiday reached out to hug me. I seized the moment. It had been a long while since she'd been so kind. I just hoped her change of heart remained the same forever. After squeezing her tightly, I was ready for another kiss.

"Boo, where's the mistletoe?" I asked.

"What mistletoe?"

"You mean you don't have any mistletoe in this house?"

"No. Do I need some?"

"Well, I just wanted a reason to kiss you all night long from head to toe."

"You have a reason. At least I thought you did."

"Oh yeah, what's that?"

"The fact that you love me, dummy," Holiday teased. "You do still love me, don't you?"

"Umm, let me see." I scratched my head and pretended I needed to think about it.

"Uhn-uhn, don't play with me like that. You love me, mister."

I pulled Holiday closer to me and gripped her butt as I passionately kissed her. To my surprise, she sank deeper into the kiss then removed one of my hands from her butt and replaced it to the middle of the heat between her thighs. I stroked her as we kissed. This was one time I wished she was wearing a dress. The jeans made it difficult to caress her, but she began to make things easier by unzipping her pants.

Suddenly a loud crash and an explosion came through the window near where we were standing. The Christmas tree became a ball of flames. Holiday and I ran to the back of the house to exit. She screamed hysterically as we watched the fire claim her home. The more I tried to calm Holiday, the more upset she became.

"Please, Holiday, have a seat on the curb, boo," I pleaded as she continued to cry and pace the pavement.

"Noooo. Leave me alone, damnit. This shit is all your fault," she screamed.

"Boo, don't say that. Please don't say that."

"Why not? It's the truth," Holiday said. "What the hell was I thinking? Somebody wanted to see you hurt for all the crap you've ever done to them, and I invited you over so they could harm me, too."

"Boo—" I started.

"Don't you, 'boo,' me! Look at my home. Where am I going? What am I gonna do about Crystal's Christmas? The gifts her father sent are in those flames! What do I say to my child, huh?"

Holiday kept ranting, stomping, and pacing in the street. In my despair, I called Lance. I hoped he could calm her down because I knew she was making herself sick. Even Lance couldn't compose Holiday, so the paramedics were called. She was given a tranquilizer and sent home with people from Crystal's father's side of the family. She had refused to go home with Lance or me. She kept screaming she didn't want to see either of us again.

I sat in my car across the street from Holiday's demolished home with my head hung low. All of my energy had been drained, and I couldn't think of anything to say or do to appease Holiday. I wanted her so much. I needed her, but not in the dissatisfied frame of mind she was in. Knowing the attack on her home was meant for me saddened me greatly. I still had a house, and it didn't seem fair, which is what probably kept Holiday from wanting to hear anything I had to say.

After sitting in the dark, smelling burnt rubble, and watching firemen dig through things for hours, I finally decided to drive home. I pulled up to the four-way stop simultaneously with what appeared to be the same dark, SUV I'd chased from Mr. Brown's shop. I tried to get a look at the driver, but all I could see was a hint of a hooded coat pulled over someone's head.

Once the truck sped away, that was my clue of this person's guilt. I drove like a wild man trying to catch up, but once again, I lost the driver. I went home anguished and distraught, but I vowed to get to the bottom of things for Holiday's sake. I knew she wanted to feel safe again, and that was going to happen. I swore it on my mother's grave.

Chapter Thirty-five

The Untold

There came another Saturday for me to have to work at the Jackson office. I was pretty cool about going there considering I knew Toriana wouldn't be present. I had enough drama in my life thanks to Lance, Holiday, and Rachel. The added pressure of having to deal with Tori would've just placed my share of troubles over the top.

Being back in Jackson was sort of refreshing because it was a different environment than to what I was accustomed. Although the office was much smaller than the Memphis location, I didn't mind the breather from my neck of the woods. Plus, I returned to Jackson as a manager, so I was in a better position to do more delegating rather than having to put actual hands onto assignments. Franklin Hubbard—once my superior, now my peer—was more laid back with talking with me. I went into his office to ask about the weekend workload.

"So, Broxton, tell me how you feel now that you're a part of the management team," Franklin asked after he told me what to expect.

"Actually, it feels pretty good. I still go into the fields almost as much as I use to, but I'm not complaining because I get paid more."

"I feel ya there, Broxton. I like making money." He laughed. "Let me ask you something though. If it's none of my business, please just say so, and I'll leave it alone."

I was curious as to where Franklin was going with this discussion. "Go ahead. Ask me," I replied.

"It's about Toriana Ponce. I'm aware the first time you visited this office that you had an eye for each other. Did anything ever come of you?"

"Man, you're nosy as hell," I responded then we both laughed.

"Just tell me it's none of my business, and I'll let the topic go," Franklin replied with his hands in the air as if he was surrendering.

"Naw. The answer is easy. Nothing ever came of us. We had an attraction to each other, but nothing more. I think she's a sweet girl though," I lied.

"Sweet, huh?" Franklin looked around the office, then leaned in closer to whisper. "Man, that girl has a reputation for not being so nice, if you know what I mean."

I shot Franklin a confused look. I pretended I didn't have a clue what he meant. "Say what? Where did you hear that?"

"C'mon, Broxton. I know she made some type of pass at you. Hell, she's made her way around this office with just about every man at least once, and even a few of the ladies, too."

"Are you serious? Even you, Franklin? Tell me it ain't so. I know you wouldn't get with a bad girl like Tori."

"Even me, but good thing I was one of the first she fooled with. I don't like going behind other guys, if you know what I'm saying. It was such a long time ago when I slept with Tori, so I hardly even remember what it was like."

"Damn. It's just a shame that such a cute woman would

play herself. I mean she's beautiful with all that long hair—"
I was cut off by Franklin.

"Long hair, that's a goner. She cut that off shortly after
your first visit to Jackson."

"Cut it off? You mean it's completely gone?"

"No, but she cut it awfully short, and had the nerve to dye
it blonde, too. Imagine that. As if she isn't fair-skinned
enough, she went and colored that beautiful dark hair. If you
ask me, that tint also brightens her complexion, making her
look like a white woman, especially at first glance or from a
distance."

I was stunned. "Where is Tori now? Does she still live in
Nashville? Last I heard she relocated to work in the office
there."

"Umm, seems I remember someone mentioning Tori
bought a new truck and moved to Memphis. A big boy,
Denali, I think. I can't confirm the SUV or that she really
moved, but I know she hasn't been around here in quite
some time."

I was speechless, and I suddenly felt sick to my stomach.
After months of harassment, I never once considered
Toriana Ponce as the culprit. She lived in Nashville, or so I
thought. Franklin was still talking, but I went into a trance,
reflecting on all the prank calls, the explosion in my face,
the keying of my car, the dent on my hood after she smashed
a beer bottle on top, and burning down Holiday's house.
The more I daydreamed, the angrier I became. Franklin had
to snap me out of it.

"Broxton, are you listening to me?" he asked.

"Umm, yeah. I hear you, man. Sorry if it seemed as
though I wasn't paying attention. It's just that all this talk
about Tori is actually making me homesick for my girl in
Memphis," I lied. "Tori is an attractive woman, but she can't
touch my boo, and I can't wait to get back to her."

"Is that right? You got any pictures?"

"Naw. I usually don't carry photos around, but I'm start-ing to think I need to reconsider. Times like this when I'm missing her, I need a picture."

Franklin pulled out his wallet. "Well, take a look at my sweetheart. She's a beauty," he said, handing me the snap-shot.

"Wow. Franklin, how'd you pull such a princess?" I teased.

Franklin obviously had a thing for Hispanic women be-cause his woman favored Toriana. He went into a spiel about how they first met, but I wasn't in the frame of mind to hear him. Although my eyes were looking into Franklin's, I was ac-tually in deep thought about what I was going to do to find Tori and put a stop to the madness she was creating. I nod-ded when I thought it was appropriate, so Franklin had no clue I was in another world. Finally, he shut up long enough for me to make an excuse to leave.

"I'm glad to hear you and your girl are happy. Let me know when you plan on jumping the broom. I just might take a drive back to Jackson for that occasion," I said, head-ing for the door.

"I don't know about jumping any brooms, Broxton, but yeah, I'll keep you posted," Franklin said, smiling.

"Good. I'm on my way back to check on things with the analysts then I'm going to do an early lunch. Hit me on my cell if you need me."

"Oh, okay. I might need you to bring me something back, so I'll call you when I decide."

"Alright, man. Peace," I said, leaving Franklin's office.

I headed straight to the team of analysts to play detective. I asked a few questions, hoping no one would get suspicious. I finally got a response from a man who told me where Tori once lived. I left for lunch on a mission.

As I pulled up to Tori's old neighborhood, I spotted children in the street playing dodge ball. I pulled over to see if they could tell me anything about Tori's whereabouts.

"Hey, kid, don't you think you hit that little girl a bit too hard with that ball?" I asked, getting out of my car.

"No, sir. You oughta see how hard she throws the ball. My legs and back be stinging!"

All the children laughed, and so did I. "Say . . . I'm trying to find someone who once lived in this neighborhood, but she moved."

"Oh, you mean Ms. Ponce who use to live in that house?" the boy said, pointing.

"Yeah. I believe that's her. Do you happen to know where she moved?"

"No, sir, but I heard my mommy say she left town."

"Okay. I appreciate your help, kid. What's your name?"

"Franklin," he responded.

I did a double take at the young boy who couldn't have been more than six or seven years old. "Franklin? What's your last name?"

"Hubbard," the kid responded.

I stared blankly at the child who was an apparent mix of my coworker, Franklin Hubbard and a part Puerto Rican, Toriana Ponce. I couldn't believe what I was seeing. I started to question the little boy again. "So do you—" I was cut off by a screaming white woman.

"Franklin, what have I told you about speaking to strangers, huh?" the woman said.

"Sorry, Momma, but this man is nice," the boy said, looking at me.

"I don't care if he's nice or not. I've told you never to speak to strangers," the woman said, grabbing Franklin's hand. She looked at me with squinted eyes. "Who are you?"

"Ma'am, I'm not trying to hurt your kid. I was just looking

for someone who lives in the neighborhood. Are you his mother?"

"Yes," she replied with an attitude. "Why do you ask?"

"I just wanted to make sure I'm making the apology to the appropriate person. That's all."

I turned to get into my car, still dumbfounded over the site of Franklin and Tori's child. I wondered if Franklin even knew about the kid, or if the only reason he made Tori sound like a whore when he talked about her was because he didn't want me to have anything to do with her.

The woman who fussed at me bared no resemblance to that kid at all. After thinking about it, I believed the woman had adopted Franklin before he was old enough to understand his true relation to Tori. The boy answered my questions as if I was just talking about someone he remembered in the neighborhood, not his mother. I had no plans to tell my coworker what I had learned. Besides I didn't want him to know where I was during lunch.

I drove around a bit more, plotting my next move. Something was gonna give. I didn't know what, but I knew that patience was going to be the virtue to getting the information I needed.

Chapter Thirty-six

Putting Together the Pieces

On the ride back to the office, Franklin called my cell. I picked up on the first ring once I noticed the familiar number on the ID. "Franklin, what can I do for you, man?"

"Roman, where are you?"

Damn! Just the question I hoped he wouldn't ask, I thought. "Umm, not far from the office. What's up?"

"You think you're gonna pass by a Wendy's? I've got a craving for a Frosty. I'll pay for your gas if it takes you out of the way."

"Oh no, I'm cool. I'll head to Wendy's now. See you when I get back," I replied.

It was a relief to me that the conversation was brief. I was afraid of getting tongue-tied about what I did on my hour off. Driving to get Franklin's dessert bought me more time to think of my next strategy for finding Tori. The answer ended up falling into my lap during a conversation with one of the analysts just before I left work.

"I really wish I could've seen Tori on this trip, and now that I know she's relocated, I don't have much hope I'll ever see her again," I said solemnly to the team.

One of the men spoke up. "Damn, man, you sound like you got it bad. Why didn't you just keep up with her phone number?"

"Stupid, I guess. I just kinda wanted to hang out with her. I thought she was cool. She was nice enough to show me a good time on my first visit here," I replied.

"Yeah, I bet she did," one of the men replied, laughing.

The cynical laughter answered my question of whether Franklin was right about Tori sleeping around the office. I should've felt sick at that moment, but the thought of all the recent destruction Tori had caused in my life kept me focused on why I needed to find her.

"Can any of you tell me anything of Tori's whereabouts?" I asked.

"Did you try the post office? I have a friend who works there. If you have her old address, perhaps she put in a change for a new one," one of the men said.

"Oh, that would be great, but isn't that information supposed to be confidential? I wouldn't want to get anyone in trouble," I lied. I could care less what happened to the postal employee. All I cared was for what I wanted: Tori.

"Well, I won't tell if you won't. I'll help you because I hate to see a grown man in need," he joked.

I hurriedly reached for a pen. "Cool. I'll write down the old information. When do you think you can have something for me?"

"Just give me a minute to make this call," he replied.

I felt like a kid who had just received his birthday present. I was excited and hopeful all at once. Within a matter of minutes, I had all I needed to know in order to find Tori. It turned out she forwarded all her mail to a PO Box in Memphis. I was hyped the remainder of our shift. Ant called just as I was walking to my car to head back to Memphis.

"Yo, Roman. Where you at, man?" he asked just after I answered.

"What's up, Ant? I'm in Jackson. I had to work today, but I'm on my way back to Memphis now. What you got up for the evening?"

"That's why I'm calling you. A brotha is ready to kick it tonight. How about we go to the Premier Night Club? Allen Iverson is going to be down there again. You know the place is going to be packed with the honeys," Ant said.

"First Los, now you? What's really going on with you two? See y'all need to be more reserved like me 'cause I only have my mind on one woman, and you know who that is, right?"

Ant tried to respond, but I couldn't hear him because of the laughter and chatter behind me. The fellas from the office were walking to their vehicles when they overheard me on the phone. One of them spoke just when Ant was answering my question.

"Yeah, Toriana Ponce," the man said, laughing. "Forget about that whore-bitch and get you a real woman."

I asked Ant to hold on before responding to the man. "Wait a minute. What's your name?" I asked.

The man looked at me with a peculiar grin. "Jeremy Frye. You mean you didn't know my name?"

"Jeremy, I just tried to prove to you that we don't know each other. And, I don't care to know you. The worse thing a man who doesn't know me can do is try to get into my business. Now the Tori jokes are cute, but if I'm not laughing, you should take that as a clue to let the shit go. Do I make myself clear?" I could feel my temper raging.

Jeremy looked around at the other men who were snickering. He responded, obviously out of pride. "Make yourself clear? I'm not some little punk." Jeremy stepped into my face. "You don't talk to me that way, pretty boy."

One of the men grabbed Jeremy's arm, but he jerked away then continued, "You bring your ass up here every other month or so thinking you're Mr. Know-It-All, but you don't intimidate me."

I could hear Ant asking me what was going on. I responded to him. "Ant, I need to call you back."

"Why? What the hell is going on, man? Who is that? You a'ight?" Ant inquired.

"I'm fine. Just give me two minutes, and I'll call you back."

I flipped the phone closed then placed it into my pocket. I never took my eyes off Jeremy who knew how to play tough guy. I was ready to break him off a taste of what it was to be rough. I refused to hit him first because if my job or the police had to come into the situation, I wanted it to look as if I had to defend myself. After a few minutes of staring, one of the men persuaded Jeremy to walk away. I was geared up for a fight, so I taunted him to return and be the first to strike a blow.

"What? You walking away now? I thought you said you ain't a punk. You could've fooled me, punk."

Jeremy stepped back to me just as I had hoped. "You think you bad, Roman?" Jeremy said, standing just inches from touching my face with his nose.

"That's one of your problems, Jeremy. You think too much. I *am* bad, and trust me, you don't want me to show the rest of these guys that you actually wear panties for drawers."

That did it for Jeremy. The fact that he punched me in the face let me know he knew how to take the hint that I was calling him a sissy again. I didn't take being hit in the face too well. Jeremy should've kept the blows coming then maybe I wouldn't have had a chance to break his jaw. I heard his face crack as I jabbed him with my right hand. I tagged him almost immediately after he struck me. Jeremy hit the ground, screaming like the bitch I knew was. The other guys helped him off the ground but none of them bothered to take me on in Jeremy's defense.

I didn't have to say anything else because all the men scattered after putting Jeremy into his car. I got in Black Onyx and laughed as I passed Jeremy, slumped over his steering wheel, holding his jaw. My hand hurt like hell, but I was sure it wasn't in as much pain as Jeremy's face. I stopped at the corner store to get a bag of ice just in case my hand decided to swell.

Driving off adrenaline, I made it back to Memphis in record time. My hand still throbbed, but I didn't let that stop me from going out with Ant. Besides, I needed to run a few things by him. I knew my boy was going to be candid and not hold out on me, so I prepared to hear his good and the not-so-good responses. I pretty much knew I was gonna do what I was gonna do regardless of Ant's feedback. Tori had it coming.

Chapter Thirty-seven

Let The Games Begin

As Ant and I headed to The Premier Night Club in his big-boy Excursion, I figured this was our quiet time to talk. I reached to turn down the volume on the radio.

"Yo, man. What's up with you? Shit, that was my song. You know how I love me some Destiny's Child. Beyonce's gon' be my baby's momma."

"Oh yeah? Too bad she doesn't know it," I teased.

"Oh, she knows," he stated confidently.

"She knows? What dream did you discuss this in?" I laughed.

"You got jokes, but I happen to be serious. See, when I took that ex-girlfriend of mine to the concert last year, we were sitting on the front row of the Pyramid. That's when I gave Beyonce that 'girl-I'm-yo'-man' look then I winked, and she threw one back at me."

I laughed even harder. "What ex-girlfriend? You talking about, Paula?"

"Yeah, you remember her, right?"

"I remember Paula. That's why I'm laughing at your ass. I know if you did something stupid like winking at another woman in front of Paula, you would've gotten your head busted."

"Man, I never said she didn't slap me." Ant laughed at himself. "I'm just saying that Beyonce and I shared a wink, and although Paula laid her hands on me, I know Beyonce got the picture of what I was saying to her."

"Dude, you can be so funny at times. I guess it doesn't hurt to live in a fantasy world every now and then. Beyonce is too young for you anyway."

"That's okay. She gon' grow up, and I'm gon' be right there waitin' for her, too."

I couldn't help laughing at Ant. He knew I always found him comical. Other than the night he and Holiday exchanged harsh words, I've never really been mad at Ant for anything. We continued to rap a little more before I told him what was on my mind.

"Man, I know Los told you about what happened to him at home, right?" Ant asked.

"No, what are you talking about?"

"Man, oh man, oh man. Los tried to sneak to the strip joint, right?"

"Yeah, I believe that's the time he called to ask me to meet him there, but I couldn't. Has he gone back to the club since then?"

"Man, hell naw. Sonia put a knot on that boy's head so big, I'm sure he gets the shakes every time he drives anywhere near the vicinity of an erotic place." Ant almost doubled over with laughter.

"Damn. No wonder I can't catch up with him. How did you find out?"

"I couldn't catch up with him either. I just happened to see him in Wal-Mart, shopping his ass off. He had a basket full of snacks for the kids. He tried to tell me he bumped his head in the shower, but you know that went in one ear and out the other. After he realized I wasn't believing it, he went ahead and confessed that Sonia had served him upside the head with a shoe."

"Oh, snap. I told that man to go home to his wife, but he insisted she wouldn't know he went to the club," I responded.

"I don't think she knows anything about the club. If she ever finds out, his ass will be outdoors and that's for sure. He told me she clocked him because he didn't come home until almost daylight."

I laughed. "Now see. Carlos not coming home is partly Sonia's fault for not letting the man out the house more often."

"Aw, man, you know that besides his kids, Los adores that woman harder than anything he could ever dream of loving. I still don't know what gave him the notion to go to the club in the first place, especially with all that Bible talking he does."

"I hear ya. I guess he just wanted to see if he could get away with it, and he pretty much did. He just got greedy, not coming home until the break of dawn. I ain't married, but even I know better."

Ant laughed and slapped five with me. "Yeah, me, too. You gotta know how to play your cards rights."

"Let me run something by you, Ant."

"Okay, shoot."

"Let's say you're in love with someone, and you know this person loves you, too, but there's no real commitment between the two of you . . . How would you convince this person to be dedicated to you?"

Ant sighed. "Okay, man, cut the shit. You know I know who you're talking about. Does this woman have platinum between her legs or what? I mean, between you and Lance, y'all about to drive me fucking crazy over this one damn woman. I'm not convinced either one of you really love her, and the charade that's going on just ain't fucking worth it."

"You don't know Holiday like I do, Ant."

"You're right in some respect because I ain't fucked her like you and Lance, but I do know she doesn't have enough respect for either one of you. If she did, she would've either chosen between the two, or let both of you go. She likes the game, man. Can't you see that?"

"Man, I don't see things that way, and for your information, Holiday and I truly love each other. I messed up when I gave Lance the opportunity to play her, but I'm gonna get back what Holiday and I had, even if it kills me."

"A'ight, but since I can't tell you anything that would change your mind, I'm gon' shut the hell up."

We drove in silence for a moment before I spoke. "Remember that person who smashed a bottle on top of my car near Mr. Brown's shop?"

"Yeah, I remember that. Why?" Ant questioned.

"Well, I found out who did it. I also know this is the same person who burned down Holiday's house. I need to find her so that Holiday will feel safe with me again."

"Say what? How do you plan to make Holiday feel safe, man? Exactly what does safe mean?"

"I don't know, but I know since Holiday lost her home, she doesn't trust being around me. She won't accept my calls or even tell me where she lives."

"Well, I can understand her on that one, but I'm still trying to figure out how you can make her feel safe," Ant replied.

"I'm going to have to find this person, and take care of the situation once and for all," I responded.

"Man, I don't think I need to hear anymore. If you're saying what I think you're saying, keep the rest of that shit to yourself. Don't be talking about committing a crime while riding in my vehicle. If the police come to question me, I want to be able to tell them that you and I had a clean conversation the last time we talked. Plus, what I think you're saying is stupid. I know you've been drinking, so I'm holding the crazy talking against the liquor, and not you."

"A'ight, I'll shut up. We're almost to the club anyway, right?"

"Yeah, we're almost there," Ant replied.

As we pulled up to The Premier Night Club, I took one look at the long line and almost turned around. Ant opted to jump in the VIP line instead, and since he offered to pay, I had no objections. We still had to wait because the line wasn't moving as quickly as we thought it would.

I glanced around the parking lot and noticed that it was full. I knew the club was about to be jumping. Hearing the music on the outside had me hyped about partying for the night. I missed Holiday so much, and I hoped the club would take my mind off her. Looking around, I noticed that the women in line were fine as hell, but I still craved Holiday.

Suddenly, I spotted what looked like a pair of spectacles staring my way. Once I realized that I was staring into a pair of binoculars and a dark colored SUV, I decided to confirm my suspicion.

"Hey, man, let me borrow your keys," I said, never taking my eyes off the utility vehicle.

"My keys? For what?"

"I think I left my wallet in the truck. I need the keys so I can go look for it. I'll be right back."

Ant gave me his keys. As soon as he passed them to me, I could see the SUV pulling away. I took off like a track star to Ant's truck. I kept my eye on the driver the whole time as I ran. I was pretty certain I had positively identified Tori as the stalker. She smirked at me as she drove away.

I made it to Ant's truck, and I sped through the parking

lot. I could hear Ant yelling for me to stop, but I was on a mission, determined not to let Tori get away from me again. I managed to stay on her tail as we headed from American Way to Perkins Avenue.

Tori decided to duck through a residential area, but I was familiar with the streets, so I wasn't worried about her getting away. I floored Ant's truck to speeds I'm sure he never dare tried. I had no time to think of possibly destroying Ant's car because I was focused on one thing: catching Toriana Ponce.

Tori made it to a stop sign where she was forced to slow down since a car was crossing. As she eased her pace, I pulled up on the left side of her truck. We made eye contact. I could see in Tori's face she was distraught over having been seen so closely. Her wheels spun as she took off, and I raced behind her.

Shortly after leaving the four-way stop, a police car pulled behind me with flashing lights. I was devastated because this meant I would be forced to let Tori get away once again. I pulled over, beating the steering wheel and cussing to myself. The officer walked up to my window just in time to catch me ranting.

"You better tell me what type of emergency caused you to speed through this neighborhood like this, and you better make it good, 'cause if you don't, I'm taking you to jail."

I didn't know what to say to the policeman. I figured no matter what I said, I was probably going to prison anyway, so I just told the truth. "Officer, I was chasing a woman who has been stalking me. She's made my life a living hell, and when I spotted her, I just sort of lost it."

The man looked at me sort of perplexed. "A woman stalking you, huh? And you mind telling me what your plans were going to be after catching this lady?"

I sighed. "Honestly, officer, I don't know. I'm sure I wasn't going to hurt her though. I just wanted her to know how it feels to be chased, I guess." This lie flowed better than I thought it would.

"I'ma tell ya something, so listen to me good," the policeman said.

"Yes, sir, I'm listening."

"I'm gon' let you go. I saw the SUV you were chasing as it sped by me. I saw you next, and I just wanted to see what you would tell me. I want to believe you, so I'm going to let you off. Don't get any crazy ideas of taking the law into your own hands with this woman. File a report the next time she does something to you. You understand?"

"Yes, sir. I understand," I replied.

"Good. Now slow this thing down, and go home. If I ever catch you out here speeding like this again, you and me are gonna take a ride downtown. Is that clear?"

"Oh, very clear, sir. You won't see me racing in the streets again. I'm on my way home, sir. Thank you."

I wiped the sweat from my forehead. My nerves were on edge, and I had a notion to comb the streets of Memphis looking for Tori. The officer drove around me, but then stopped alongside Ant's truck. I let down the window to see if there was something wrong.

"Is there a problem, officer?" I asked.

"That's what I was about to ask you. Why are you still sitting here?"

I couldn't respond right away. I just looked at the policeman because I feared saying the wrong thing. I noticed that he put his car in park and was about to get out to chat with me again, so I interrupted him before he stuck his foot out the door.

"Umm . . . officer, I was just taking a deep breath. It's been a long night, but I swear I'm on my way home."

"Something isn't right with you. I don't know what it is,

but I can feel it. Take your deep breath or whatever you need to do. Just know that I meant what I said a minute ago about hauling you off to jail," he said as he closed his car door.

"Yes, sir. I understand."

I waited until the officer drove away, then I headed back to find Ant. Once I returned to the club parking lot, Ant was pacing the sidewalk, ranting into his cell phone. He didn't see me as I pulled up, so I got out the truck and walked over to him. His back was to me as he continued to cuss.

"And then he ran off after some bitch in my muthafuckin' truck. What kinda shit is that? I'm telling you . . . something's not right with his ass. All I want is my damn vehicle back in one piece," Ant vented into his mobile phone.

"It's back, man, and it's unharmed," I said.

Anthony turned around to face me. His eyebrows looked as if they had grown together he was so angry. He quickly hung up on whoever was on the phone, and immediately began to rip into me.

"Yo, man, what the fuck is up with you?"

"Ant, man, I apologize. I had to do that. I know you're not going to understand—" I was cut off.

"Hell, nah. Hell, nah. I don't want to hear some kind of bull about Holiday and all this mess going on. Are you fucking losing your mind? That's all I want to know." Ant and I stared at each other as I remained silent. He began to speak after he realized I wasn't going to respond. "We're boys, man. You know I got your back on just about anything, but this Holiday chick seems like bad news for you. You're not thinking rationally these days. I don't like what's going on with your behavior."

I took a deep breath. "Listen, I understand your concern, but I'm fine. When you fall in love, perhaps you'll understand why I'll do anything for Holiday. But, until then, I need you to just stay out of this."

"Stay out of what, Roman?" Ant yelled. "You drove my truck out of here like a bat flying out of hell, and you don't expect me to be upset or worried?"

I had already lost the cat-and-mouse game with Tori, and then Ant wanted to make me out to be a madman. I began to yell back out of frustration. "Yeah, well your truck is alright, now what? What other excuse you got for not trying to hear me out?"

Ant hissed then snatched his keys from me. "Give me my damn keys. Either you can come or you can stay, but I'm not going in the club. I've had enough embarrassment for one night. Make up your mind what you want to do."

Frustrated, I spoke through my teeth. "Take yo' ass on. I got money. I'll catch a cab if need be. Fuck you and that big raggedy-ass truck."

Ant looked around at the crowd standing in line, eavesdropping then got into his truck and drove away. He shook his head as if to say he thought I was pitiful. I waited until Ant's SUV was out of sight before I called a taxi to pick me up. I didn't feel much like partying. All I wanted to do was find Tori, so I could make Holiday feel safe again.

Chapter Thirty-eight

Make a Way Out of No Way

I returned home to an empty house and a lonely bed. I checked my voice mail and was saddened by the absence of Holiday's voice. I wanted her to understand how much I missed her, but I couldn't tell her if she wouldn't have anything to do with me. Holiday had even stopped taking my calls on her job. I would leave messages on her answering machine there, but she'd never return my calls. I felt mistreated for no good reason.

Day after day, I couldn't stop thinking of Holiday, and I just wanted a part of her in my life. I began thinking of creative ways to capture her attention. I knew I needed to find a way to get hold of Holiday's new phone numbers and home address. One day, I called her office, and her assistant didn't realize it, but she gave me everything I needed to know. After the fire, I figured Holiday would look for a new place, so I used that to my advantage.

"Hi, I'm Holiday Simmons's real estate agent, and I was wondering if she's available," I said after the assistant answered.

"No, I'm sorry. Ms. Simmons is not available at the moment, but is there a message I could take down for her, or would you like her voice mail?" the woman asked.

"Umm, well, I'm sort of in a bit of a crunch for some information from her regarding her new home. I was able to arrange things so she could get the necessary repairs done to the home for free, but she left part of the form blank, and it's already overdue. I need to turn in this paperwork by 1:00 P.M.," I lied.

"Oh gosh, and it's ten minutes till that time now. I don't know what to do. I wish I could help you."

My plan started to come together. I began questioning the assistant extensively. I was careful not to let her detect my deceit.

"Well maybe you can help me, Ms . . . Ms . . . Ms . . . ," I repeated, waiting for the woman to give me her name.

"Dodson. I'm Ms. Dodson," she replied.

"Oh great. Ms. Dodson, maybe you can help me fill in some blanks here. Has Ms. Simmons gotten her new home telephone number yet?"

"Well, I do know that she has a new home number, but I don't have access to that information. She only gave me her new cell number, which I'm sure you have already."

I smiled inside because I knew I was about to get the answer to one of my questions. "Oh yes, you're right. I do have her new cell number. Let me pull it out. Let's see . . . 901-491-6—" Ms. Dodson cut me off.

"Oh no, you're reciting the old mobile number. I knew that when you began with 901 for the area code," she stated.

"Hmm. I recall Ms. Simmons giving me that new cell listing, but I can't find it anywhere right now."

"It starts with area code 662," Ms. Dodson said.

"Oh, now I see it," I pretended. "Area code 662 . . . oh no, this is hard to read. Her pen must've run out of ink as she jotted this down," I lied.

"Here let me help," Ms. Dodson said just before giving me Holiday's number.

"Yes, yes, that's it. I can see that now." I was ecstatic. "By the way, have you had a chance to get by Ms. Simmons's new home?"

"Oh yes, it's gorgeous. I'm so happy for her and her little girl. They had a rough time after losing their last house to that fire."

"So what do you think of my abilities? Based on what you saw of Ms. Simmons's home, would you choose me as your real estate agent?"

"Yes, I most certainly would. I knew when she told me she lived on Cherry Lane that you had helped her find a good home. My sister lives in Southaven, too, so I'm familiar with the area."

If Holiday knew all the information Ms. Dodson willingly gave me, Ms. Dodson would be in a world of trouble. I didn't even have to pull out my old charming ways to get Holiday's business. I was so happy that I thought about anonymously sending the assistant some flowers.

I decided to hold on to my newfound info until I had my approach well-thought out. In the meantime, I still had other unfinished business to handle. Toriana Ponce remained a threat, and a visit to her was well overdue.

I rented a car so Tori wouldn't recognize me upon pulling into the lot of her post office center. I had to stake out the post office several times, and the rental car expenses were escalating. No matter what the cost, I wasn't going to give up.

My adrenaline began to flow once I spotted her getting out of her truck about a week later. She looked like a tanned white woman with bleached-blond hair just as my coworker Franklin said. I couldn't believe how short she had cut it. I thought maybe trimming and dyeing it must've been part of her plan to disguise herself as she attempted to destroy my life.

Tori spent about twenty minutes in the post office before coming out. She never bothered to look around, so getting caught was the least of my worries. In fact, since I was driving Black Onyx, I pretty much new that being discovered would never be an issue. I waited until she was out of the parking lot and through the intersection before I pulled out to trail her.

I slowed as Tori turned into the driveway of a small home in the Parkway Village area. She jumped right out of her truck and went inside without ever looking around. I pulled up to the front of the house to get a closer look at the address. I figured returning late at night would be best in order to remain unseen.

I went home and pulled out a pair of black jeans, a long-sleeve black shirt, and black gym shoes. I looked all over for the necessary tools that would help me break into Tori's place. Deep down, I couldn't believe I was actually plotting to do Tori harm, but this was something I knew had to be done.

I picked up a picture of me and Holiday. I smiled at the miniature framed likeness of us. I stared into Holiday's eyes and made a promise to the photo to make her safe again. I felt it was my responsibility to protect her. I headed to Tori's house on a dangerous mission.

Chapter Thirty-nine

What You Won't Do for Love

I parked my car several blocks away from Tori's house. I watched from behind a shrub as she entered her home around nine o'clock that night. Again, Tori didn't bother to note her surroundings. She stood at the door several minutes, yakking on the phone, and fumbling with her keys before finally stepping inside. I couldn't believe how careless she was by not paying closer attention. This just didn't seem like the behavior of a woman who could stalk and plot against me for several months.

The fact that her neighborhood was poorly lit worked to my advantage. I tipped to her back door to see if there would be an easy way in. I saw a partially raised kitchen window. The paneling was sheer, and I saw Tori as she headed to the refrigerator, talking on the phone. I stooped at the window, listening to Tori as she poured herself a glass of water.

"No, Franklin," I heard Tori yell, "I'm not saying that at all. I just want you to understand that our son is better off where he is. Dana's a great lady. I know she'll continue to take good care of him. He knows you well as his father, but he's never known me as his mother. Why would I wanna come back to snatch his life from under him?"

I knew it. That boy I met in Jackson is Tori and Franklin's child. I guess no one ever figured out Franklin and Tori's little secret. Though it was a trip to discover such information, about I wasn't interested in spreading their business. I came focused on sweeping the dirt named Toriana from under my own feet. She had become too much to ignore.

I could see frustration on Tori's face as she continued to talk to Franklin. "Franklin, I don't want to hear any more. I've told you already . . . I'm not in Memphis for that. All I want to do is continue to give that man hell. He needs to learn he shouldn't play with other's feelings." Tori paused. "I know there's no way Roman could have known the story behind my whole life, including my tough upbringing, meeting a self-centered man like you, birthing your child to only have you deny and hide him for years, and the other men at the office who used me to no end. I realize Roman didn't know all of that before breaking my heart, but I made myself a promise that the next man to use me would have hell to pay."

I wanted to come through the window on Tori right then. Her words were confirmation that she was trying to ruin my life due to a grudge. I tried hard to maintain my composure. I listened closer.

"What?" Tori screamed. "Why did you even tell him the kind of vehicle I was driving and that I had a haircut? This explains why he knew me when he saw me the other day. But, your blabbing is all my fault because I shouldn't have come to see you last month." She paused, looking at the floor as she listened to the voice on the other end of the phone then Tori responded. "So, what? I didn't have to tell you anything.

It wasn't your business that I had slept with Roman, and I'm sure as hell glad I didn't tell you my motive for moving to Memphis. You probably would've blabbed everything to him before I could get my revenge."

The more I listened, the more enraged I became. I had brought my gun, but I figured it would make too much noise, causing a difficult getaway. I looked on the ground for some sort of weapon, but then I realized I needed to wait and just use my hands. I wanted to hurt Tori bad. I remained quiet and waited patiently.

I slowly raised up to peep once again. Tori removed her platinum wig and her long, black hair bounced as it fell down her back. Tori began to walk in my direction. I dropped flat to the ground and listened. I heard some type of crumbling, and I eased back up to look through the panel, flinching at Tori's closeness. She sat at a small table near the window, digging through her purse. She pulled out some type of wet wipe or cleansing cloth and began to wipe it across her face. The white toilette seemed to change colors as she continued to rub her skin. Before long, the cloth appeared to be tan. Suddenly things started to make sense. Tori used a foundation color to enhance the illusion that she was a Caucasian woman. I smirked at the thought that Tori had everyone, including me, fooled with her new look.

She got up from the table to throw the toilette in the trash. I eyed her from behind as she headed to the other side of the kitchen. I have to admit I was turned on by the sight of her. She was wearing a pair of jeans that fit tight like the ones she wore the day I met her. When she turned to head back to the table, I got a glimpse of her naturally creamy vanilla skin. She had on a black blouse that rose above her navel just enough so her silver belly chain could be seen. I continued to look on as Tori headed to the table. Suddenly, it appeared she was looking straight into my eyes. She began to walk toward me. I quickly dropped down and balled up for fear she would take a peep out the window. I could see the shadow of her curtain moving to and fro and the light from the kitchen flickered on the ground as Tori looked outside. I heard her shut and lock the window.

I was relieved once Tori began to turn off her lights. I eased up once again to see what she was doing. I could see her heading up a set of stairs. I remembered she had told Franklin she was getting ready for a shower, so I waited before attempting to enter her home. Anthony once worked for a home security company, doing installations, and he had told me every detail of what he did to deactivate his exgirlfriend's alarm so he could surprise her on her birthday. I never thought I'd come to use the information he had given me, and I'm sure neither did he.

My timing was excellent because I could hear water running as I cracked the door to go inside. I sneaked into Tori's bedroom, looking for a place to hide. I panicked when the faucet shut off. I still hadn't found a good place to duck. Tori came out the bathroom, and I jumped behind the door as she flung it open. She didn't see me or detect my presence, so I still had time to plot.

I leaned around the door a bit to see what Tori was doing. She had a towel wrapped around her body, covering her upper torso down to her butt. She stood in the mirror, caressing her arms with lotion. Once she finished, I had to hide back behind the door when she came toward me to enter the bathroom. I knew when I heard her hair dryer she would spend quite a bit of time in there. I had to remain on the back side of the door because Tori didn't close it behind her.

Approximately twenty minutes later, Tori shut off the dryer and returned to her bedroom mirror. I continued to peer around the door at her—until she spotted me. Her face filled with fright. I lunged at Tori, tackling her before she had a chance to scream. Though clearly frightened, Tori surprised me once again with her will to fight back. She kicked, scratched, bit, and even punched me. We scrambled to the floor with me on top of her naked body. I knew this was my chance to gain control.

I attempted to pull her up, and when I did, she raised her foot to kick me. I grabbed her ankle before I was hit. I punched Tori in the midsection, knocking the wind out of her. She fell to the floor, gasping for a breath. I picked her up by her hair and dragged her over to the bed. She was limp like a rag doll. I threw her onto the bed, where I parted her hair in half to tie her to the headboard with it. I made certain the knot was tight. All the squirming in the world wouldn't have released Tori's head. She was too weak to protest anyway. She attempted to speak.

"Shut the fuck up! I knew I'd catch you, tramp," I yelled.

I don't know where Tori muscled the strength, but she caught me off guard when she whisked a glob of spit in my face and glared at me. I looked into her eyes and thought of Holiday's horror and how unsafe she'd been made to feel after her home was burned down. Then I had flashes of the harassing calls, the damage to my car and to my eyes. I lost control and began to strangle her. Tori tried to push me off her, but she was too weak. I choked her with my right hand and covered her mouth and nose with my left. Soon, there was no sigh from Tori. I didn't stop until I was confident she was dead. Tori's eyes and mouth were still open.

I looked at her lifeless body as she stared blankly at me.

Then I began to feel sorry for her. I reflected on the phone conversation I'd overheard about her son, and I wished I had maintained better control of my temper. I closed Tori's eyes and did something I hadn't believed in doing in a very long time. I said a prayer for her.

Chapter Forty

Just One More Chance

After taking Tori's life, I realize my gratification hadn't come yet. I still hadn't convinced Holiday she could be happy, in love, and secure having me as her man. Although Holiday was on my mind, I sat on my couch in deep thought about the sin I'd just committed hours before.

I was very careful about not leaving evidence and certain no one saw me. Still, I was depressed. I wasn't so sure anymore that Tori deserved to die, but there was nothing I could do about what was already done. I lay on my sofa for most of the night, sulking and contemplating my next move. A notion came to me that I should change clothing and go pay Holiday a visit. I felt enough time had passed since I first got information on where she lived, and since Tori was out of the picture, all I had to do was convince Holiday she could live comfortably with me.

I put on my best white Oxford shirt and a pair of Tommy Hilfiger blue jeans Holiday had once complimented me on, and then I went for a drive. My heart began to beat rapidly as I approached her neighborhood. Lights were on outside of her place, and I spotted a small sign on her mailbox that read SIMMONS RESIDENCE. There was no hint of her Mercedes anywhere around. I wondered whether I should wait for Holiday to return home then decided against it. I was content with having seen her home at least, and I knew I still had things to sort out in my head.

Having killed Tori proved I was crazy, but who could I tell? Who would I tell? No one. That was a secret I was prepared to take with me to my grave. I wasn't going to spend time in jail if I could help it. Keeping my mouth shut about Tori's death would definitely ensure I remained prison-free.

I took the lonely drive back toward my home, but then I figured I'd use the number Holiday's assistant had so graciously helped me discover. I stopped at a payphone to call so Holiday wouldn't see my number on the caller ID. My fingers trembled as I pressed the keys. I wondered if Holiday was finally ready to accept my call and listen to me. I needed to hear Holiday's voice—nice or nasty. She answered sweetly as I remembered her once.

"Hello," she said.

"Holiday, boo, it's me. Don't hang up. I miss you."

"Roman, how is it that every time I get my number changed, you still manage to gain access to it?"

"Look, let's not argue. It's been almost two months since we've talked, and I just want to come see, hold, feel, and kiss you. Don't you miss me, too?"

"You know what, Roman? I do miss you. I miss you like I miss having a bad cold. Quit finding my numbers. Stop calling me," she said just before hanging up.

I was crushed. I decided not to call Holiday back. I got in my car and went straight home. I resorted to my couch for the next few days, barely even taking restroom breaks. I had enough sense to call in sick on my job, but I couldn't bring myself to speak to anyone else. I don't ever remember being so sad before in my life.

When Rachel and my sister, Sharonda, called me, I ignored them. I felt too bad about having killed Tori for Holiday's sake, only to have my love rejected. Once I finally felt like turning on the television, my mind began to play tricks on me. I listened to commercials and watched shows that reminded me of Holiday. Then, an idea dawned on me.

Without thinking, I jumped up, grabbed my wallet and keys, and headed out the door. I decided that I could make Holiday want to see me with what I had up my sleeve. She loved to be spoiled, and that's exactly what I was going to do.

I drove down Holiday's street and saw that her car was sitting in the driveway. I kept driving toward the nearest grocery store. I was excited because I knew within a matter of minutes I would see my boo.

I parked along the sidewalk in front of Holiday's house. I snatched the groceries out of the car and ran to her door. I could barely ring the bell because I had a sack in each arm. I wondered if Holiday had been expecting someone because she answered on the first ring. We both stood silent, at a loss for words. I could only tell myself how sexy she was looking. She finally spoke.

"Roman, what are you doing here?"

"I came to kick it with you like old times, boo," I stated, making my way into the house.

"Uh, I don't remember inviting you in." Holiday placed her hand up to my chest, preventing me from moving any farther than the doorway.

"C'mon, boo. You know I hate it when you treat me this way. You're acting like I'm somebody you never cared anything about." I tried playing on Holiday's emotions a bit. "Holiday, I just want to see you and spend a little time with you."

"How did you find me?"

"Boo, you know me. I have my ways of getting what I want.

Now quit standing there asking questions. These bags are weighing down on a brotha's arms. Let me in, boo." I tried to enter her home once again, but she blocked me once more.

"Roman, you can't come in," she said.

"Why? Who's in there?"

"Nobody. This is my home, and I say you're not welcome here."

Anger set in quickly as I thought Holiday might be refusing to see me because of another man, probably Lance although I didn't see his car. I closed my eyes and bit my bottom lip as I attempted to silently count to ten. I don't think I made it to seven before I pushed past Holiday, making my way into her house. I could hear Holiday yelling for me to get out, but I kept on. I searched high and low, and I wasn't satisfied until I finally discovered no one was there with Holiday, not even Crystal.

It wasn't until I was back out on the porch that I realized I had dropped my groceries, ruining the hundred-dollar bottle of champagne, which was her main gift.

I guess it turned out that Holiday's top surprise was actually an unwelcomed one—my knowledge of her new residence. Even though she wasn't pleased by the time I left, neither was I. It was time to start handling things the way I felt they needed to be handled. It had become obvious Holiday wasn't going to accept my love easily, so I decided she was going to get it the hard way. One way or the other, she would be mine—mine alone.

Chapter Forty-one

A Close Call

Another month went by as I continued to have dreams of Holiday. I thought of how she was meant to be my woman. I just knew it. I could feel it. I made a few more attempts to see her, but again and again, she rejected me. She did accept except a few of my calls on her job and on her cell phone, but I felt like she was just trying to pacify me to keep me quiet. Speaking to her through a phone line just wasn't enough.

Rachel was getting on my everlasting nerves. As she got closer to her due date, she became the bitch from hell. She was very demanding, so to shut her up, I was nice and even took her shopping for the baby. I preferred spending a little money on a few baby things rather than having to keep repairing my car or having to explain my way out of her temper tantrums at work.

One Saturday morning Rachel and I came face-to-face with Lance and Holiday at the mall. I was fuming to see them there together, but there wasn't anything I could say. Holiday was angry at seeing Rachel with me, which let me know she still cared. She ranted and even called Rachel out of her name. I knew then that all of the pressure I'd been placing on Holiday to be with me wasn't in vain. By this time, my mind was made up that I would let her play hard to get, but I would never stop chasing her.

I got a phone call from the hospital, letting me know Rachel had the baby. I showed up, pretending to be interested. After she returned home from the hospital, I didn't waste any time having a blood test performed. When, the long-awaited mail finally hit my doorstep. I was so relieved to read the words *zero probability*, I took a leap into the air, clicking my heels before hitting the ground. After the exciting news of my non-parental obligation, I felt I had another reason to see Holiday. It was time to celebrate.

It was Saturday before I decided to show up at Holiday's place unannounced. I knew she would be angry at first, but I also knew that all I had to do was flash that piece of paper with the written answer to all our troubles. Holiday opened the door with a look that said she was prepared to cuss out whoever was on the other side so early in the morning. I almost froze, but then I waved the paper in her face.

"Boo, what's yo' man's name?" I brushing right past Holiday.

"Huh?"

"I said what's yo' man's name? Boo-yow! Peep this out," I said, handing her the paper.

Holiday began reading out loud. "Zero probability . . . could be produced by Mr. Roman Broxton." She smirked at me. "Hmph. So you weren't lying to me, huh?"

"Naw. I told you I used a condom," I lied.

"Well, I guess this is congratulations to you, but you really didn't need to bring this for me to see. I'm no longer your woman."

"Yes, you are. We're just going through some rough times right now, but you are my woman."

"No. I'm not, and I'm gonna have to ask you to leave now."

"W-W-Why? Who? Who's here?" I wondered if she had male company, and my temper began to flare.

"No one, Roman. I swear to you, no one besides Crystal. I don't want her to wake up and find you here. Please leave."

Then as quickly as my temper flared, I regained my composure. "I'll leave, if you say my name first." I began to snap my fingers and dance. I loved having the upper hand. "Say my name. Say my name. C'mon, boo, say my name," I continued to chant, doing my best James Brown impression.

"Why do I need to say your name? Just leave, Roman."

"Uhn-uhn, boo. That ain't it. Say my name."

Holiday sighed, looked around then whispered, "Rome."

"What is it? Let me hear you say it again. Say my name," I repeated.

This time said it louder. "Rome."

She might have only obliged in order to get me to leave. It didn't matter to me though. She did what I told her to do, and that was sign number two that I had some control on her. I felt Holiday was just using Crystal as an excuse. She could've called the police if she really wanted me out of there, but she didn't because she still loved me. I knew the real reason she asked me to leave is because she was just pacing time for us to get back together. The Holiday I first dated didn't want to rush things between us.

I stopped dancing and took my DNA results from her. "Thank you. Now you gon' learn to believe your man," I said as I turned to leave.

Holiday was my woman. She just didn't know it. It was my responsibility to help her know it and love being my woman at the same time. This I promised on everything I owned.

Chapter Forty-two

Never Giving Up

Mr. Brown had men lined up, wall-to-wall, waiting to sit in his barber's chair, and I just happened to be the last one for the night. I have to admit, it felt awfully strange being there on a Friday evening without my old crew. Ant wouldn't hang out with me anymore since our argument about me chasing Tori in his truck, and he even had Carlos's feelings of me twisted. I stopped by Carlos's place to see if he wanted to go have a drink with me, but he cut me off each time I opened my mouth to begin a new sentence. I felt pretty bad at first, then I thought, who needs half-ass friends? Carlos never even bothered to hear my side of things. Sonia probably wasn't gonna let him go out the house anyway. I walked away from Carlos's place without looking back or even saying good-bye.

I finally got my turn in Mr. Brown's chair. One thing about Mr. Brown, he loved to talk. Although I was the last customer, Mr. Brown still had plenty of conversation. He even asked about my father and sister. The shop was empty, so I spoke freely about my family.

"My sister is doing well, Mr. Brown. I need to catch up with her and take her out sometime. She really tries to reach out to me and be close. I owe her a dinner at least. Thanks for asking about her."

"Oh sure. I remember her to be a sweet young lady. Sharonda, right?"

"Yes, sir. That's her name. My father is still the same as he was years ago. I just don't think he'll ever change, and we will never understand each other. As a matter of fact, we're not speaking to each other."

"Not speaking? Wait a minute. We are talking about your father, right?"

"Yes, sir."

"Then I'm confused. You say the two of you aren't speaking as if he's just one of your boys or something. Your father is your blood. I remember how stupid he could act, but he and your sister are all the family you've got. No matter how crazy that man acts, he's your father, and you should be able to forgive him every time."

"But, Mr. Brown, he makes me so angry."

"Get mad. Then get glad. Be glad you got a father. There are a lot of people around here who wish they ever knew their fathers. Yours could've pushed you away after your mother died, but he didn't. As a matter of fact, I remember that he took great care of you."

"He did, Mr. Brown. He was there for me. I can't deny how much responsibility he took on with me."

"I'm not going to pretend like your father doesn't have issues, but we all know how his problems started. Everyone handles death differently. Although he had an outside child during his marriage, your mother meant a hell of a lot to your dad. Don't hate him, Roman. Just try to understand him. Then forgive him."

"I don't know, Mr. Brown. It's been a long time since I last visited him."

"Don't waste any more time, Roman. If you need me to, I'll go with you tonight. I can't be over there long because the Mrs. is looking for me home before nine o'clock."

"That would be great. I'd love for you to go with me. Maybe you could help be the ice breaker."

I waited around as Mr. Brown packed up. It was dark out, but I knew my father was probably up watching some of his favorite shows before the late-night news since this had been his routine for years. Mr. Brown locked up his shop, and we started toward our cars. Suddenly, my mind began playing tricks on me. I saw a dark SUV speeding toward the shop. The person on the inside was hard to make out, until the truck came to a screeching halt and parked diagonally in front of Mr. Brown's barbershop. For a brief minute, I swore I was looking at Toriana Ponce, but then reality hit me. I shook off the daze and noticed a very fair-skinned male getting out of the truck.

"Mr. Brown . . . please don't close up the shop yet. I need my fade tightened up. See here," the man said, pulling off his cap and pointing to his hair.

"Aw, Leon, man, I gotta go home to the Mrs. You understand what I'm saying?" Mr. Brown smiled and made his eyebrows dance.

"I'll pay you double, Mr. Brown," the man said. "Okay . . . listen, I'll pay you triple. Just don't leave a brotha hanging like this. I've got big plans tonight."

"Aw, shoot. Son, come on here," Mr. Brown said, unlocking the door to the shop. "Now don't you make this no habit, you hear?"

"Yes, sir, Mr. Brown. Thank you, sir. You just don't know how much I appreciate you," the man said.

"Roman, you go on. Go make that visit to your father. Be sure to tell him I said stop acting like an old fool. Life is too short to be so stubborn." Mr. Brown shook his head. "Umph

. . . and tell him my shop is still in the same spot . . . I ain't going anywhere, so I'm looking forward to seeing him again real soon."

"I sure will, Mr. Brown. Have a great evening. I'll see you next Friday."

I got in my car, thinking about the flash I'd had of Toriana. I wondered what, if anything, had been done about her sudden disappearance or if her body had been discovered. I stared at the SUV parked outside the barbershop, contemplating taking a ride over to Tori's to see if her truck was still in her driveway. I decided it would be a good idea then headed toward her house.

I didn't make it far when I spotted Holiday driving past me. Her hair was flowing down her back, and she looked pretty made up. I dropped all plans of going over to Tori's house to see what Holiday was up to. I followed her all the way downtown to the Peabody Garage.

I decided to wait around in my car to watch for Holiday's return. I fell asleep a few times, but when I'd awaken, Holiday's Mercedes was still parked. I was finally awakened by Holiday's laughter. I remained slouched in my seat as I watched Holiday and some guy, apparently her date, giggling and holding hands. I was furious. I'd gone through too much and had done some horrible things just to be with Holiday. I would never see her happy with anyone else. Only I deserved her love.

I wanted to jump out of my car and confront them, but I held my composure instead. Holiday was wearing the same black dress I'd seen her wear the first night she went out with me and Lance. Two years later, she still looked good in that dress. I continued to watch as she gave this man a hug then drove away. He walked another direction, and I finally left the garage. I called Holiday's home to leave a few messages,

careful not to alert her that I'd been following her. I just
wanted her to know how much I needed her.

I knew I could make Holiday love me despite her not
wanting to be involved with me or Lance. It would only be a
matter of time. I called her a few days after her date with that
guy to see if she'd go out with me. She didn't sound pleased
to hear my voice.

"Hey, boo. I need to ask you something," I said just after
she answered the phone.

"Need to or want to ask me something?"

"I need to. I need you. Don't you know that by now?"

"Roman, why are you calling me? I know you have some
other woman you can contact. You don't need me. You just
think you need me," Holiday said.

"Boo, I thought you knew that you're mine forever. I'm
never gonna let go. If only you knew the lengths I've gone in
order to make our relationship better, you'd straighten up
and realize you do want me. I can't share some of these
things with you now, but perhaps later."

"Perhaps never. What I need is for you to move on," she
responded coldly.

"I can't move on. You're mine, and I expect to see you this
weekend."

"Expect all you want, Roman. That's not gonna happen. If
I tell you I won't be with you then lovin' me is wrong."

"Well, I don't wanna be right. I just don't see how you can
say that you ever loved me and you can refuse to see me,
even if it's just for one minute. If I show up on your job, you
treat me as if I'm a stranger and just about jog to your car."

"That's because when I get off work, I'm in a hurry. You
don't need to keep popping up on my job, trying to see me
before I get to my car. You have my cell phone number. Call

me and ask if I'm busy and if I'll meet you somewhere. It'll save you a lot of time and keep you from getting your feelings hurt."

"Holiday, how am I gonna ask you something if you won't answer your phone? I know you look at the caller ID. Come on now, boo."

"You don't know what I do, Roman."

"Oh, I know what you do. I know plenty about what you do."

"And, what is that supposed to mean?"

"You just better not go anywhere with that nigga this weekend."

"What?" Holiday sounded stunned.

"You heard me."

"Roman, you're sounding real silly right now. How do you know who I'm seeing? It's none of your business anyway. I'm getting ready to hang up if you don't stop talking foolish."

"I'm foolish? I tell you what. You can hang up. Don't go out with that muthafucker Saturday. If you do, you'll be the foolish one. I've already said it: you better not go out with him Saturday!" I hung up before she could respond.

If Holiday didn't get the picture after that conversation, it wasn't because I didn't make myself clear. I was at my limit, and it was time out for cutting her some slack. She was going to play by my rules and my rules only.

Chapter Forty-three

Time Out

Lance contacted me trying to make amends. He told me he was no longer dealing with Holiday on an intimate level and that he wasn't interested at that point. Since I knew he was no longer sleeping with my woman, I felt there was no harm in hanging out with him again, especially since my boys, Ant and Carlos wouldn't have anything to do with me. Lance and I made plans to hook up that weekend.

Holiday went against my advice by going out with that guy again. Lance and I happened to show up at the same restaurant, and I spied Holiday with that dude as they were leaving. I tried to break that dude's neck, but Lance kept me back. I picked Holiday up, forcing her to go with me. She broke loose and got away, thanks to Lance. Needless to say, I ended up on Holiday's doorstep banging and yelling for her attention. She wouldn't let me in, but that didn't mean I would never get my way. I became mentally prepared to make Holiday's life a living hell. I felt if I couldn't be happy, then why should she.

Over the next couple of months, I stuck to my game plan to make Holiday miserable. I made harassing phone calls,

made unannounced visits to her home and her job, and I followed her through the streets of Memphis, including a high
speed chase, which landed me in jail. One of the officers on
the scene happened to be the one who pulled me over after
I chased Toriana in Ant's truck. I knew when I saw his face
my hands would be cuffed behind my back.

A weekend in jail didn't stop my determination to see
Holiday suffer. I wasn't gonna let up on her until she decided she would accept me in her life. It soon became evi-
dent she wasn't gonna change her mind, so I decided if I
couldn't have Holiday, no one could.

My last straw was after I witnessed Lance moving into
Holiday's home. He told me things were over between
Holiday and him. I couldn't understand why he would betray
me after saying he missed our friendship. The only thing I
could come up with was that Holiday was dreadfully afraid of
me, so Lance was supposed to be her protection. The only
problem with that was Lance was in the way, so I'd have to
kill him, too.

When I had first purchased the replica of Lance's gun, I
knew it would come in handy. I knew that if I ever had to do
something drastic, I could set things up so that Lance could
take the blame. I thought a few days on the perfect way to ex-
ecute my plan, then when the mood hit me, I packed my gun
and headed to Holiday's.

I waited until I knew Lance and Holiday would be asleep
before going into her neighborhood. I tried to take a peek
into her windows, but she had them all covered with curtains
and blinds. There was no way I could see inside, but since it
was the wee hours of the morning, I knew Lance and
Holiday should've been in the bedroom. I walked around
her house several times trying to decide which window
would be best for the disturbance I was about to cause.

I brought along a canvas bag, which held the perfect instrument—a two-pound stone to carry out my plan. I tossed it through a window in the front of the house and jumped over Holiday's back fence as her alarm blared. I left the area for a while. Once I returned, I noticed the police leaving.

I let a little more time go by, then I went onto Holiday's property again, fishing for a way to get to her and Lance. I choose what appeared to be either the back door or an entrance to the kitchen. I thought about Lance being inside holding my woman, and then I used all my might to kick in the door. Again the alarm blared. I knew I had to do what I came to do quickly and get out of there.

I stepped inside the kitchen, coming face-to-face with Lance. He yelled out to Holiday.

"Holiday, it's Roman. Get down."

I shot at Lance, but he saw me draw my gun, so he was able to duck. He headed farther into the house, and I ran behind him. I was determined to finish both him and Holiday off before I left. I was greeted by gunfire when I entered the great room. I took cover behind a closet door until I heard the clicking of Lance's gun. He was out of ammunition. I slowly came out from behind the closet, ready to take care of business. As I got closer to Lance, Holiday sprang out from behind the couch on top of me.

I wrestled with Holiday and Lance for a while before I was able to gain full control. The two of them struggled to get away from me, but I knew I had won. I quickly took aim at Lance, then fired. He laid motionless as I stepped over him to get to Holiday.

Holiday had backed against a wall, her eyes filled with terror. Since no one had picked up the phone to speak with the alarm company, I knew the police were on their way. But, I didn't let this stop me from saying my last words to Holiday.

"I loved you with everything I had in me. And I told you, if you can't love me, then you won't love anybody else," I said.

"Roman, think of how upset this is going to make Crystal. Why would you take her mother from her?" she responded, obviously stalling me.

"That ain't my kid. Did her mother think of how upset she was making me when she refused to let me back into her life?" I looked at Holiday as tears filled her eyes and her chest heaved. "No. I don't wanna do this to you, boo, but right now I feel I have no choice."

I lifted my arm to aim at Holiday, but she distracted me by glancing behind me. I noticed Lance had inched to grab another gun from a table drawer. He pulled the gun out, but I shot him first. Lance once again lay motionless. I turned to Holiday to finish her off. She raised her arms to her face in an attempt to block whatever was coming her way. I took aim, but then I heard shots that I knew I hadn't fired. I couldn't look around because my back felt like I had been hit over and over with a large hammer.

Suddenly, my knees buckled. I was on the floor, face-to-face with Holiday. She looked at me with a great sadness yet she seemed so terrified. I wanted to tell her I loved her, but I couldn't form the words. Finally, I was too weak to sit up any longer. The next thing I remember was falling over on Holiday.

I woke up and noticed Holiday passed out next to Lance. Blood was oozing from every direction. My vision was blurry, and I couldn't tell if either of them was breathing. I was too injured to move, so once I spotted my gun, I managed kick it over in the near Lance and Holiday. It landed at Holiday's feet. I wanted to set Lance up as planned, but that meant I needed to place my gun closer to him and retrieve his gun to hide it.

I tried to get up, but I couldn't. I didn't move again. I could hear the police entering the house. I felt someone standing over me, and without checking for a pulse, he announced to everyone in the room that I was dead. Soon after that, I slipped out of consciousness.

I awakened in the hospital with IVs in me, cuffed to a bed. The doctors were in the room with me at the time. As soon as they saw me open my eyes, they called the police into the room. The officers questioned me, but I didn't part my lips to say a word. They all assumed I was too weak to speak and that I needed time to recuperate from my wounds.

I was told Lance had placed four bullets in my back, none of which caused permanent damage, and the surgeons were successful in removing all of the bullets. Four days went by before the police tried to question me again. I lied and told them I was a little groggy, and that they'd have to help me remember some of the events of that day. They told me Lance only suffered minor wounds and was released from the hospital. I was furious.

"That man tried to kill me," I yelled to the police detective.

"Mr. Broxton, that's why we're trying to get more details from you. We don't have enough information to prove you're the innocent one in this whole ordeal."

"It must've been a set-up."

"What was a set-up, Mr. Broxton?"

"Holiday called me to come over there. She said Lance had gone crazy and was trying to fight her, so I went over there thinking she was in trouble."

"Did you kick the kitchen door in, Mr. Broxton?"

"Yes, but only because I heard Holiday screaming. Once I got inside, Lance aimed a gun at me, but I shot at him first. I was only defending myself and the woman I love. Am I in trouble?"

"You might want to get yourself a lawyer, Mr. Broxton.

There are still some things that aren't unclear, and you could find yourself in a great deal of trouble," the detective replied.

"Wow. I never thought things would end up this way. I need to get well first then I'll find an attorney. In the meantime, will you do me a favor and take these handcuffs off? I'm in too much pain to cause any harm, and besides, it's a real trip trying to get someone in here to take them off so I can use the bathroom."

"Isn't there an officer outside your room at all times?"

"No, actually there isn't. These people around here know I'm no threat. They only call an officer to come in and remove the cuffs when I need to get up or use the restroom."

"Okay. I'll see what I can do about that."

The detective left the room, leaving me cuffed to the bed, and about an hour later, an officer returned to remove them. I thanked him and smiled innocently. I was told by the cop that I'd only be relieved from the cuffs for a few hours, but by ten o'clock that night, I was still free. I plotted to runaway when there were fewer staff members on my hall. I sneaked out of the hospital wearing doctor scrubs. Lance and Holiday were meant to die, and it was my duty to carry that out.

Chapter Forty-four

No More Strain, No More Pain

I knew that whatever I was about to do, I would have to do it quick. The hospital would soon miss me and report the disappearance. I stopped by my house to retrieve some money I kept hidden in case of an emergency. I had to break into the window because the police still had my keys and my car was impounded. Once in my home, I decided I should at least change my appearance somewhat. I went into the bathroom and shaved off all my hair, then I shaved the beard I'd being growing since being in the hospital and shaped it into a goatee. Lance had one, so I figured I would make Holiday drool over mine before she died.

After collecting my money, I reached into the nightstand drawer to retrieve my extra gun. Then, I walked to the corner store and called a taxi from a payphone to take me to Lance's home. The driver arrived, but he almost didn't let me inside the cab because I was carrying a heavy stick that I'd found not far from the hospital. I explained I needed the stick for protection from big dogs when I walked back home late at night. I actually needed the weapon because I had intentions of beating Lance to death with it. I didn't want to make his death quick and easy. He deserved to suffer. After a flash of a hundred-dollar bill, the man finally agreed to let me in the cab.

I asked the driver to wait as he dropped me off around the corner of Lance's house. He was a little leery.

"What am I waiting for?" he man asked. "You said you'd walk back."

"Just hold on for me. My friend might not be home, and I could need you to take me somewhere else."

"You mean, just sit here and wait on you to come back? Where are you going?"

"Not far from here," I answered.

The driver looked back at me, glancing at me from head to toe then over at the big stick. "No. I'm not going to be able to sit here and wait. I suggest you find another way home."

I reached into my pocket and pulled out a fifty-dollar bill and handed it to the man. He still seemed a little bit reluctant at first, but then he went ahead and took the money.

I opened the car door and eased out careful not to re-injure the wounds in my back. I made my way to Lance's porch and rang the bell. I held my head down so he wouldn't be able to get a good look at who was standing outside his door, but then turned and realized that his truck wasn't parked outside. After standing there a few more minutes, I walked away. I took a glance back, and that's when I noticed Lance standing barefoot and shirtless on his porch. His head had a white bandage wrapped around it, and he had a large patch on his shoulder. He looked at me as if he was staring at a ghost.

Just then a crowd of teens rode by on their bikes, so I didn't draw my gun to shoot at Lance for fear I would hurt the innocent kids. I was too far away to lunge at Lance, so I turned and kept walking. I looked back and saw Lance rushing to get inside his home. He didn't even close the door behind him, which led me to believe he was grabbing some shoes and a shirt to chase me. I hurried back to the cab as much as I could without causing myself more pain. I asked the driver to speed away.

"Go . . . go . . . go," I yelled, looking back.

"What? Where am I going?" he asked.

"Go . . . just drive!"

The man sped away as I had requested. Since there was no vehicle outside Lance's home, I didn't fear he would follow me, so it was on to the second phase of my plan. I remembered that Holiday once told me her medical insurance would only pay if she visited Methodists hospitals, so I tried my luck downtown first. I gave the driver a twenty-dollar bill and told him there was no need to wait on me. He gladly accepted the money then pulled away.

Again, I knew I needed to move quickly. Not only had I been missing from the hospital for a couple of hours, but I had also been spotted by Lance. If he called Holiday's room, he would ruin my entire plan.

I walked inside the hospital and blended right in with the rest of the medical staff since I was still wearing scrubs. I wondered how I could get someone to give me information regarding Holiday's stay, but as I walked toward the nurse's station, the answer practically fell in my lap. I heard a doctor instruct a nurse to get the night medication for Ms. Simmons up in Room 516. The nurse agreed and headed inside an office.

I went to find the elevator, but I had a little trouble. I stumbled upon a doctor standing in a hallway, writing on a memo pad outside of an office. He was apparently dressed for surgery because his hair and feet were covered. The only confusing thing about his attire was the fact that his garments underneath his lab coat didn't appear to be scrubs.

Last thing I remembered, doctors didn't wear black into surgery or in a hospital at all. I didn't want to give the doctor any suspicion that I didn't belong there so I stopped staring as I approached him. I continued to walk as I asked him for directions.

"Excuse me, doctor. I'm new here, and I'm having trouble locating the elevator," I innocently said.

"Down the hall and to the right," the man answered in a mild tone, never looking up from his memo pad.

I found the elevator and jumped on, anxious to see my love.

Once I got off the elevator, I was surprised to see there wasn't a security guard around, and no one was sitting at the nurse's desk either.

I entered Holiday's room and noticed her lying in bed with her back to the door. I could tell she heard me enter because she moved a little in the bed. I stood silently, thinking of how much I was going to miss her. I reminisced for what seemed like forever on the years we had, but then I snapped back into reality. I was standing in Holiday's room to complete a much needed task. I couldn't let Holiday live.

I noticed her room was filled with fresh flowers, even roses like the ones she'd once received from Lance. Then it hit me—Lance had sent her some more roses. I became angrier and realized I had better handle my business before Lance alerted people that he'd seen me. I began to walk toward Holiday. She caught me off guard when she spoke.

"Is it time for my antibiotic or is it that nasty liquid stuff Dr. Chambers prescribed for me?" she asked.

Holiday obviously thought I was her night nurse. She was startled when I responded, "Neither."

She quickly turned to see me standing in her presence. I went over to her bedside and leaned over her to muffle her mouth.

"Don't bother screaming, boo. No one will hear you in time," I said, staring into her tear-filled eyes.

As her tears fell, I heard her mumbling something. I briefly removed my hands from her mouth to hear what she was saying.

"Did I really cause you so much pain that you feel I don't deserve to live?"

"Yes. I ached for you every day. Right now, I love you so much, I hate you. I know now that I can't have you, but I won't see you be happy with anyone else—especially not Lance."

"Roman, I'm sorry," she cried.

"I know. And I'm sorry, too," I whispered.

Then I placed my hand over her mouth and nose just in time to muffle her screams. With my other hand, I squeezed on Holiday's neck, just like I did with Toriana. She tried to pry my hand from her face, but I was much too strong for her. I was interrupted by the same doctor I'd asked for directions along with Lance.

"Roman, cut it out, man. The police are on their way," Lance said.

Immediately, I drew my gun. "I don't give a shit. You two mutherfuckers have caused me a lot of pain, and somebody has to pay for it. Why not the two of you?"

"You think you're the only one who has experienced pain, Roman? C'mon, man, no one ever told you that life isn't supposed to be filled with trials. Killing Holiday or even me won't get rid of your pain. You need to get some help, man."

"Who are you to tell me what I need? Your presence is enough grounds to shoot both of you and get the hell out of here," I said, lifting my gun.

Lance jumped, but to my surprise, he didn't run. Neither did the doctor. At that moment, another doctor and nurse entered the room.

"What's going on in here?" the nurse asked.

"Dr. Chambers, this is Roman Broxton. He's trying to kill me," Holiday yelled. "Somebody get the police."

"Don't worry. They're on their way, Ms. Simmons," the nurse responded.

"You all apparently don't understand. Holiday and Lance aren't meant to live, and I am not going to jail. I'll die first," I threatened.

Just then the doctor I'd seen downstairs spoke out. "Ms. Simmons and Lance Ferrell aren't the ones who aren't meant to live. Mr. Broxton, you're the one who deserves to die," the doctor said, pulling off a fake mustache, then removing the net from his head.

I wondered if my eyes were playing tricks on me as I watched long dark hair fall from underneath the doctor's net. Standing before me was Toriana Ponce. I felt sick to my stomach. I realized I hadn't carefully checked for a pulse the day I thought I had killed her.

"Jail is the least of your worries. Right now, hell all you need to worry about because that's exactly where I'm about to send you," Tori stated, pulling out a gun.

Before I could react, I felt a heavy pounding in my chest. She fired another shot, and the next one knocked me to the floor. I looked at Tori in disbelief. Her face housed a lot of anger, and I suddenly felt sorry for her. I looked around the room at everyone else standing there. Lance seemed shocked, the nurse was holding on to the doctor screaming, and Holiday was on her knees in the bed, holding her ears, crying. I couldn't take my eyes off her. She seemed so sad. I opened my mouth to tell her everything would be okay, but I coughed up blood instead. Someone turned me over, and I noticed Toriana had disappeared. The sounds in the room became faint, and I could hear someone yelling for help. I lay on my side with my life flashing before my eyes.

I thought of the good times I shared with my boys, including Lance. I thought of the womanizing ways I once had, Mr. Brown, and the things he'd taught me, Rachel Clark and the close call with parenthood, my sister and how much she loved me, and I even thought of my father.

What would my father think of me now? I became the opposite of the man he raised me to be. If I hadn't cared so much for one woman, I wouldn't have been in the predicament I was in. It was too late, but I didn't regret having cared so much for Holiday. She only wanted to be loved, and I only regretted that I never knew how to give her the affection she needed. Now it's too late. It's too la—

Discussion Questions

1. Do you feel this was an ideal situation? Why?

2. Did either Lance or Roman love Holiday?

3. What did you think of Rachel Clark? Did you feel sorry for her? Why or why not?

4. Were Roman's friends, Carlos and Anthony true to him?

5. Who was your favorite character and why?

6. Who was your least favorite character? Why?

7. Who did you believe was responsible for harassing Roman?

8. Was Roman crazy to want Holiday so much?

9. What could've been done differently between Lance and Roman about their attraction for Holiday in the beginning?

10. Which character did you empathize?

11. What was your favorite scene? Why?

12. Was the ending surprising, and did you find it justified?

About the Author

Alisha Yvonne is a native Memphian and a rising new voice in the world of African American fiction. She is the author of *Lovin' You Is Wrong*, and the dynamic follow-up title, *I Don't Wanna Be Right*. Alisha is currently working on her next other project.

Alisha is a member of several online literary groups, including R.A.W.4ALL, ReadersandFriends, and FictionFolks. She is President of the R.A.W.SISTAZ Memphis Chapter Book Club, and she is an avid supporter of local anti-domestic violence charities.

Visit Alisha online at *www.alishayvonne.com* or email to *author@ebonyliterarygrace.com* .

IN STORES NOW

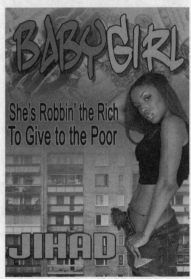
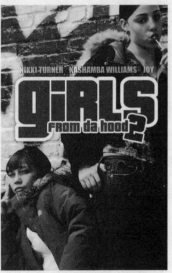

1-893196-25-9

0-9747025-9-5

1-893196-27-5

1893196-30-5

OTHER URBAN BOOKS TITLES

Title	Author	Quantity	Cost
Drama Queen	LaJill Hunt		$14.95
No More Drama	LaJill Hunt		$14.95
Shoulda Woulda Coulda	LaJill Hunt		$14.95
Is It A Crime	Roy Glenn		$14.95
MOB	Roy Glenn		$14.95
Drug Related	Roy Glenn		$14.95
Lovin' You Is Wrong	Alisha Yvonne		$14.95
Bulletproof Soul	Michelle Buckley		$14.95
You Wrong For That	Toschia		$14.95
A Gangster's girl	Chunichi		$14.95
Married To The Game	Chunichi		$14.95
Sex In The Hood	White Chocalate		$14.95
Little Black Girl Lost	Keith Lee Johnson		$14.95
Sister Girls	Angel M. Hunter		$14.95
Driven	KaShamba Williams		$14.95
Street Life	Jihad		$14.95
Baby Girl	Jihad		$14.95
A Thug's Life	Thomas Long		$14.95
Cash Rules	Thomas Long		$14.95
The Womanizers	Dwayne S. Joseph		$14.95
Never Say Never	Dwayne S. Joseph		$14.95
She's Got Issues	Stephanie Johnson		$14.95
Rockin' Robin	Stephanie Johnson		$14.95
Sins Of The Father	Felicia Madlock		$14.95
Back On The Block	Felicia Madlock		$14.95
Chasin' It	Tony Lindsey		$14.95
Street Possession	Tony Lindsey		$14.95
Around The Way Girls	LaJill Hunt		$14.95
Around The Way Girls 2	LaJill Hunt		$14.95
Girls From Da Hood	Nikki Turner		$14.95

Girls from Da Hood 2	Nikki Turner		$14.95
Dirty Money	Ashley JaQuavis		$14.95
Mixed Messages	LaTonya Y. Williams		$14.95
Don't Hate The Player	Brandie		$14.95
Payback	Roy Glenn		$14.95
Scandalous	ReChella		$14.95
Urban Affair	Tony Lindsey		$14.95
Harlem Confidential	Cole Riley		$14.95

Urban Books
74 Andrews Ave.
Wheatley Heights, NY 11798

Subtotal: _____

Postage:_____ Calculate postage and handling as follows: Add $2.50 for the first item and $1.25 for each additional item

Total: _____

Name: _____

Address:_____

City: _____ State: _____ Zip: _____

Telephone: (   ) _____

Type of Payment (Check: ___ Money Order: ___)

All orders must be prepaid by check or money order drawn on an American bank.

Books may sometimes be out of stock. In that instance, please select your alternate choices below.

Alternate Choices:

1._____

2._____

PLEASE ALLOW 4-6 WEEKS FOR SHIPPING